Her Masked Identity

A Story of Survival, Strength, and Starting Over
by
LK Menzies

"Sometimes the bravest thing you can do is let yourself be seen."
— Unknown

LKM Story House, LLC

Dedication

For the young who have ever felt unseen,
for every heart that had to grow up too soon,
and for every child who learned to be their own
hero—
this story is yours.

— LK Menzies

First Edition
Printed in the United States of America

ISBN: [979-8-9913232-9-1 Hardcopy]

ISBN: [979-8-9990665-1-0 Paper Back]

Prologue

People wear masks for fun.

Makenzie wore hers to survive.

It was not made of glitter or plastic, not a festive disguise for a night's revel. Hers was woven from silence—of perfectly timed smiles and careful stillness, of eyes trained to never betray the tremor inside when someone asked, "Are you okay?" Because no was not something Makenzie ever felt safe saying- Not after they left.

They did not leave in a storm. No screaming, no suitcases, just... gone. One morning, she woke up thirteen and alone. The coffee pot was still warm; the air scented faintly with the last traces of cinnamon and grounds. Her mother's slippers—soft, faded terrycloth—waited by the door, and when Makenzie crouched beside them, her fingers brushed their worn edges, cool and foreign in the hush of that abandoned morning. They were gone like the milk in the refrigerator gradually became sour over time.

There were no notes. No goodbyes, just emptiness— and Makenzie in it.

She waited three days, listening to the tick-tock of the kitchen clock, the distant drip from the bathroom faucet, the sound of her own breath echoing through rooms that seemed impossibly large to fill without voices. Then she stopped waiting. Because no one was coming.

So, she did what she had to do. She vanished—in plain sight.

Makenzie learned how to blend in—how to make herself invisible. She identified safe places to sleep, which questions to dodge, and how to lie with a straight face. She learned how to hide her hunger and her fear and the part of her that still hoped. Hope, she decided, was a luxury she could not afford.

And yet the world would not let her stay hidden forever.

One afternoon, at school, when her stomach gnawed hollow and her hands shook as she clutched her notebook, someone offered her a sandwich. She stared at it—a simple gesture, white bread, and peanut butter—and felt a war inside herself. Should she refuse? Was kindness a trick? The smell was sweet and sticky, and when she finally accepted, the first bite was a revelation: salty, familiar, achingly good. Tears she hadn't known she was holding threatened to spill as she realized the taste was not just food, but the possibility of comfort and friendship.

That moment cracked something inside her—just enough for light to seep through. She remembered how it felt, the warmth of hands passing her the sandwich, the teacher's gentle voice asking quietly, "Are you sure you're alright?" Her instinct was to retreat, to wrap herself tighter in invisibility. But kindness, persistent and soft, kept coming. A blanket left on her desk. A smile in the hallway. Each gesture chipped away at the mask she wore.

Makenzie's trust did not blossom overnight. It grew in small, trembling increments—a nod in response to kindness, a whispered thank you, a new willingness to linger in the warmth of someone's concern. The silence of the empty house faded, replaced by the subtle rhythms of hope: the scent of clean laundry, the hum of voices in a crowded lunchroom, the security of routine.

This is not the story of a perfect girl who found a perfect ending. This is Makenzie's story the girl who wore a mask for years who learned, in the smallest moments and through the gentlest touches, that sometimes, believing in others was the first step to believing in yourself.

And this is what happened when Makenzie finally let her mask slip and let the world see the hero she was becoming.

Table of Contents

Chapter One:

Left Behind

I was thirteen when I woke up to an empty house.

There was no note, no goodbye, they both simply left in the middle of the night. They were gone!

The lights were still on, the TV humming in the background—a constant, tiny murmur that made the silence sharper, as if someone might walk back in at any moment. But they did not. My mom's favorite coffee mug was on the counter; lipstick smudged at the rim. My dad's boots were gone. So was his truck and so were they.

I sat on the floor for hours, knees hugged to my chest, listening to the tick-tock of the kitchen clock and the distant drip of water in the bathroom sink. At first, I thought maybe there had been some kind of emergency—maybe they'd just stepped out, maybe the phone would ring, and I'd hear my mom's voice saying, "Baby, we'll be home soon." That hope was a warm ache in my gut, thick and stubborn.

The phone stayed silent. Only then did I notice the missed signs—packed suitcases, empty closets, and boxes marking where dust had settled.

By the third day, the fridge was nearly empty, and the power had already been cut off. The air grew heavy with the scent of spoiled milk and damp bread. I scavenged what I could: a stale loaf, a jar of peanut butter, a few warm cans of soda. I kept expecting someone to show up—a neighbor, a teacher, maybe someone from Child Protective Services—who noticed the shadows shifting behind the curtains. But no one did. Maybe no one cared.

I went to school that Monday. I wore the cleanest shirt I had, combed my hair with my fingers, and tried to patch together a sense of normalcy. I even remembered my lunch card, though there was no money left on it and no appetite in my stomach. Everything appeared normal as I sat through class, but routine felt brittle and forced. I smiled at the right moments, answered questions when called, and slipped the mask into place when needed.

That night, I walked home under a bruised violet sky, unlocked the front door, and stepped into the same unmoving hush. This time, though, the air felt hollowed out—like the house was already forgetting I'd ever lived there. The scent of burnt toast still clung to the walls, mingling with the cold draft that crept through the back door. I remember sitting on the bottom stair, feeling a bitter mix of anger and disbelief—resenting how quickly an ordinary life could become a memory.

By the end of the week, the water was shut off. I filled every cup and bottle I could while the last trickle sputtered out of the tap, then sat on the porch and watched the rain tap softly against the mailbox. When the landlord came knocking the next morning, I didn't answer. I just grabbed my backpack, stuffed it with what I could, and climbed out the back window. The world smelled of wet earth and rusted metal. I never looked back.

The days blurred into weeks, then months, as I learned to survive on the edges.

At first, the streets were terrifying.

The first night, I wandered in circles downtown until I found an all-night laundromat. The harsh scent of detergent and the whir of machines made the place feel almost safe—anonymity and warmth rolled together. I pretended I was waiting for someone, sitting in a hard plastic chair with my backpack clutched tight, the vinyl sticking against my skin. Eventually, I curled into a corner behind a row of dryers and slept with one eye open, the steady heat humming against my cheek, drowning out my thoughts.

In the morning, I brushed my teeth in a gas station bathroom, the water startlingly cold, and the fluorescent lights buzzing overhead. I watched the condensation on the mirror gather and slide, tracing lines down my face. I learned to move early, to avoid questions or suspicion. I became just another kid with a hoodie and a backpack, blending into the city's grey morning shuffle.

That became my goal: look like you belong.

Nights spent behind the hardware store, inside a broken-down van that reeked of oil and mildew, or under a church awning, where the sweet, yeasty scent of baking bread from a nearby bakery drifted through the air in the early hours. Sometimes I'd wake to rain tapping against my jacket, the water seeping in and chilling me to the bone, and I'd listen to worship songs drifting through the walls, wondering if anyone inside had any idea a girl was sleeping just feet away. I stayed quiet. I stayed hidden.

I figured out which convenience stores had free coffee if you brought your own cup—a battered, plastic thing I found in the park—and memorized every public restroom with a sturdy lock and a warm hand dryer. I learned which dumpsters were worth checking for food that wasn't too far gone, and how to ask for leftovers at closing time without meeting anyone's eyes. Hunger sharpened my senses; survival dulled my shame.

I also learned not to make friends, never to share my story.

At school, I was still Makenzie Rowe—at least on paper. I kept my head down and my grades up. Clean meant baby wipes instead of showers, changing clothes in bathroom stalls, timing it so I'd never be late. I spoke only when called on. I turned in my work early, always neat, and precise. I avoided the counselor's office as if the linoleum itself were radioactive.

Teachers liked me because I was quiet and smart. It was my armor. The quieter I was, the more invisible I became.

Still, there were moments that pressed in, crushing and suffocating. Sometimes I envied the girls after gym class, laughing with friends, showing off phones, complaining about curfews. I'd sit with shoes untied and a knot in my stomach, longing for what they had: the certainty that someone would notice if they didn't come home. The knowledge that their absence would matter.

Fear and loneliness became old companions, but beneath them, I felt flickers of anger and resentment—toward my parents, toward the world, and sometimes even toward myself. There were nights when hope seemed more dangerous than despair, and I wondered if trusting anyone ever again was worth the risk.

There were close calls, reminders of how quickly things could get worse.

Once, I fell asleep behind the gym and woke up locked out until sunrise, the dew seeping through my jacket.

Another time, a man tried to follow me when I slipped behind a building, his footsteps echoing on wet pavement. I ran for six blocks, adrenaline burning cold in my veins, the city's neon glow blurring past. I didn't feel the cold until hours later when my hands finally stopped shaking.

I saw what happened to kids on the streets, to girls who traded pieces of themselves for warmth, and to boys who started running errands for dealers just for a place to sleep. I watched, I listened, and I promised myself: no matter what, I wouldn't become one of them.

Time slid by this way—days into weeks, weeks into months, until…

Three years later, I am still here; still hiding, still pretending.

No one knows I am homeless…at least I hope not. Maybe a few teachers suspect—especially Mr. Danner, the new art teacher, whose eyes linger a little too long—but I've learned to bat away questions with a joke or a smile. People don't ask if you make it easy for them not to see.

And I always, always make it look easy.

But some days, the mask feels too heavy, like it's cracking at the edges, threatening to shatter. On those nights, the silence settles thick as dust, and I remember the first time I opened that door and felt everything I knew slip away.

It was the moment I stopped being a daughter and started fading into the background—a ghost learning how to survive.

Chapter Two:

The Ones Who Vanished

Even now, years later, I can feel the silence in that house—the walls humming with emptiness, the cold floor pressing against my bare feet as I wandered room to room, searching for a sign that my parents were just out of sight. The air hung heavy, filled with the lingering scent of burnt toast and the metallic tang of fear. I remember gripping a chipped mug in my hands, the ceramic icy against my fingertips, waiting for the phone to ring. Each tick of the clock was a needle pressed into my skin; every silent moment stretched longer than the last.

Some people say time heals everything. They are wrong. Time does not heal—it hardens, it silences, and it pushes the memories deeper, where they burrow under your skin like splinters: invisible, yet sharp enough to stab when you least expect it.

Looking back, I realize I replayed that day in my mind, hoping for a different ending. My dad pacing in the kitchen, his shadow flickering against the linoleum as he muttered about bills. My mom is folding laundry; her jaw is set, and her hands work steadily. I asked if I could go to the library after school. She nodded, eyes fixed on a stain in my shirt, never meeting mine. That was our last conversation—the ordinary moment before everything changed.

The worst part? There wasn't a single sign that they'd thought twice about leaving. They left no bag of food for their only child, no whispered goodnight, no apology. There was only emptiness—a silence so loud it throbbed in my ears, drowning out hope.

It's a strange thing, being left by the people who are supposed to love you most. First, you don't believe it. The house feels haunted, not abandoned. You tell yourself there's been a mistake, that maybe they're in trouble or have no choice. But after the second day, when the phone doesn't ring and no car pulls into the driveway, hope curdles inside you—thick and sour, like milk you keep drinking because it's all you have left, even though it makes you sick.

I used to dissect every detail, searching for clues. Was I too loud? Too quiet? Did I push them away, or did they simply stop holding on? Sometimes, I wondered if I was the glue holding them together longer than they wanted, or if my presence was just another weight.

Loneliness settled over me like a chill, a physical ache that pressed against my chest and made it hard to breathe. I felt it most in small moments—the way every sound echoed against the walls, magnified by the emptiness. At night, I lay awake, the sheets cool against my skin, listening for footsteps that never came. My hands gripped my pillow so tightly my knuckles burned, wishing for comfort that was out of reach.

When you're alone long enough, you start to believe you deserve it. You begin to think there's something broken inside you, something others can see that makes them turn away. If your own parents didn't think you were worth staying for, why would anyone else?

But even as I tried to wall myself off, survival forced me forward. I learned small tricks: how to stretch a can of beans over two days, how to patch up holes in my sneakers with duct tape found behind the hardware store, how to fake laughter in front of teachers so they wouldn't ask questions. Independence became my armor, forged not by choice but by necessity.

One night stands out—the first time I decided that being entirely on my own was not how I wanted to live. My stomach was hollow with hunger, my hands shaking as I counted each rough-edged coin I'd scavenged from the bottom of my backpack. The metal felt cold and small against my skin, a reminder of every moment I'd spent searching for what I needed. I chose to buy a loaf of bread instead of another bus ticket, weighing the comfort of food against the fantasy of escape. Sitting on a curb beneath flickering streetlights, I tore off pieces of crust and ate slowly, trying to let the taste fill more than just my stomach, hoping it might patch the emptiness inside me. As I chewed, memories pressed in—the scent of burnt toast in the kitchen, my mom's steady hands folding laundry, and the silent ache that followed their disappearance. That was the night I realized I could survive, even when it hurt. Looking back, I see how that moment shaped me: I stopped waiting for rescue and began searching for ways to take care of myself, one small decision at a time. The resolve I found beneath those streetlights became the thread I held onto in the hardest days that followed.

The worst is when people say, "You're lucky you're so independent." No, I am not lucky. I am abandoned. There is a difference. Independence chosen is freedom. Independence forced is survival!

Occasionally, I dream that my parents might come back. In the dream, I am sitting at the kitchen table, hands wrapped around a mug, the cold seeping through my fingers as the door creaks open. My mom stands there, tears on her cheeks. "We made a mistake," she says. But even in dreams, I stay silent, the pain too real to forgive.

They did not just leave me; they erased me. They built a new life somewhere; one I was not part of. People may have been told I ran away. Maybe they called me troubled. Or maybe no one said a word.

If I ever saw them again, I wonder what I'd say. I imagine myself wanting to scream, demand answers, but I know their words wouldn't fix anything. So instead, I picture myself turning away, walking past them like they are strangers—strangers who once knew my name.

There is still a part of me that aches for them—not for the people they were, but for the parents I imagined. The bedtime stories, the peanut butter sandwiches cut diagonally, the belief that I was loved. I miss those illusions more than I miss them, because missing them would be too much to bear.

Now, late at night, when the world is still and the air presses in, I let myself feel it for a moment—the weight of their absence, the cold that seeps into my bones, the anger, the sadness, the guilt. Then I pull my hoodie tighter, wipe my eyes, and remind myself: They left, but I stayed. They walked away, but I kept going. They quit on me, but I will not quit on myself. Each day, I choose to survive—and, slowly, to become someone in whom I can believe.

Some people say time heals everything.

Chapter Three:

Shelter in Shadows

My parents did not make a sudden decision to leave rather it was a gradual process marked by subtle changes. Disagreements began quietly and were discussed privately. Over time, financial difficulties intensified, leading to increased tension within the household and then they left. I found myself waiting for someone to return for me, but no one ever arrived. I packed my belongings when the landlord knocked and left, entering a world where my presence went largely unnoticed. I was helpless, homeless, and alone.

The first night I slept in the all-night laundromat on Fifth Street. The cold seemed almost secondary to the fear that crept into every corner of my mind. Each unfamiliar sound—a distant car horn, the click of a door, the clatter of coins in a vending machine—felt like a warning meant only for me. I pressed my back against the wall, clutching my backpack to my chest as if it could make me invisible. The cardboard beneath me was damp and curling, but its roughness was small comfort, a reminder that I still took up space in the world. I lay awake, eyes wide, trying to listen past my own heartbeat echoing in my ears. The night was alive with the mingled scents of detergent, machine oil, and the metallic tang of city air.

In those restless hours, I wondered what safety meant. Was it a locked door, a familiar voice, or simply a place where I could close my eyes without fear? My idea of safety had unraveled with my old life, thread by thread. I thought about the way I used to trust the world, how adults noticed and cared, that home was a certainty. Now, I questioned everyone's gaze—was its indifference, suspicion, or pity? Sleeping under the humming fluorescents, I realized I'd begun to see people not as helpers, but as unpredictable variables, sometimes kind, sometimes cruel, mostly just busy with their own lives.

When morning came, I peeled myself off the cardboard, blinking at the too-bright lights, and wandered toward the library, hoping for warmth and a corner to disappear into. The city was gray and slow to wake, the sidewalks shining with last night's rain. At the library, I sank into a battered chair between the stacks of books, the scent of old paper and floor polish grounding me.

The days blurred together in a rhythm of searching and hiding. Each place had its own textures, its own soundtrack: the scratch of paper towels in the school bathroom as I scrubbed my face, the click of my little deodorant stick, the taste of a stale granola bar scavenged from the sidewalk—sweet, gritty, and gone in a rush. The laundromat on Fifth Street became my nighttime shelter when the weather turned bad. Sometimes, I sat beneath the whir of dryers with a dog-eared paperback, pretending I was waiting for my mother to finish laundry. No one asked. The machines filled the silence with their steady hum.

I collected small things to survive—a hoodie left on a park bench, half a granola bar, a nearly empty bottle of apple juice. People didn't notice what they left behind, but I did. Each item became a piece of my armor, a way to carve out comfort in a world that no longer guaranteed safety.

School became my anchor. Most kids dreaded it, but for me, it was a safe zone. Seven hours to feel normal. I became Makenzie Rowe again—quiet, smart, always early with homework. No one knew about my nights behind strip malls and laundromats.

My routine was muscle memory. Go in early. Use my little deodorant stick. Blend in. Swipe food when no one's looking. Try not to be noticed.

No one saw. Or maybe they did and chose not to.

One morning, I arrived at school with a split lip and muddy knees from having tripped and fallen on my way there. My morning was challenging, as my normal routine was disrupted by a disagreement between two newcomers to the homeless community. Ms. Crane, the music teacher, stopped me in the hallway. Her eyes were kind. She smelled like lavender. She asked, "Makenzie, are you okay?" For a second, I thought about telling the truth. I almost did.

But I smiled. "Tripped on the sidewalk. I'm fine." She gave me a look—half-believing but let it go. I learned how easy it was to lie if you packaged it with a smile.

Nights were the hardest. After sunset, the city changed. It got louder, meaner, hungrier. I never stayed in one place for long. Staying invisible was safer. I did not want to be a problem or a target.

I stashed an old, rusty pocketknife under a rock in the park. Holding it made me feel a little safer. Not really, but enough to where I was able to sleep.

I never used it. Didn't want to. But I slept better knowing it was there.

There were moments of grace, small and unexpected. A woman at the convenience store who looked the other way when I took a banana. A janitor who let me linger in the hallway after hours while he mopped the gym floor. An old man who pressed a crumpled dollar into my palm and smiled.

Those moments changed nothing. But they reminded me I wasn't invisible. Sometimes, that was enough.

One night, I made a list in my notebook. It was dumb, but it helped.

Things I Will Do Someday:

1. *Have a room with a door that locks.*

2. *Take a real shower with shampoo and conditioner.*

3. *Eat hot food I didn't steal.*

4. Go to college.

5. Stop crying over people who left.

6. Forgive, but don't forget.

7. Make my life count.

8. Be seen. Truly seen.

I tore the page out and kept it in my backpack, tucked behind a photo—old, from sixth grade, before everything changed. Before I became the girl with no address.

Looking at that photo reminded me of who I used to be and who I was determined to become. Not the broken girl behind the dumpster, not the ghost in the back of the classroom.

Someone who mattered. Someone with a future.

And no one—not even those who abandoned me—could take that away.

Chapter Four:

The First Glimpse

School felt like a performance—a daily ritual where I memorized my lines, avoided any spotlight, and kept my edges blurred. I'd learned early that attention came with questions I couldn't answer, and questions led to places I wasn't ready to revisit. I became an expert at blending in the girl with the silent shoes, the backpack with nothing but essentials and memories.

Until, one day, I slipped.

It was second period—Art with Mr. Danner. I hadn't wanted the class, but speech would have meant standing before people, letting them judge what they couldn't see. I'd spent too long that morning in the gas station bathroom, scrubbing at my hair with cold water that left my fingers tingling and raw. The mirror reflected someone I barely recognized.

I slid into my seat late, hoping no one noticed. Mr. Danner—always ink-stained, always a little apart—didn't turn around. "Makenzie," he said, "pick any medium from the back table. Today we're drawing truth."

Truth. The word pressed against me, heavy and uncomfortable.

He finally looked my way. "Truth as it feels—not as it looks. Use whatever speaks to you. There's charcoal, paint, pencil, even scraps. Make it yours."

I hesitated, then reached for the charcoal. It felt honest: messy, impossible to hide, hard to erase. As I shaded the corner of my paper, my hand trembled, not just from the cold but from something deeper—an old fear of being seen for what I really was. I drew a shadow in the vague shape of a girl, her mouth a blank space where words should have been.

Halfway through, I sensed someone watching. Not the usual passing glance, but something intent and searching. I looked up.

Mr. Danner was neither grading nor speaking; rather, he observed me with a measured curiosity, as if he had experienced a similar situation before. He commented thoughtfully on my drawing: "It is interesting," he noted, acknowledging my work. "While most individuals seek to make themselves visible, you appear to be doing the opposite."

I shrugged, unsure how much to reveal. Invisibility was armor, born of necessity.

He didn't push, just nodded and returned to his desk. The silence he left behind felt like understanding—a rare gift.

During lunch, I sat at my customary spot at the far end of the cafeteria, my back against the chilled wall. I did not have a tray; instead, I brought a bruised apple and a slice of bread. The room buzzed with voices and the clatter of trays, but I floated on the outside, drawn to the comfort of isolation.

That's when I saw her approaching—combat boots scuffed from too many sidewalks, purple hoodie pulled tight, red glasses framing eyes that missed nothing. Lila Moreno. She dropped her tray across from me with an air of belonging that made it seem like we'd always been friends.

"Mind if I sit?" she asked, already settled.

I blinked. "I guess not."

"Cool. People remember my boots before they remember me," she said, tearing into her sandwich. Her honesty was sharp, but not unkind a shield she wore openly.

Lila had a way of talking that made the world seem ridiculous, but survivable. She didn't expect anyone to keep up, but she didn't mind if you tried. "You're in my Art and English class," she continued, mouth half-full. "You drew that ghost girl today, right?"

I stiffened. "She's not a ghost."

"Didn't say she was." She grinned, a flash of mischief and solidarity. "I liked it. Felt like what a secret feels like."

Her words landed somewhere deep. I'd worked hard perfecting my disguise, believing no one could see the cracks.

"You're weird," I said, not unkindly.

"Thank you." She flashed a grin that was all teeth and spark. "So are you."

I didn't know how to respond, but for the first time in a long time I didn't want to be alone.

We sat in companionable silence. The cafeteria's air was thick with the scent of old fries and the hum of fluorescent lights. Lila slid her chips across the table. "Not charity," she insisted. "I don't eat fake cheese. Gives me weird dreams."

I laughed—a sound that startled me, as if laughter had become a stranger lately. The sensation was so unfamiliar, it felt like sunlight cracking through a window I'd forgotten existed.

Lila noticed. "See? You are human." Her eyes softened, and I felt gratitude flicker inside.

When the bell rang, she hefted her backpack with practiced ease. "You ever need someone to walk with after school," she said. "I've got nowhere to be."

"I'm good," I lied, instinct taking over.

"I know." She studied me for a moment longer, then sauntered off, boots echoing on the linoleum.

I stayed seated, feeling something brittle loosen inside—a thaw, fragile and bright. It was as if warmth had crept in when I least expected it, and I didn't trust it, not yet anyway. But it was there.

Two people had seen me—really seen me—and for a
moment, the world felt a little less shadowed, a little
more possible.

Chapter Five:

A Crack in the Mask

Trust was dangerous.

It was something I had locked up so tightly that even I had forgotten where I put the key. Every part of me was trained to run—run from questions, from kindness, from anything that felt even remotely like safety. The last time I believed someone would stay, they did not. They packed up their lives and drove away during the night. So now, kindness did not make me feel warm—it made me feel nervous. Like the second I reached for it, it would vanish.

That's how I felt after the conversation with Mr. Danner. After Lila sat across from me—like she knew, somehow, that I needed someone even when I acted like I didn't.

But I didn't want it. Or maybe some part of me, small and stubborn, did.

That afternoon, I walked out of school at my usual careful pace. My head was down, hoodie up. The sun was sharp, casting long shadows that made everything feel harsher. I crossed behind the gym, took the alley behind the dollar store—my shortcut to nowhere, where there were no cameras, no eyes.

But this time, someone followed.

"Hey!" Lila's voice called from behind. "Slow down, track star!"

I froze. My heart slammed into my ribs. Instinct told me to run. But she was already jogging up, her bag bouncing against her hip—a denim patch sewn on, "Property of Nowhere High." She caught her breath and grinned. "Didn't mean to scare you," she said. "You just vanished."

"That's kind of the point," I muttered.

She raised an eyebrow, mouth quirking in a half-smile. "You serious? You live in a spy novel or something?" She didn't ask to tag along; she just matched her pace to mine. She fiddled with a keychain—a tiny wrench— hanging from her backpack. "My stepdad fixes cars. Used to drag me to the garage, teach me how to listen for what was off. People are kind of the same, you know? You just got to listen."

I turned away, trying not to let her words land. "Why are you following me?"

"I'm not. I just figured we'd walk together." She glanced over, then added, "Anyway, the cafeteria is brutal after lunch. I'd rather be anywhere else."

Her honesty threw me off. For a moment, I couldn't find a reason to push her away.

I shook my head. "I've got somewhere to be."

"Okay," she said, softer now. "Is it somewhere important?"

I nodded.

She tucked a strand of hair behind her ear, shrugged. "See you tomorrow, maybe?"

Her boots scuffed the pavement as she turned back, and I stood there long after she was gone, wondering why it suddenly felt so hard to breathe.

That night, I did not sleep.

I curled under a tarp near the loading dock behind a mattress store, the cement still warm from the day, the air turning cold fast. I stared at the sliver of sky between rooftops and tried not to think about Lila's face, or the way Mr. Danner looked at my drawing like it meant something. Like I meant something.

That was what I didn't know how to handle. Being seen.

Being invisible was painful, but at least it was safe. No one could damage what they couldn't touch. But what if I let someone in—would they leave, too?

The next morning, I sat on the library bathroom floor, cleaned up as best I could. I'd found a pair of clean socks at a donation box—thick, mismatched, but they felt amazing. I redid my braid, used a little lip balm, and forced myself to smile in the mirror.

It's just another girl going to school—not a big deal.

The bell rang, and I slid into art class right before the tardy bell. Mr. Danner glanced up, gave a small nod.

He handed out sketchbooks. "Today's exercise: self-portrait, no mirrors. Draw how you feel, not how you look. No one else will see it unless you want them to."

He moved through the room, pausing by a kid who never spoke and murmuring, "Try using color, Will. You might like the chaos." It wasn't just me he noticed; he had a way of making everyone feel less alone, whether they wanted it or not.

I stared at the blank page. How did I feel?

Lost, tired…small, but still fighting!

My pencil moved before I could think. I drew my outline first—slumped shoulders, oversized hoodie, sharp lines where soft ones used to be. Then I sketched flames behind me, like I'd walked through fire and come out the other side. Charred but standing.

When I looked up, Mr. Danner caught my eye. He gave me the faintest nod of respect, then drifted to the next desk, encouraging, never lingering.

At lunch, Lila showed up again. Of course she did.

"Thought I'd find you here," she said, dropping into the seat across. She pushed a plastic baggie toward me. "Brought you a peanut butter and banana sandwich. Don't judge—my mom used to make them on rough days."

I blinked. "I didn't ask for this."

"I know," she said. "That's what makes it not charity."

I stared at the sandwich like it might explode. It was still warm, carefully wrapped, so different from the cold bologna sandwiches handed out at shelters. My stomach twisted—part hunger, part caution. The last time someone gave me food like this; it was followed by expectations I couldn't meet.

This was different, but I couldn't trust that yet. It was just a sandwich, but it felt like more—a dare to believe in something good, even for a second.

So, I hesitated, then took a bite.

Lila's grin was wide, teasing. "Progress!"

We ate in silence. She glanced at her phone, then at me. "My mom works double shifts, so I'm on my own most nights. Not as glamorous as it sounds. That's why I hang around after school."

I nodded, understanding more than I wanted to admit.

She asked, "So, where do you go after school?"

I froze as if my secret was written on my forehead. She held up her hands. "Hey, I'm not following you. I just... I notice things."

I swallowed. "Nowhere in particular."

She gave me a long look. "You don't need to tell me. But if you ever want to, I'll listen. Ask no questions, make no judgments that's my motto."

I wanted to believe her. More than anything, I wanted someone to know. But not yet. Not today.

So, I just nodded. She seemed to understand.

That night, under the streetlamp's buzz, I opened my notebook and added something to the list I kept tucked in the back:

Things I Will Do Someday:

9. *Tell someone the truth.*

Only once, without fear, and maybe, just maybe…let them stay.

Chapter Six:

Rules of Survival

Survival had rules.

They weren't written, handed to me like a map when I was thirteen and left suddenly adrift in an empty kitchen, wondering what invisible mistake I'd made. I pieced them together through experience—sometimes painful, always instructive.

Rule One: Don't trust anyone, no matter how gentle their words.

Rule Two: Don't linger anywhere for too long.

Rule Three: Blend in, even if it means hiding yourself behind a practiced smile.

Rule Four: Never cry in front of others.

Those rules kept me safe, but they also kept me alone. Most days, loneliness was better than being discovered.

After Lila's unexpected kindness and Mr. Danner's searching glance and the memory of my sketch—flames swallowing a girl—I felt an unfamiliar ache. It was the sensation of something shifting inside me, a slow, persistent leak in the roof I'd tried so hard to waterproof.

Trust, I'd learned, always started small. A drip, a crack, a whisper of hope.

The person I used to be—the one who watched movies with her mother and sang along to her father's off-key tunes—would have reached for help. But that version of me had vanished, replaced by someone careful and silent.

Rain hammered down as I left school that afternoon, each drop cold against my skin as I hurried through alleys and bus shelters, checking my usual spots for the night. All were either too exposed or flooded.

By dusk, I was outside the old laundromat on 9th Street. It felt safer than the one on fifth, and the owner had quietly given me a key to its broken back door months earlier. I slipped inside, greeted by the humid air, the sour-sweet scent of soap and mildew. The warmth wrapped around me like a worn blanket. I tucked myself behind the dryers, knees to chest, listening to the hum and clatter of the machines.

Even here, I couldn't let myself settle. My rules reminded me—never too long, never too comfortable.

As the night deepened, I let myself cry, silent and hidden. The sound of rain on the windows mingled with the steady thrum of the machines, and for the first time in a long while, I wished someone would notice.

Dawn crept slowly, gray, and hesitant. I woke to the soft clink of quarters in a distant machine and the gentle warmth that lingered in the steam-filled air. My limbs were stiff, my eyes gritty. I listened to the city waking: delivery trucks rumbling, birds chattering, the distant echo of lives I wasn't part of.

Stepping outside, the morning felt like a shock—fresh, damp, and alive with the scent of wet pavement and blooming weeds. I paused in the alley, breath steaming, and let the cold bite of the day remind me I was still here.

School was another world, sterile and bright. In the bathroom, I changed into clean clothes, wiped away the night's tears, and tried to smooth my hair into a braid—each gesture an attempt to rebuild the mask. The hallway buzzed with voices and the clang of lockers. I moved quietly, the ache of last night echoing in my chest.

Still, something was different. The mask felt thinner—like it might slip if I didn't hold it tight.

At lunch, Lila sat across from me, her presence determined but gentle. She set down two juice boxes and granola bars without a word, her nails chipped from nervous picking, her gaze steady but wary. She toyed with the wrapper, glancing at me, then away, lips pressed together in thought.

"You look tired," she said softly.

"I'm always tired."

Her brow furrowed, and her fingers fidgeted with the edge of her sleeve. "Do you ever think about telling someone?" she asked, voice almost a whisper.

I stiffened. "Telling them what?"

She shrugged, but her eyes held something more— a quiet worry, a hope she couldn't quite voice. "That you're not okay."

I forced a brittle smile. "I'm fine."

She hesitated, searching for my face. "Mak—"

I cut her off, my words a wall. "I said I'm fine." My voice was sharper than I intended, and I watched her flinch ever so slightly, shoulders hunching in retreat. She nodded, pressing her lips together, the granola bar untouched between us. We finished lunch in silence, the distance between us stretching wider.

I saw the way she lingered at the table, how she glanced back as she left—uncertain, maybe hurt, maybe just trying to understand. I hated that I'd made her doubt, that I'd pushed her away.

After school, I slipped into the library. The warmth, the hush, the gentle shuffle of pages—it was the closest thing to comfort I had. I retreated to the back corner, surrounded by tall shelves and the scent of old paper.

There, I pulled out my notebook-the one with the list.

I found #9: *Tell someone the truth.*

I crossed it out, my hand trembling.

Then I wrote it again, the ink darker this time.

My thoughts spun: Did I want to be seen, or did I just want to disappear? It appeared that there was an internal conflict developing within my thoughts.

Night returned, and with it, the laundromat's familiar hum. As I curled behind the dryers, I thought about Lila—her red glasses, her stubborn kindness, her quiet concern. I wondered if, after today, she'd ever try again.

I remembered Mr. Danner too—his attentive eyes as he watched me draw, the way he lingered after class, offering extra supplies or a wordless nod.

Once, he had pressed a note into my palm: "Art can say what words can't. You don't have to be alone with it."

I clung to that line, wondering what he saw, how much he understood.

Would either of them look at me differently if they knew where I slept, how I lived? Would they see me as broken, or would they still try to reach me?

Rule Five: Don't let hope in. It hurts more to lose than never to have.

I held my notebook tightly, pressing it against my chest as if it could shield me from my own longing. For the first time, I allowed myself to imagine breaking the rules—just enough to let someone in.

But for now, I remained hidden, the mask safely in place.

Still, somewhere inside, a fragile hope persisted that someone might tear down my walls and say,

"I see you"

Chapter Seven:

The Essay

It started with a worksheet, a blank page with just a prompt printed at the top in bold letters:

"Write about a moment that changed your life."

I stared at it for five straight minutes during first-period English, my pencil still on the desk. Around me, the steady scrape of lead filled the silence, punctuated by the occasional cough or shuffle of sneakers on linoleum. Everyone immediately began writing, but I hesitated, needing a moment to think.

Only one moment came to mind. The moment when my parents stopped being my parents.

However, I am unable to address that subject currently or in this context.

So, I sat there, paralyzed, hoping the bell would ring before I had to pretend.

Mrs. Callahan circled the room like she always did, her steps muffled by the thin, industrial carpet. She peered at notebooks, offered nods or whispering suggestions. When she passed my desk, I angled my page away, feeling the rough paper graze my wrist.

She stopped. "Makenzie, is everything okay?"

"Fine," I said, my voice flat. "Just thinking."

She smiled gently. "You're allowed to write fiction if that helps. Just as long as it's something meaningful."

I nodded as she moved on.

I recognized that my experiences did not resemble those found in fiction, and I was uncertain about how to fabricate stories in writing.

After class, students mingled in the hallways talking about football, homework, games, and parties. I slipped away to one of my usual hiding places—under the staircase near the science wing. The concrete was cold against my legs, and the faint scent of cleaning fluid mixed with something musty lingered in the air. The distant clang of lockers slamming echoed through the empty corridor above. I took out my notebook, which had a list on the last page, and a drawing of a girl surrounded by flames.

I flipped to a blank page.

"A moment that changed my life..."

I wrote the words, then stopped.

My hand hovered over the page. The truth screamed to get out, but I still did not trust the sound of it.

So instead, I wrote around it..." No explosion, no sirens—just silence."

It wasn't everything, but it was my story and a beginning.

Later, when I handed it in, I folded the paper tightly, the edges creased and softened by my anxious fingers. It was anonymous—like a confession I could not undo.

Mrs. Callahan reads our papers aloud every Friday. I wished she'd skip me. I hoped she would see the weight of it and decide to protect whoever had written it.

Friday morning came, bringing with it the smell of burnt coffee from the faculty lounge and the sleepy shuffle of students settling into their seats. She stood at the front of the room with a stack of papers in her hand.

"Today's essays were some of the most honest I've seen all year," she said. "I'd like to read a few—anonymously, of course. I think you'll see yourselves in each other's words."

I shrank in my seat, tracing the chipped edge of the desktop.

She read one about a broken arm at summer camp. Another story was about a father returning home from overseas deployment. Then she unfolded mine.

Her voice was steady, even as the words wavered.

"No explosion, no sirens—just silence."

The class fell quiet. There were no whispers, no snickering; just silence, the kind of silence I felt. And now, they were all standing in it too.

She finished and paused.

"Whoever wrote this—thank you."

My stomach twisted. My cheeks burned. I looked down and counted the stitches in my hoodie cuff just to stay grounded.

No one knew it was me. And somehow, that made it worse.

At lunch, I tried to hide in my usual corner of the cafeteria, beside a rattling vending machine and a window that fogged up from damp boots tracking in melting snow. It didn't work.

Lila found me.

She stood across the table, arms crossed, instead of sitting down immediately.

"That was yours, wasn't it?"

I didn't answer.

"I knew it," she whispered. "I could feel it. It sounded like you."

Still, I stayed silent.

"I get it," she added. "You're scared someone will see too much. But... you want to be seen, too. Don't you?"

I looked up. I didn't smile.

"I don't know what I want."

She finally sat, opened her apple juice, took a sip. The scent of tart apples lingered between us.

"I do. I want you to have a day where you don't have to hide from everyone."

I blinked hard. "That's never going to happen."

"Why not?"

I shook my head. "Because even if I told the truth, it would change nothing. It would not give me a house, or parents, or a normal life."

"No," she said. "But it might give you someone who doesn't walk away."

The words hit me so hard I forgot to breathe.

As night fell, I couldn't find a dry place to sleep. The all-night laundromat was closed for repairs, and the mattress store's loading dock was blocked by construction tape. The 9th Street laundromat now had a fixed door secured with a new padlock beneath the streetlights. I checked two other spots. One had police officers near it, the blue and red lights flashing against the brick. Someone had taken the other bigger, spot, he was bigger, older, with a Pitbull at his side, its low growl warning me away.

So, I wandered the streets for hours, the cold biting through my jacket, searching for a new safe place. My breath rose in silver clouds as I made my way past shuttered shops and puddles reflecting neon.

I ended up behind a church near the freeway, half-sheltered by a stone wall slick with moss. The traffic thundered overhead, a constant low rumble. I huddled beneath my tarp, the plastic crinkling in the wind, notebook cradled like a heartbeat.

And for the first time in a long time, I whispered something out loud:

"I don't want to do this forever."

The next morning, bleary-eyed and stiff, I went to the library as soon as it opened. The warmth hit me as I stepped inside, the faint scent of old paper and brewing coffee wrapping around me. I found a quiet corner, pulled out a clean sheet of paper, and wrote something different:

"My name is Makenzie Rowe. I am sixteen years old. I go to Eastside High. And I am homeless."

Then I stared at it. Read it. Read it again.

I folded it, put it in my backpack, and didn't throw it away.

It was not a plan.

It was not a scream.

But it was a voice.

My voice.

For now, it remained silent.

Chapter Eight

Unwanted Attention

It started with a knock at the classroom door. I was halfway through second period—Biology—watching Mr. Jensen sketch a sloppy heart on the whiteboard trying to stay awake. My head felt heavy, my eyes gritty from lack of sleep. When the knock came, the whole class froze and looked towards the door.

The assistant principal, Mrs. Danvers, stood in the doorway, clipboard in hand, her gaze sweeping the room. I felt her eyes snag on me and a chill ran down my spine.

"Makenzie Rowe?" Her voice was calm, measured.

I swallowed, pulse hammering, and nodded. "Yes?"

"Could you come with me, please?"

Every set of eyes followed me as I gathered my things. I tried to walk steadily, arms closed, resisting the urge to shrink into myself. Don't panic. Don't show it. Smile if you must.

The hallway was colder than the classroom, and each step sounded louder than the lastl. Mrs. Danvers didn't speak as she led me past the trophy cases and locked doors, her heels a steady metronome to my nervous thoughts.

"Have a seat," she said, gesturing toward the soft chair outside the counselor's office. The air inside prickled against my skin—too much artificial brightness, the hum of the copier, the faint scent of lemon from a nearby cleaning cart. I clung to my backpack and tried to slow my breathing.

Time seemed to stretch. I studied the framed affirmations on the wall— "Your story matters." "Kindness is strength." "Speak your truth."—but the words felt distant, like they belonged to someone else.

Ms. Hill opened her door, her smile gentle but searching. "Makenzie, come in."

I sat across from her. She folded her hands together, as if bracing herself for something delicate.

"I want you to know," she began softly, "you're not in any trouble."

My heart squeezed tighter. If I wasn't in trouble, why was I here?

She took a breath. "Your English teacher shared a writing assignment you turned in this week. It was raw, honest, and… it raised some concerns."

Heat rose in my cheeks. I glanced at the wilting plant on her desk, at the clock ticking slow above the door. "I didn't put my name on it."

"I know," she said gently. "But the details felt personal. Your teacher asked me to check in."

"It was fiction," I said quickly, voice catching.

Ms. Hill didn't move. For a moment, she let the silence settle, her eyes steady on mine. "Makenzie, we attempted to contact your parents at your previous address, but it appears they no longer reside there." There was a brief pause before continuing: "Have you relocated? What is your current address?"

The question hung in the air—sharp and heavy.

I paused, then replied casually, "With a friend."

"Can I ask for the address?"

I hesitated. "She moves a lot. Her mom's got custody issues."

Ms. Hill nodded, jotting something on a pad. "Do you feel safe there?"

"Yes."

"Are you able to get food, clothing? Do you have a place to sleep?"

I nodded—too quickly, betraying myself.

She studied my face. "Makenzie, if things aren't okay, you don't have to deal with it alone. We can help."

But help was a trap. Help meant paperwork, visits, group homes, strangers. Help meant losing the scraps of life I'd pieced together.

"I'm fine," I said, almost whispering.

Ms. Hill's sigh was soft, but it lingered. "If you ever need anything—anything at all—come straight to me. My door is always open."

Outside the door, I paused. The hallway seemed endless. I paused, leaning against the cool wall with my eyes shut, as the faint scent of floor polish and coffee lingered. My hands trembled, and I wished I could disappear.

Eventually, I slipped into the bathroom, locking myself in a stall. I sank onto the closed toilet seat, pressing my forehead against the metal. My thoughts spun, too fast and too loud. They know—maybe not everything, but enough. I'd broken the rule: no attention, no exposure.

For a long time, I stayed there, listening to the muffled sounds of footsteps and voices echoing through tile. When the final bell rang, signaling the end of school, I waited until the traffic outside faded and the building quieted. Only then did I emerge, blinking into the late afternoon light.

Instead of my usual routine—heading straight to the library—I wandered. The hours blurred together as I drifted through the city, past the skate park with graffiti-stained ramps, down cracked sidewalks, past the boarded-up gas station and the thrift shop where the neon sign flickered out most of its letters. The world felt too big, and I felt too small inside it.

Later, I found myself on a park bench near the river, the wind snapping at my hoodie, the water glinting cold. I watched the ripples move and tried not to cry.

I'd spent so long working to stay invisible. Why did writing the truth—just a few sentences—feel like I'd set everything on fire?

That night, sleep didn't find me in the laundromat or behind the mattress store. Instead, I curled up under the awning of a bus stop, backpack clutched tight, listening for footsteps as the city slowed around me.

Ms. Hill's voice echoed in my mind. "We can help."

But help came with consequences. If I let someone in, I'd have to be ready to lose everything I'd built.

Yet, as I lay there listening to the distant hum of traffic, I realized I wasn't carrying it all alone anymore. For the first time since my parents vanished, the truth was no longer mine alone to bear.

And I wasn't sure if that was terrifying—or something like hope.

Chapter Nine:

Fractures

The next morning, I didn't want to go to school. My body was heavy with exhaustion, my mind running through half-remembered dreams of doors closing and voices fading. But I went anyway—because school, because of all its fluorescent chill and echoing hallways, was the only place left where I belonged to something, even if only on a roster.

My steps echoed on linoleum. The city outside felt indifferent, the sidewalks glazed with last night's rain and the air was sharp enough to sting my nose. I tried to breathe slow and steady—the way Dad used to tell me, "Count your breaths when you're scared, Mak. Give your heart something to hold on to." I remembered sitting on our old couch, tracing the constellations in the popcorn ceiling, listening to the television murmur in the next room. That was before everything changed.

Now, someone had read my words—words I'd meant to bury, not share—and I was left exposed, nerves raw and aching.

When I reached the front steps, I spotted Lila perched on the railing, orange juice in hand, swinging her legs like she didn't have a care in the world. The sight of her, so nonchalant, ached somewhere small and secret in my chest.

She smiled as I walked toward her, yet there was also a fleeting look in her eyes—something gentler, perhaps a bit cautious. "Hey there! Thought you'd pulled a Houdini yesterday."

I hesitated, rubbing my palm against the cold stone. "Can I ask you something?"

"Sure," she said, lowering her drink.

"Did you… say anything? To anyone about my essay?"

Her eyebrow arched in genuine confusion, then dropped. "No. I wouldn't. That's your story, not mine."

I searched her face for any sign of a lie, but all I found was a flash of hurt. She looked away, picking at the corner of her juice carton. "Mak, you don't have to trust me. But I'm not here to break you open."

"I'm sorry," I stammered. "I just—someone knew. I thought maybe—"

She interrupted, her voice quiet but steady. "My mom left when I was twelve. I know what it's like to feel like the floor's going to drop out from under you. That's why I stuck around. Not because you need to be saved. Just… sometimes it helps to know someone won't leave."

The words hung between us, delicate as spider silk, and for a moment I saw her—a person with her own fractures, not just the girl with jokes and orange juice.

But the shame pressed in. "I shouldn't have accused you," I said softly.

She shrugged, her hands trembling. "It's hard to trust people who stay. I understand."

A sudden urge to bolt seized me, like the ground was tilting beneath my feet. The school doors loomed, the crowd inside a blur of noise and movement. I needed space.

So, I turned away. The cold bit through my hoodie as I stepped off the path, every footfall a pulse of adrenaline. The world narrowed to the rhythm of my breath, the slap of my shoes on wet pavement. The confrontation with Lila crackled inside me—anger, regret, fear—and I let the city absorb it.

I walked. Past sagging bus benches and the smell of wet concrete, past the old playground where I once spent a summer afternoon spinning in circles, dizzy on laughter and sunlight. Back when my parents' laughter filled the air and home wasn't just a word that ached.

I made it to the bridge by the train tracks before my legs buckled. I dropped my backpack and folded into myself, letting the wind gnaw at my knuckles. The water below was dark with morning shadow, flecked with silver from a rising sun.

I pulled out my notebook, fingers stiff and ink smudging as I flipped to the list:

#1   Have a room with a door that locks

#2   Take a real shower

#3   Eat hot food I did not have to steal

#4   Go to college

#5   Never cry again over people who left

#6   Forgive, not forget

#7   Make my life count

#8   Be seen

#9   Tell someone the truth

In the hush of the riverbank, memories surfaced—my mother's humming as she made eggs, the warmth of her hand on my forehead when I was sick. I pressed my thumb to the paper, wishing I could press those memories into the present.

I added another line:

#10   Don't hurt the people trying to help.

Lila's face came back to me—not the grin, but the softer look I'd seen that morning, the one that said she was fighting her own battles too.

When I returned to school, the halls were mostly empty, haunted by the scent of pencils and floor wax. I drifted to the library, tucked myself behind a stack of outdated encyclopedias, and let the minutes bleed away until the bell rang.

When the corridors flooded with noise, I moved with the crowd, invisible as smoke. At her locker, Lila was shoving books into her bag, a frown creasing in her forehead.

I moved in quietly, heart hammering. No rehearsed apology, just the truth, raw as a scraped knee. "Hey."

She didn't look up. "What's up?"

"You were right," I said, voice ragged.

She paused, one hand still on her backpack. "About?"

"That I didn't trust you. I'm not used to people sticking around. I panicked."

She finally met my gaze, searching for my face. "You pulled it loud yesterday," she said, a ghost of a smile tugging at her mouth.

I nodded. "If I do it again, you can steal my hoodie."

Her smile grew, small but real. "Deal."

In the quiet that followed, I noticed the faded friendship bracelet on her wrist—a single blue bead missing. "You know, sometimes I think about leaving," she said suddenly, so soft I almost missed it. "But then I remember how it felt when no one stayed for me. I'd rather be here."

Something loosened in my chest.

That night, I curled up under the metal awning behind the mattress store. The wind rattled the side, and the city's glow painted the sky a dull orange. I listened to the hum of distant cars, the shifting quiet that settled near dawn.

I pulled out my notebook again, put a check by #10, and underlined #9.

For the first time, the truth was not just a burden. It was a promise, fragile but real. And in the hush between memories and morning, I let myself hope.

Chapter Ten:

Smoke and Mirrors

The fire alarm went off during third period.

One moment, I was taking notes in history; the next, a piercing wail shattered the classroom's quiet. My pencil slipped from my fingers. Desks scraped, books snapped shut, and Mr. Reyes shouted something over the noise, but no one listened—we were already halfway out the door.

I kept my head down in the surge of students, blending into the current as we spilled into the hallway. Outside, the wind slapped cold against my cheeks, biting through my hoodie. On the soccer field, everyone clustered in loose knots, laughing, scrolling their phones. Most treated it like another break from class. But I could never relax when alarms blared.

Since my parents' departure and my subsequent life on the streets, the sound of sirens has become a persistent aspect of my daily experience. It's like a flame burning each time they wail, and I'm reminded of all I lost; fear rises, sharp and insistent, echoing through the hollow spaces where my life used to be.

"You okay?" he asked, voice nearly lost in the wind.

I nodded, not trusting myself to speak. He studied me for a moment, patient.

"You sure?"

I nodded again.

Mr. Danner didn't press. We stood side by side in silence, letting the cold and the noise settle around us like a second skin.

"I read your last self-portrait," he said after a while," the one with flames flickering behind the figure."

I stiffened. "You said no one else would see it," I managed, my words sharper than intended.

He nodded. "I didn't show it. I just wanted you to know it mattered. It said something real."

"It's just a drawing," I muttered, turning away.

"No," he replied quietly. "It's a voice."

That word again. Voice. I didn't know what to do with it.

When the alarm finally ended and teachers began herding us back inside, I lingered on the field, letting the crowd thin. Mr. Danner didn't follow. He just let me be. That meant more than I could say.

I moved through the rest of the day in a haze. In our old house, alarms meant a fight or a fire, my mother's shouts, my father's silence, the crash of something breaking. Back then, they'd pick up the pieces. That hope was dangerous—too sharp, too bright.

During lunch, I spotted Lila across the cafeteria with the theater kids, her laughter bright and easy. I didn't join her; I didn't want to intrude on her happiness. She caught my gaze anyway, lifted her chin as if to say-I see you, but I won't make a scene. Somehow, that was enough.

I sat alone, but this time, it felt like a choice instead of a sentence.

Later, in study period, I slipped into the art room. Mr. Danner was sorting canvases. He glanced up as I entered.

"No class now," he said, not unkindly.

"I know."

He gestured to the open table. "Want to paint?"

I nodded. I let my hands find a brush, dipped it in blue and black, and let color spill onto canvas—stormy sky, no sun, a small, faceless girl standing in the corner.

When I finished, my fingers smeared with paint and my heart thudding, I slid the canvas away. Mr. Danner came closer to look.

"She's still there," he murmured." Despite everything, she stands."

"I didn't want her to disappear," I said quietly.

He met my eyes. "Neither do I."

Something tightened in my throat; I turned away before it could show.

After school, the weight of the day lingered as I wandered through the city, searching for somewhere I could breathe.

That night, I didn't sleep in any of my usual spots. Instead, I walked south—toward unfamiliar blocks, a little more dangerous, a little less forgiving. But I needed the distance, the edge. I needed to prove I could still manage unpredictability, that I hadn't gone soft just because someone noticed my pain.

In an alley behind a music store, I huddled beneath my tarp and coat. Cold, uneven ground pressed into my legs; the air was thick with smoke, rust, and rain.

As I drifted toward sleep, I thought about the fire alarm, the red lights, the shouting, and the chaos. And how, even in all that noise, someone had found me in my silence.

Chapter Eleven:

Before the Silence

The situation evolved over time. There was no single moment when the decision was made to leave; rather, it occurred through a series of subtle changes and understated shifts. The deterioration was not dramatic but rather marked by quiet resignation.

When I was twelve, the nature of my parents' arguments changed. Previously, their disagreements were vocal and intense, typically concerning matters such as bills, groceries, and chores. This indicated ongoing engagement between them. Over time, the arguments lessened, and family dynamics shifted at home.

My father increasingly arrived home late, carrying the scent of alcohol. My mother often sat at the kitchen table, coffee untouched, focused on the same page of the newspaper for extended periods. They interacted minimally, passing each other without engagement. I simply occupied the space between them, present yet largely overlooked.

I did chores without being asked, hoping they'd notice. They didn't.

I made my own lunch, stopped asking for help, and quit reminding them about meetings—each reminder seemed to hurt my mom. They were drifting away, and no matter what I did, I couldn't hold on.

The week before they left, I came home from school one day and found the hallway closet open. Empty hangers dangled in the half-light. Dust outlines showed where boxes used to be. The air felt heavier—still holding the faint scent of my dad's aftershave, sharper in the emptiness.

I walked through the house slowly, heart pounding, each room quieter than the last. Their bedroom was still full, but less so. My dad's guitar was missing and so were the framed photos from the bookshelf. I opened the bathroom cabinet; her makeup bag was missing, but the toothbrushes remained—a pair in the cup, side by side, like nothing had changed there.

Two nights later, I sat at the kitchen table, pencil tapping against my notebook as I stared at the half-finished math problems. The hum of the refrigerator filled the silence, and the scent of lemon soap lingered in the air as my mom scrubbed the same dish for the third time, her movements slow and deliberate.

I looked up. "Are we moving?"

She blinked, not meeting my eyes. "Why do you ask?"

I shrugged, forcing my voice to sound casual. "Because the hallway closet 'is empty."

She glanced over her shoulder, gaze skimming past me before settling back on the sink. "We're just cleaning out some things."

"Are you and Dad okay?"

Her fingers tightened on the dish, knuckles pale. Another pause.

"We're fine."

That was it.

Not "yes." Not "of course." Just fine.

A word that meant nothing and everything.

I tried to convince myself it was true, but the tightness in my chest wouldn't let me believe it. I focused on the kitchen light reflecting off the soap bubbles, willing myself to accept her answer, to ignore the way she avoided my eyes and how the conversation slipped away like water down the drain. Instead, I felt the space between us fill with everything unsaid, thickening the air until I could hardly breathe.

The last night I saw them, I don't think I slept at all.

I got up around 2 a.m. and walked quietly to the living room. The TV was off. The lights were low. My dad sat in the recliner, staring at nothing. My mom stood by the door, her purse on her shoulder.
I stayed still, unnoticed.

She looked at him. "We should leave tonight."
He didn't answer at first.

She glanced at me briefly, surprised, then looked away without acknowledging my presence.

"I'm not ready,"
"Get ready," she said, her voice flat—gritty as sand.

I waited for him to stand up. He didn't. I waited for her to walk out. She didn't. They just sat in silence. A cold knot tightened in my stomach as the silence stretched on, making me feel forgotten, small. I wondered if they felt it, too—the quiet so thick it pressed in on my chest, each second dragging out until even the sound of my own breath seemed too loud. Still, neither moved. The room was full of words left unsaid, and I stood there, hidden afraid to break the spell.

I returned to bed, telling myself it was just another argument, and they'd be there in the morning. But when I woke, they were gone, leaving only the smell of coffee and an empty toothbrush cup by the bathroom sink.

I made my own toast, the scent of scorched bread lingering in the air, and ate it in silence. The taste was bland, but each bite felt heavy, almost like I was swallowing the quiet itself. As I stared at the empty kitchen, for the first time I felt truly alone. I didn't call anyone for help. I didn't cry. Instead, I sat listening to the emptiness, feeling as it smothering me— frightening, unfamiliar, and somehow, full of possibility. Whatever came next, was on me.

People imagine abandonment as a storm—doors slamming, voices cracking, engines roaring down the street, dramatic, messy, impossible to ignore.

But for me, it crept quietly. No footsteps down the hall. No car peeling off. Just the silence, cold and dense, settling around me like a heavy blanket. It pressed against my chest, thicker than any shouted word.

Others expect chaos, the kind you can hear echoing through the house. But all I felt was emptiness—deafening and absolute. No note, No explanation, just absence.

And somehow, that made it worse.

Because they didn't even give me the dignity of an explanation.

As I lay behind the church remembering that day I slowly woke up with tightness in my chest. The pavement beneath me was cool, gritty against my palms as I pushed myself upright. A faint smell of damp earth mingled with the metallic tang of morning air. The sun was slowly rising, and the streetlamps were flickering off, their light giving way to a bruised, blue dawn. Somewhere beyond the fence, sparrows shrieked at the world to wake.

I reached into my backpack and pulled out my notebook, its edges softened from being handled so often and flipped to the list. My fingers hovered over the page, but I didn't write anything new this time.

I just sat there, feeling the weight of everything I hadn't said. A memory rose—my mother's laugh echoing down the hallway, the warmth of her hand steadying me before sleep. I wanted to hold onto it, but it slipped away from me like water.

Regret prickled at the edges of my mind, sharp and persistent: What if I'd asked them to stay? What if I'd spoken up, instead of shrinking into the background? The possibility of forgiveness, of closure, felt impossibly distant. I pressed my thumb to the paper, wishing it could absorb my hope, my anger, my longing.

Thinking about the girl I used to be, and the version of me they never got to meet because I'd grown up without them. And whether they ever came back or not—I wasn't their little girl anymore.

Chapter Twelve:

The Ask

It did not happen in some big, cinematic moment.

There was no crash, no scream, no dramatic fall to the floor.

It happened in the hallway—on a Tuesday—when my body just gave out on me.

I had made it halfway through the day on a stale granola bar and three hours of sleep. The cold had crept into my bones overnight, and it had not left. I could feel it in my spine, in the heaviness behind my eyes. I kept blinking, trying to stay sharp, trying to stay there.

But between third and fourth period, the hallway started tilting sideways.

It started with the edges of my vision fuzzing out—just a little. Like my eyes were fogged glass.

I leaned against a locker, hoping no one noticed. Students passed me, laughing, bumping shoulders, scrolling through their phones. My backpack felt heavier than usual, straps biting into my tired shoulders.

I breathed in, then out, focused on the floor tiles, the pattern, and the rhythm. But my legs did not get the memo. My knees wobbled. my hand grabbed the metal handle of a locker and clung to it as my backpack slipped from my shoulder.

Someone brushed past me. They muttered "Watch it," but I could not hear them clearly. The world seemed to fade out at the edges.

And then… Mr. Danner was there.

"Makenzie?" His voice was low, urgent.

I looked up, blinking slowly. "I'm okay."

I wished I could tell him the truth—that I was anything but that every part of me was tired and scared. But the words jammed, lodged behind my teeth. What if he saw right through me? What if he thought I was weak, or worse, a burden? For a split second, I wanted to disappear; to shrink so small nobody would ask anything at all.

He did not believe me. I saw it in the set of his jaw—a softness mixed with worry.

"Come with me," he said, already guiding me by the elbow; not pulling, just steadying. As we left the hallway, I felt an odd mix of relief and embarrassment. Passing through the school's clamor into the quiet of his classroom, I realized how tense my shoulders had become, how much I'd been holding together.

He did not take me to the nurse's office. I do not know why—he saw in my face that I would not go. Instead, we slipped into his classroom. It was empty, the lights dim, the walls papered in art and brushstrokes. The room smelled faintly of old paint and pencil shavings.

He pointed to a stool by the sink, so I sat. He provided me with water.

"Drink slowly," he said.

I sipped, my hands trembling slightly.

"I didn't eat," I mumbled.

He nodded, crouched in front of me. "When's the last time you did?"

I looked away, shame curling in my stomach. I wanted to say "yesterday," but I wasn't sure it was true.

I didn't say anything and that was answer enough.

He did not speak right away, just let the quiet hang between us. I liked that about him. He did not rush to fill silences the way most adults did. I remember a time, years ago, when my mother would sit beside me in the dark, saying nothing, and somehow her presence was enough. I miss that.

Finally, he said, "You don't have to tell me anything. But if you need help, I'm listening."

I stared at the floor, searching for words that wouldn't betray me. A memory flashed—me clutching my notebook, scrawling wishes I'd never say aloud, wanting so badly for someone to notice but terrified they would.

"I don't want to go to a shelter," I whispered. "Or some system, or a stranger's house."

He nodded. "I'm not here to force you anywhere."

Tears sprang up in my eyes without warning. I blinked fast, furious at myself.

"It's just… I'm tired," I said. "I'm tired of acting like I'm okay with waking up cold. Of wondering where I'll sleep next. I keep waiting for it to get better, but it doesn't."

He did not flinch. He did not look away.

"Makenzie," he whispered, "that's not weakness. That's survival. But you don't have to do it alone anymore."

I shook my head. "I don't want to be someone's charity case."

"You are not," he remarked. "You are entitled to stability, as I was—a secure environment, suitable accommodation, and meals that do not come from discarded sources."

I clenched my jaw. The words cut close to home because they were true.

"I just don't want to lose school," I said finally. "It's the only thing I have."

His face softened. "We are going to make sure you lose nothing." He paused, searching my eyes for understanding. "I never told anyone this, but I was placed in a home as a teenager. At first, I was scared. I didn't know if I could trust anyone or if things would ever feel normal." He gave a small, reassuring smile. "But it gave me a sense of belonging I never expected. The people there made me feel safe. It became the most fulfilling event in my life." He gently leaned forward. "So, what do you say? Let's take one step at a time."

My eyes widened in astonishment as tears started streaming down my face. "Yes, of course!"

He made a call, but not with me in the room. He gave me space, kept his voice low, professional, calm. But when he came back, his eyes met mine with something I had not seen before- certainty.

"There's a program," he said. "It is called 'Youth Housing Partnership.' It is run through the district, quiet, respectful. There are no group homes. It is for students like you—who just need a little time and safety to breathe."

"What's the catch?" I asked, suspicion prickling at me. What if there was paperwork, or rules, or things I'd have to give up?

He shook his head. "You stay in school. That's it. They'll help with food and accommodation. They even keep your school info confidential."

It sounded too good to be true, so I did not stop him.

That night, I did not sleep behind the mattress store.

I did not sleep behind anywhere.

I was placed in a temporary host home—just for the night, they said. A quiet apartment with a retired teacher named Mrs. Grant, who did not ask any questions. She indicated a guest room with a prepared bed and stated, "You may shower first if you wish. Soap and towels are provided, and dinner is on the stove."

I wasn't sure if I should trust this kindness—if it would last beyond tonight. I lingered in the doorway, uncertain, my mind circling the possibility that it might all disappear by morning.

The room was small, but warm. Clean, soft lights illuminated the space; a lavender candle burned on the dresser, its scent mingling with the hush of the apartment. My backpack landed on the floor with a dull thud, a sound swallowed by comfort I didn't know how to name. I walked to the bathroom like I was moving through someone else's life, each step slow, deliberate, uncertain.

The hot water nearly broke me. I stood under it until my skin turned red, until the grime of months peeled away.

As the steam curled around me, I tried to make sense of the quiet. The mask I'd worn for so long began to slip just a little bit and washed down the drain with everything I'd carried. My thoughts pressed in, half-hopeful and half-afraid: Could this be real? Did I deserve this softness, this moment without fear?

That night, I lay in bed, feeling the unfamiliar weight of safety settle over me. The blanket smelled of fabric softener. The pillow was gentle, not crinkling with plastic. I listened to the hush of the apartment, my chest tightening, afraid to let go of vigilance.

For a long time, I lay still, uncertain what would happen if I allowed myself to believe.

And then, quietly, tears came. I cried silently, the release slow and aching—because for the first time in a long time, I had asked for help.

And the world had not collapsed.

Chapter Thirteen:

Borrowed Warmth

I woke up and, for a moment, the hush felt foreign. I lay still, heart pounding, as if the safety of the blankets might be revoked at any second. Sunlight slipped in through the gauzy curtains, brushing pale warmth across the unfamiliar room. Beneath the soft weight of the quilt, I felt both grounded and adrift. Was I allowed this peace? Or was it another borrowed thing, destined to dissolve with the dawn?

The clink of dishes and the scent of toast drifted through the crack beneath the door—evidence that the world continued outside my temporary sanctuary. I drew the blanket close and let myself imagine, just for a heartbeat, that I could stay. That safety might stretch into tomorrow. But the thought felt dangerous, so I pushed it aside, the old fear pressing against my ribs.

My feet found the floor cool and solid. I moved quietly, as if not to wake the spell, noticing the faint trace of lavender that lingered in the air—remnants of the candle Mrs. Grant had lit the night before. My clothes were folded neatly at the bed's edge, and as I dressed, I wondered if I'd ever feel like I belonged in spaces so carefully tended.

In the kitchen, Mrs. Grant's faded blue sweater matched the morning light. She hummed along to a jazz song on the radio, soft and meandering notes.

"Morning, dear," she said, her voice gentle as the steady rhythm of her movements. She nodded at the table, where a plate waited for me, steam curling from freshly toasted bread and oatmeal. The scent of strawberries and brown sugar mingled with the sharper tang of marmalade, bright and strange.

I hesitated at the threshold, a surge of longing mixing with caution. "You don't have to—" I started.

She cut in with a wave of her hand, "I know, but I want to." Her gaze didn't demand anything in return.

I sat, feeling the chair's cushion yield beneath me, the anticipation of the toast and oatmeal grounding me in the present. The silence between us was not empty, but full of possibility. Each bite tasted like something I didn't dare name—hope, maybe, or the memory of home. The jam was sweet on my tongue, and I let myself savor it, afraid to trust that it was meant for me.

After we'd eaten, she pressed a small plastic container into my hands. "Lunch," she said, her tone light. "Take it or leave it. It's there if you want."

My hands trembled as I accepted it. I wanted to speak, to thank her in a way that would convey how much this kindness ached, but my voice caught. "Thank you," was all I managed. She just nodded, already absorbed in her crossword, the tip of her pencil tapping softly against the page.

The short walk to school was spent with my senses heightened, as if the world might snatch this security away at any moment. Each breath of crisp morning air made me aware of how recently, every step had been a calculation—a search for exits, a catalog of risks. Now, with a full stomach and clean clothes, I felt exposed, as though having less fear made the possibility of loss more acute.

School was unchanged—lockers slammed, voices echoed—but something in me had shifted. I caught myself flinching less. There was food in my bag, a bed waiting for me. The knowledge felt both miraculous and precarious, and I guarded it like a secret.

In between periods, Lila appeared at my side. "Hey," she greeted, eyes scanning my face with a searching intensity. "You look… not terrible."

Her casual words made me smile despite myself. "Thanks," I said, my voice small.

She tilted her head slightly. "You're staying somewhere, aren't you?" I froze, but she didn't press. "You smell like real detergent," she said, "and you're not wearing the same hoodie as yesterday."

I said nothing, afraid that speaking the truth aloud would ruin it.

She leaned closer, lowering her voice. "I'm glad," she whispered, sincerity thrumming beneath the bravado. Something in me softened. I almost laughed. "Don't get used to it," I tried to joke.

She only grinned. "Too late."

By Art class, the tentative comfort was already thinning, replaced by the familiar tension of waiting for the worst. Mr. Danner handed out blank canvases and a set of acrylics. "Today's theme is memory," he announced. "Paint a moment that changed you."

I stared at the canvas, hands tingling, thoughts colliding. Around me, the classroom filled with stories told in color—laughter, summer, family, and trophies. I painted a hallway, long and dark, the door barely ajar, winds seeping in. In its center, a girl stood, back turned, gripping a chipped mug like it might shatter if she breathed. The silence of the brushstrokes felt raw and honest. I left it unsigned, a small act of defiance, before placing it on the drying rack.

Walking home was tense; I didn't know if I'd still have shelter or end up on the streets again. The November air nipped at my cheeks, carrying the faint promise of rain, and my anxiety mounted in time with the rhythm of my shoes against the pavement.

Mrs. Grant was out when I returned—probably at the market, or walking her little dog, Boots, who'd barked a single gruff hello and then fallen asleep on my sneakers. The apartment was hushed, the air tinged with the last traces of that lavender candle, and I paused in the entryway, listening to the stillness.

I wandered to the couch, fingertips tracing the texture of the well-worn throw blanket draped over the armrest. The bookshelf overflowed with hardback mysteries and family photos, the puzzle on the table half-finished, its edges carefully aligned. For a while, I stood there, heart full of longing and fear, afraid to let my guard down in a place that felt like someone's home.

In the guest room, I found my notebook and opened my list:

#1   *Have a room with a door that locks.* ☑

#2   *Take a real shower.* ☑

#3   *Eat hot food I did not have to steal.* ☑

Three check marks, as if proof I'd been here, proof I'd been cared for. I stared at them, half-hopeful, half-terrified that they might vanish if I turned away. Good things didn't last. Borrowed things didn't stay.

That evening, the apartment glowed gold in the light of the lamp. Mrs. Grant sat across from me, her hands careful as she pressed puzzle pieces together—smooth cardboard clicking into place, one after another. The faint scent of lavender drifted from the dresser, mingling with the earthy aroma of Boots, curled up beneath her chair.

She looked over, her gaze steady but not unkind. "I'm not keeping you," she said quietly. "You'll move on soon—that's how it works. But while you're here, this is yours."

A sharp ache bloomed in my chest. "What if I mess it up?" The question escaped before I could swallow it, fear sharpening my voice.

She smiled, soft and certain. "Then you try again."

Her words settled in the air, simple and impossible. I opened my notebook and wrote them beneath my list, pressing my pen into the page until the impression bled through.

#11 *Try again, even if it breaks you first.*

Chapter Fourteen:

On Borrowed Time

It started with a phone call.

I was sitting at the small kitchen table in Mrs. Grant's apartment—Mrs. Grant, my foster guardian, the woman who had taken me in for the past few months. I was supposed to be working on homework, but mostly I was just letting the pencil roll between my fingers, listening to the rhythm of her quiet humming as she chopped vegetables nearby. The golden light made the place feel impossibly safe, as if the warmth itself might keep me here.

The phone rang, slicing through the calm. Mrs. Grant picked it up in the other room. Her voice became low and careful—gentle in a way that made my heart pound. I couldn't make out the actual words, just the cadence, and suddenly I was a kid again, clinging to overheard snippets of adult conversations, trying to guess what would happen next.

My mother used to do the same. She would answer the phone in the kitchen, her lips pinched and her voice tight, and by the time she hung up, our bags would be packed. That was how I learned to listen for changes I couldn't control.

When Mrs. Grant came back, she looked tired—not upset, not angry, just worn thin around the edges. She set her hands on the table and sat across from me, like she was about to deliver news I'd heard too many times before.

"That was the program coordinator," she said, her tone as soft as the lamplight. "Just checking in." She paused, searching my face, as if gauging how much I already understood.

"They're trying to make room for another student in the system. They asked if I'd be open to rotating placements."

The words landed heavily. My hands went cold on the table, fingertips tingling. I felt my chest tighten, as if the walls were closing in. I tried to keep my expression even, but I could feel my jaw clenched. "What does that mean?" I managed, though the answer was already forming in the pit of my stomach.

"It means… your stay here might end soon. Maybe in a week or two."

I stared at the notebook in front of me. The algebra problem swam on the page, the numbers blurring together. I tried to steady my breathing, counting each inhale and exhale. "Right," I said finally. "It makes sense."

"Makenzie—" she started, using my name the way only people who really cared did.

"It's fine," I cut in, too quickly. "It was never going to last forever."

Her eyes softened, and for a moment, I hated how much I wanted to believe her when she whispered, "I wish it could be."

But I'd lived through enough goodbyes to know better. Everything good in my life had come with a time limit. No matter how long I stayed, I was always preparing to leave.

That night, I lay in the borrowed bed, under the borrowed blanket, everything here was borrowed, even the silence. I stared up at the ceiling, listening to the pipes creak and the wind rattle the windowpane. Each sound reminded me this wasn't really mine to keep. It was some else's home.

I listened as the wind slipped through the window frame, carrying the faint scent of rain on concrete and the distant hum of passing cars below. The pipes rattled softly, a homespun symphony, and I counted each sound as though it might anchor me to the room. I curled deeper under the blanket, tracing the frayed edge with my thumb, willing myself to feel present—to believe the borrowed warmth could last.

And I waited.

The next morning, uncertainty pressed down heavy, but I tried to move through the day as if I belonged. At school, I wore my usual mask, careful not to let the cracks show. Safety here felt conditional, as if the walls might fold up and vanish the moment I let myself relax.

Lila noticed. She slid onto the bench beside me at lunch, her tray clattering against the tabletop. She pierced her fruit cup with her straw, then looked over, lips pursed.

"You're quiet," she said, peering at me over the rim of her juice box.

I shrugged, focused on the way the sticky sweetness clung to the plastic.

"Quieter than usual."

"Just tired," I replied, glancing at the clock.

"You're always tired."

I managed a half-smile. "Then maybe I'm always quiet."

She gave a soft laugh, the kind that seemed to push back the noise in the cafeteria. After a moment, she leaned in. "My mom messaged me last night. Said she might move cities for a job. I don't know what it means for me yet." Her voice trembled like she was letting me peek behind her own mask. "I hate not knowing."

I nodded, surprised by the offering—her uncertainty, so much like mine. She didn't press me for more, just sat close, eating crackers one at a time, waiting for me to speak if or when I was ready.

In art class, Mr. Danner handed out clay. The room smelled faintly of dust and linseed oil, the sunlight turning each moted particle golden.

"Todays about form," he said, rolling up his sleeves. "It isn't perfection. I want you to sculpt something that feels like you."

I pressed my fingers into the cool, damp clay, feeling its resistance and give. It was cold, almost gritty, with the faint earthy tang of riverbanks after rain. The clay yielded in places and cracked in others, as if it, too, was not sure it belonged.

Everyone else molded familiar shapes—flowers, cats, stars, initials.

Mine became a house—small, uneven, fragile. One wall split down the middle, the roof a little caved, the doorway pinched too tight. I smoothed the sides, trying to make it seem sturdy, but my hands shook.

Mr. Danner lingered by my desk, his gaze gentle. "Does it feel like home?" he asked.

I hesitated, unsure how to answer.

He smiled, kneeling beside me. "When I was a kid, home meant wherever we landed for the month. My father traveled for work, so I made little houses out of whatever I could find—sticks, shoeboxes, old tins. None of them lasted, but I remember how much I wanted them to."

His words settled into the soft place beneath my ribs—
a brief warmth, like the sunlight shifting across my
clay. I realized, for a moment, that I wasn't alone in
wanting something permanent.

That afternoon, I skipped the short walk back to Mrs.
Grant's and took the long route through the city. The
air was heavy with the smell of fried onions from open
windows, mingling with the metallic tang of rain on
pavement and the sour exhaust of buses idling at the
corner. Pigeons fluttered up from the sidewalks, their
wings beating a rhythm with the distant clang of
bicycle bells. Each step made me more aware of the
world's textures—the roughness of brick against my
fingertips as I passed along the stores, the warmth of
late sun prickling my skin, the distant echo of
children's laughter in a courtyard.

I walked along the streets where I used to sleep, by the
benches and, the alleys, the closed-up storefront with
the rusted-out dumpster I'd hidden behind in storms. I
didn't linger, didn't let myself imagine going back, but
I needed to see them. To remember what waited if
safety disappeared again.

As I drifted along daydreaming I began to think - was
it possible I could belong somewhere for more than a
few weeks? Could the stability I felt now, however
tentative, become real if I allowed myself to hope?

I kept my posture straight, breathing deeply against the
rising anxiety, reminding myself—sometimes aloud,

sometimes silently—that moving forward had always been my way.

When I returned, Mrs. Grant had left a note on the table.

"Went to book club. I left dinner in the refrigerator. See you in the morning—G."

I lingered over the paper, tracing the letters with my finger. It meant she still expected me to be there, at least for the night.

That evening, I opened my notebook. The list was still there, a private catalog of promises and hopes for the future:

#1   *Have a room with a door that locks* ✅

#2   *Take a real shower* ✅

#3   *Eat hot food I didn't have to steal* ✅

#4   *Go to college*

#5   *Never cry again over people who left*

#6   *Forgive, not forget*

#7   *Make my life count*

#8   *Be seen*

#9   *Tell someone the truth*

#10   *Don't hurt the people who try to help you*

#11   *Try again, even if it breaks you first*

I paused at number four: *Go to college.*

It felt less impossible now. Maybe because Mrs. Grant had started asking me about my favorite subjects, or teachers had noticed me in class; maybe because Lila had shared her own uncertainty, and Mr. Danner had told me his story. All these moments knitted together, loosening old fears and making me wonder if hope could one day become a reality.

Maybe the hardest thing was not surviving the streets but allowing myself to imagine a future where I deserved to stay.

Chapter Fifteen:

The Meeting

I'd never met her in person.

Everything had been done over the phone—
voicemails, paperwork, quiet updates passed through
Mrs. Grant or the school. Just enough contact to make
the program feel real, but never enough to make it feel
personal.

Her name was Janelle Carter. She was a case manager,
a district liaison, with a friendly voice and calm words.
I hated her before I ever saw her face. Not because she
had done anything wrong, but because she held the
power to send me packing, to undo the one good thing
I had.

So, when Mrs. Grant said, "Your caseworker's coming
by tomorrow," I did not sleep. I stared at the ceiling all
night, rehearsing everything I would say—and
everything I was afraid to hear.

She arrived after school with a blazer and a clipboard.
An oversized purse slung over her shoulder, she looked
like she was ready for any emergency. "Makenzie,"
she said with a wide, practiced smile. "It's so good to
meet you finally."

I stood in the hallway like a guest in my life. "Hi."

She reached out her hand, and I shook it briefly, my
palm damp with nerves.

Mrs. Grant made tea, then left us alone in the living room.

Janelle sat across from me, crossing one leg over the other, flipping open a folder I could not see. "I just wanted to check in," she said. "You have been here for a couple of weeks now. Mrs. Grant has given positive feedback, your school reports are solid, attendance, grades, and behavior are all strong."

I nodded. "Okay."

She smiled again. "That's good, Makenzie. That's superb."

I waited, the air heavy between us. And waited. My fingers found the edge of my notebook on the coffee table, tracing the corner as if touching it could steady me.

Finally, I asked, sitting like a stone in my throat, "Am I leaving?"

Her smile faltered, then returned—too bright, too quick. "We're exploring options," she said carefully. "There are other students who need placements, and host homes like Mrs. Grants are in limited supply. It's possible we'll need to move you—temporarily, of course."

A chill skittered up my arms. In that moment, I remembered the last time I had to pack up overnight— stuffing everything I owned into my backpack, my clothes wrinkled and cold, the sound of the door closing behind me echoing for days. I'd promised myself I wouldn't let hope in again, not if it meant hearing that echo again.

"Where to?" I asked, my voice small.

She glanced down at the folder. "There is a group housing apartment run through a partner nonprofit. It is structured, but independent. There are multiple girls your age who have private rooms."

I pressed the spine of my notebook into my palm. "Is it foster care?" I asked flatly.

"No, this isn't foster. It's transitional housing."

"That's just a prettier way of saying temporary." I clenched my fists under the table, trying not to let my voice shake.

She softened her voice. "Makenzie… I know this is hard. But the program isn't permanent. It was never meant to be."

I looked away, blinking fast. "Then what's the point of it?" My words came out sharper than intended. "What's the point of putting me somewhere safe, giving me a bed, food, school—and then ripping it away?"

Janelle blinked. "No one's trying to take anything from you."

"But you are," I said, my throat tightening. "I finally stopped sleeping with my shoes on. I finally started doing homework at a table instead of on the sidewalk. And now I must start over?" My knee bounced beneath the table, the only part of me that wouldn't stay still.

She shifted, tucking a strand of hair behind her ear. "We're trying to serve as many students as we can."

"I'm not a number." My words were barely more than a whisper.

Her eyes softened. "No, you're not. That's why I'm here. I wanted to hear what you wanted."

I let out a bitter laugh. "What I want doesn't matter. You've already decided."

She leaned forward, resting her elbows on her knees. "Makenzie, you matter, and this isn't about punishment—it's about progress. You're thriving. You've already come so far."

"That doesn't mean I'm ready to lose everything again."

And there it was. The sentence I hadn't said out loud. The truth about the anger is... the fear was that this little patch of peace was not mine. That I would get used to it, love it—and then must watch it vanish, like my parents did. Like everything else had.

Janelle did not speak right away.

She reached into her folder and pulled out a form. "There's a scholarship application attached to this program," she said. "This is for students in housing transition. If you apply and keep your grades up, you may qualify for a longer-term solution. The college provides housing, meals, and stipends."

I stared at the form as if it were in another language.

"Is this real?" I asked.

She nodded. "Yes It's competitive, but you are already on track. You need to complete only the application and essay."

Another essay, another piece of my truth I'd have to give away. But this time, maybe it would be worth it.

She stood up. "You don't have to decide tonight. But I think you should go for it."

I did not respond.

She left the form on the table, shook my hand, and said goodbye to Mrs. Grant. As she walked out the door she left a breezy promise of, "I'll check in soon."

The door clicked shut, leaving behind a hush that felt almost sacred. I sat, tracing the edge of the application with my thumb, the paper smooth and cool beneath my touch, as if holding its own quiet promise.

My name was already there, printed in neat black letters at the top.

That night, I lay awake, the soft cotton of my blanket pulled up to my chin, the familiar scent of Mrs. Grant's laundry soap lingering in the air. My notebook was pressed close to my chest—a shield, a lifeline. I opened to where I'd scribbled my list and stared at line #4: *Go to college.*

I remembered my mother once telling me, "College means doors opening that you never knew existed." I imagined myself, years ago, walking across a campus in autumn, the leaves bright and spinning, the world feeling wide and full of hope. But that dream felt borrowed—something built from movies, from overheard stories, not real life.

Now, staring at the words, I felt pulled forward but also held back. What if I wasn't good enough? What if I left and there was nothing waiting for me but empty rooms and unfamiliar faces? I'd moved too many times already—each goodbye left a shadow.

But maybe—just maybe—the world was offering me a way forward. Maybe, for once, I could let myself imagine staying somewhere long enough to belong. Maybe this is how hope feels.

Chapter Sixteen:

What Happened

Sleep eluded me, fluttering just beyond reach. The idea
of packing up again coiled around my ribs like barbed
wire, each breath snagging. Even with the blanket
pulled close, the familiar scent of Mrs. Grant's
lavender candle could not soften the ache in my chest.
When I closed my eyes, I saw the bed evaporate
beneath me, the room dissolving into boxes and
borrowed spaces—my name vanishing from the door
as if it had never belonged.

By morning, I felt small and hollow, a shell polished
smoothly by tides of uncertainty. Still, I moved
through the halls of school, backpack heavy on my
shoulders, each step echoing in my bones. I didn't
know what else to do.

Lila was already at my locker, a bright splash of color
against drab linoleum. She leaned with casual
defiance, chipped blue nail polish wrapped around a
battered thermos, her presence grounding me like a
stone in a river.

Her gaze scanned my face, and her brow furrowed.
"Whoa," she said, voice half-teasing but gentle at the
edges. "You look like a human version of static—like
someone unplugged you in the night."

I gripped the cool metal of my locker door, knuckles pale. "Thank you," I managed, the words falling out flat.

She waited, her silence patient and steady.

Eventually, I found my voice, though it trembled. "The caseworker came last night." My fingers fumbled with the zipper on my backpack, searching for something solid.

Lila's posture shifted, tension flickering in her jaw. "Did she…?"

"They're moving me," I said, my throat tight. "Not today. Maybe next week."

She exhaled slowly, shoulders sinking. "Where?"

"It's some group apartment thing. Transitional housing." The phrase tasted foreign, clinical, on my tongue.

"Is that code for 'crammed in with four strangers and a roommate who steals your socks?'" she asked, trying for humor, but her voice had lost its usual spark.

"Probably." I tried to smile, but it slipped away too easily.

She didn't fill the space with jokes. She responded, "That's unfortunate."

I nodded; eyes fixed on a chipped tile. "Yeah."

A silence hovered, thick and humming. My heartbeat fast and wild, like a bird against a window. I hugged my backpack closer, searching for any anchor.

"Are you okay?" she asked quietly.

"No." My voice trembled, and I pressed my thumb into the seam of my backpack, searching for steadiness.

Lila leaned forward, her brows knitting together. "What can I do?" Her words came out fiercely, almost desperately sparked underneath the exhaustion in her eyes.

I blinked, taken aback. "What?"

"I mean it," she insisted, a stubborn fire igniting in her voice. "I'll talk to the principal. I'll draft an email. I'll get signatures. I'll chain myself to your locker if that's what it takes." Her hands fluttered, punctuating each possibility, and I caught the way her nail polish was chipped—glitter flecks dulled by worry.

A laugh escaped despite everything: small, shaky, but real. "You don't have to chain yourself to anything."

She grinned, that hint of mischief resurfacing. "But I look good in protest gear. Neon paint, picket signs, the works."

I tried to hold onto her humor, but anxiety gnawed at me. The thought of leaving Mrs. Grant's felt like stepping off a cliff; I wasn't sure if the scholarship would catch me. I ran a thumb over my backpack's zipper, feeling the rough plastic edge. "There's a scholarship for housing. If I apply, maybe I can stay in the system longer—through college."

"Then apply," Lila said, her voice softening, but her determination unwavering. "I'll help. We'll figure it out together."

"I don't even know where to start," I admitted, my chest tight.

She squeezed my hand. "You started the day you didn't give up."

Later, the sharp tang of acrylic filled the air as I stepped into art class. My hands were clammy with anticipation, my heart pounding as voices drifted in from the hallway—half-laughed jokes, the thud of lockers shutting. Mr. Danner was at the sink, sleeves rolled, swirling brushes in cloudy water. The sun caught on his glasses, and the smell of turpentine mixed with the chalky dust of old sketches.

He looked up when I entered, his expression gentle. "You all right?"

I hesitated, with words heavy and uncertain. "No," I finally said. "They're moving me from Mrs. Grant's. Maybe next week."

Mr. Danner set down his brush and wiped his hands on a paint-splattered rag, coming to stand beside me. "I'm sorry," he said, voice low and steady. He offered a mug of tea, steam curling in the air—comfort given wordlessly.

I swallowed, nerves prickling under my skin. "There's a scholarship for housing, food, and college help. But I need an essay."

His eyes lit up, and he nodded with a smile. "You're applying?"

I nodded, anxiety and hope battling inside me. What if my story wasn't enough? What if I disappeared from Mrs. Grant's walls, leaving nothing behind?

"You should," he said, his encouragement as solid as the warmth from the mug in my hands.

I hesitated. "Would you… read it? When I'm done?"

He didn't miss a beat. "Of course. Bring it to me."

Something inside loosened, just a little. Not gone—but lighter. Someone believed I could write a future, even if I were still searching for the words.

That afternoon, I sat in the school library, the white glow of the Word document both an invitation and a challenge.

Describe how your life experiences have shaped your goals and values.

I stared at the prompt, trying to see my life as more than a string of disconnected scenes. Because my answer wasn't just a sentence—it was a girl standing at a crossroads with a backpack that carried more than notebooks. It was a list in a battered journal, not of dreams, but of places to sleep one more night. It was a drawing of a house with one wall missing—a picture I drew in the sixth grade without realizing how much it mirrored my own feeling of instability, a wish for shelter that was whole and mine.

Each of these fragments—hallways echoing late-night footsteps, libraries full of strangers' warmth, empty walls that let in too much wind—are pieces of a journey that shaped me. They're not just images; they are the evidence of what I've endured and the source of my resilience.

I remembered the first night I slept in the all-night laundromat on Fifth St. with the fear buzzing in my veins, how I promised myself I'd keep moving. I remembered Mrs. Grant making cocoa and not asking questions, how quiet kindness helped me believe I could trust her. These moments, small and large, have built in me an independence I didn't choose, but now claim as my own.

So, when I began to type, the sentences came slowly. Yet, for the first time, I realized my story was not something to hide, it was something I could offer— honestly, without apology. I do not want pity, only to be understood for the strength I found in learning to exist in the in-between.

I am ready for someone to see the whole story because I am finally learning to accept every part of it, even the unfinished walls.

Chapter Seventeen:

The Essay

Scholarship Essay Prompt:
"Describe how your life experiences have shaped your goals and values."

When people ask where I'm from, I simply say "here"—it's much easier than explaining I've had no fixed home.

I used to think I had to lie to be safe. If anyone knew the truth—that I have been homeless since I was thirteen—they would look at me differently. Like I was damaged, or dangerous, or someone who did not belong. The ache of hiding settled in my chest, heavy and constant, like the chill that seeped into my bones each night spent beneath flickering streetlights.

But I am tired of lying. Each time I hid my story, the weight of it grew heavier, pressing against my ribs until I could no longer carry it alone. I realized that silence kept others comfortable, but it kept me isolated, unable to breathe fully.

So, here's the truth.

When I was thirteen, I woke up and found my parents gone. They had packed up and left without telling me. Just... gone. The silence in the rooms was deafening.

Dust motes hung in the beams of the early morning light; the fridge hummed but held only the echo of old groceries.

For days, I stayed in the house pretending it was a mistake, that they would come back. I made toast, the aroma lingering in a kitchen that felt hollow. I sat on the couch, tracing the pattern of its worn fabric with my fingertips, as if nothing had changed. I even went to school, because it was the only place that still expected me to show up.

Eventually, the lights shut off and the water stopped running. The landlord came to the door, his footsteps heavy on the warped wood. I crawled out the back window the scrape of glass against my palm sharp and real. That was the day I abandoned my home. That was the day I went into survival training.

I slept in an all-night laundromat and behind dumpsters, the sharp smell of rotting food clinging to my clothes as I curled up, the cold concrete pressing against my back. I learned the rhythms of bus stations—the buzz of neon, the echo of footsteps, the metallic clink of coins dropped by strangers. I found food in places that others overlooked, and warmth in the thick embrace of secondhand hoodies. I learned how to be invisible, blending into crowds, the hum of the city masking my fears. Being invisible kept me safe.

But it also kept me from living.

I kept going to school. That was the one rule I gave myself: stay enrolled, stay quiet, stay unnoticed. And I did…for years.

I got good at pretending. I learned to keep my head down, to disappear into the pattern of cracked linoleum and faded bulletin boards. I was the quiet girl in the back, always turning in her assignments, never raising her hand. The one who wore the same shirt four days in a row and tried not to flinch when classmates joked about the smell of old clothes.

Somewhere along the way, I stopped expecting anyone to see me. It felt like years before that changed before anyone noticed I was more than the shadow at the edge of the room.

During those days, I lived without heat, shivering under thin blankets as frost crept across the window, my breath fogging the glass. I I occasionally slept with my shoes on, sometimes finding rest in laundromats or curled up on the loading dock behind a grocery store, listening to the distant sounds of delivery trucks. Meals were often cold noodles served in a worn plastic bowl, and I learned to ration food carefully, making a single can of soup last for two days.

But then, for the first time since that night in the empty house, someone did see me. A teacher looked past the silence in my eyes. A classmate handed me half a sandwich, the bread soft and fresh in my hands. A counselor didn't write me down as a problem to be solved, but asked, gently, "What do you need?" I remember the exact quiet in the room when she waited for me to speak.

For the first time, I believed I might be more than the worst thing that happened to me. I found out that I could hope for more, even if it hurt.

I have learned how to stretch a meal and keep my backpack dry in the rain. I know how to blend in when I am breaking inside, and how to love people who damage me and still choose not to follow them.

The biggest thing I have learned-I want more than just survival. I want to live!

I want to graduate.

I want to go to college.

I want to study psychology and work with teens who feel like no one sees them.

There's one night I always go back to—the night I sat behind a shuttered bakery, shivering in the dark, listening to rain thrum against the metal lid of a garbage bin. My stomach churned with hunger, and I pressed my knees to my chest, whispering promises to myself: "Keep going. Don't disappear." That promise became my anchor, the quiet determination that shaped my goals and kept me showing up, even when everything told me to quit.

I have experienced being in that situation myself—often overlooked by others, and my circumstances not readily apparent. Despite lacking stable housing, I continued to attend, complete assignments, and interact positively, hoping that my efforts would be recognized and my challenges acknowledged.

Even if I do not win this scholarship, I need to say this: kids like me exist.

We are not statistics. We are not broken. We are not invisible.

Instead, we fight every day for a future. For a chance to be meaningful, it must have significance. For a life that does not start and end with pain.

I used to think I had no family, no home, no future. But I have something now: I have me!

I have grit. I have goals. I have a story that's mine to write, not theirs to erase.

Sometimes, the hardest lessons are learned in silence, in the shadows. But in those moments, I found strength and a sense of belonging that came not from others, but from within.

So, when people ask where I am from, maybe I will stop saying "here." Maybe I will say, "I'm from second chances." "I'm from streets I no longer sleep on." "I'm from the list I wrote in a notebook under a streetlamp." "I'm from everywhere I survived."

And now—after every setback, and every moment of doubt—I am going somewhere. Not because someone gave me permission, but because I chose not to quit.

I am proof that determination can overcome circumstance, and I want to help others discover their inner strength.

Chapter Eighteen

Boxed Up

I handed in the essay first thing Monday morning. Mr. Danner accepted it, his hands steady as he slipped it into a folde,r a simple gesture but for me, it felt monumental. The paper's edges brushed my fingertips, the faint scent of ink lingering as I let go, almost like releasing a piece of myself. He met my gaze and nodded, a silent acknowledgment that meant more than words.

Leaving his classroom, I felt an unfamiliar lightness—like my chest had been hollowed out and filled with possibility. For once, I had acted, not just survived.

I told myself-I want this.

But want alone never guarantees anything. Life has a way of reminding you of that.

After lunch, the school's corridors were filled with the lingering smell of chicken strips and the slamming of lockers closing. Mrs. Grant found me beneath the flickering lights, her face gentle but her hands restless, twisting the silver ring she always wore—a habit I'd come to recognize as worry.

"Makenzie," she said softly. "Janelle just called."

My heart thudded. "She's fast-tracking the move to tomorrow morning."

It took a moment for the words to land. The world shrank in the echo of footsteps and the faint scent of her floral hand cream. "Tomorrow?"

"She said a space opened earlier than expected. They want you settled by the end of the week."

I stared at the dull blue lockers, at their chipped numbers, at the ceiling tiles dappled with water stains—searching for an escape that wasn't there.

"Can't I just—stay? Until I hear about the scholarship?"

"I asked," Mrs. Grant replied, her voice thickening, "but they said no."

Of course they did.

That evening, the guestroom was bathed in golden twilight. The bed smelled of lavender and fresh laundry, a comfort that had become familiar. Boots, was curled in his usual corner, his fur blended into the color of the faded carpet. He blinked sleepily, but his eyes were watching my every movement, as if he understood things were changing.

Mrs. Grant handed me a small cardboard box with the edges frayed from past use. "Need little," she joked, trying to lighten the mood. "You travel small."

I looked around—the pale-yellow walls, the stack of novels she'd left by the window, the family photos on the dresser. They told stories I'd only just begun to understand.

The box stayed mostly empty: my battered notebook, several clean shirts, a toothbrush, and the envelope containing my essay. As I packed, the whispered scuff of the box's bottom against the bedsheet felt impossibly loud. My stomach ached with the familiar dread of leaving behind something good.

I wanted to tell Mrs. Grant how much I'd needed her quiet reassurance, her bad jokes, the way she left little notes in my lunch. Instead, I just nodded, words tangled and heavy. She hovered by the door; hands folded over her apron.

At dinner, the kitchen was warm, the air thick with the scent of simmering tomato and garlic. Mrs. Grant made spaghetti, serving it in chipped bowls she'd used for years. The silence between us was gentle, not awkward, punctuated only by the clink of forks and the soft whir of the dishwasher. She passed me the breadbasket and said, "Remember, leftovers are in the blue Tupperware. You know how to find them, right?" Her voice barely wavered.

As we cleaned up, the steam rising from the plates fogged the window, blurring the outside world. She broke the silence, "You know, it's okay to be scared." She paused, her eyes reflecting more than words. "It doesn't mean you're weak. It just means you've had to be strong for too long."

I gripped the countertop, searching for something steady. "I thought I might stay."

"I know." Her voice caught. "And now you have to go again I'm sorry."

She dried a dish, then turned to me, her expression fierce and gentle. "But you're not starting over, Makenzie. You're carrying something with you now—a story, a name, a plan—and that makes you unstoppable."

I nodded, blinking away tears I'd promised myself not to shed.

The next morning came too fast. Sunlight spilled through the curtains, painting gold stripes on packed boxes. I put on my jacket, the fabric stiff and cold against my arms. Mrs. Grant stood at the doorway, trying to smile, her eyes rimmed red. Boots barked once, sharp, and insistent seeming to say goodbye—a small sound that felt enormous.

Janelle arrived right on time, her car engine humming outside. She wore a crisp blazer, her posture straight but her eyes darting, taking everything in. She smiled, wide and practiced. "Ready?" she asked, her voice brisk but not unkind. Her key chain jingled—a tiny lighthouse, bright and hopeful. I wondered where she'd gotten it, if she kept it as a reminder to guide others home.

I tried to steady my breath, the morning air sharp in my lungs. "Not really," I admitted.

Janelle softened. "That's all right. Most people aren't." She glanced down, fiddling with the lighthouse. "You're not alone, Makenzie. I'll walk you in."

The new place was not a house but an apartment, on the third floor, with no elevator. The stairwell smelled faintly of old paint and distant cigarette smoke. My box thumped against my hip with every step.

Inside, the rooms were bright but spare—metal-framed beds, wide windows smudged with fingerprints, drawers with mismatched knobs. There was a shared kitchen, the linoleum floor faded beneath humming fluorescent lights, and a bathroom with shelves lined by other girls' bottles and brushes.

A staff member named Mrs. Lang lived down the hall. Her shoes squeaked on the tile as she gave a quick tour. "Just in case you need anything I'm in 301", she said, her accent soft and unfamiliar. "I'm here most evenings."

Cheyenne barely looked up from her phone, thumbs flying, music leaking out in a steady stream. Talia gave me a slow once-over, then grinned. "You eat meat? We do Taco Tuesdays," she said, her voice playful but guarded. She wore three layers of eyeliner and a hoodie with fading band logos.

I set my box down, hands trembling. The bed was firm, the blanket scratchy. I tried not to compare it to the softness I'd just left.

This was not awful. It was clean, warm, quiet enough but unfamiliar. But the air tasted different, tinged with bleach and spices. The hum of the fridge filled the silence that had once comforted me.

That night, under a blanket that itched at my skin, I listened to the apartment's sounds—the distant voices, the buzz of pipes, Cheyenne's muffled music. I ached for lavender and lit windows, for Boots nudging my knee with his nose.

I wanted to scream or cry or walk out into the street and keep walking until no one saw me again.

Instead, I pulled out my notebook. The paper felt rough beneath my fingers; my handwriting, sharp and cramped, was a map of all I'd survived.

#12   Learn how to live like you are staying, even if you are afraid, you won't.

I added a new line beneath it, the graphite smudging as I pressed too hard.

#13   Keep going, nevertheless. This is not the end. It is another stop on the road.

I was still moving forward, even if I was scared and hated it and it hurt.

Chapter Nineteen:

Thin Walls

The first thing I noticed about the apartment was the sound.

It wasn't loud—not exactly—but it never stopped. Pipes tapped and clicked inside the walls, a ceaseless rhythm that sometimes felt like a heartbeat I didn't own. Talia whispered into her phone at midnight, the glow of her screen flickering against the ceiling. Cheyenne's music—always present, even when she slept—spilled through thin headphones and into the dusky quiet. The fridge hummed in the corner, a small mechanical guardian whose drone sometimes soothed and sometimes grated.

At times, these noises felt overwhelming, weaving together into a web that left me restless, pressed against the mattress and straining to listen for something familiar. When the voices from upstairs rose in anger, or a baby wailed across the hall, my body tensed, waiting for someone to shout my name or bang on my door. I wondered if I would ever feel safe enough to let go, to trust that the lock on my door was enough.

Other nights, the sounds became a familiar and strange comfort. They meant people were nearby—living, breathing, moving through their own routines.

Sometimes, the murmur of life through thin walls was easier than silence.

As I lay awake, I couldn't help but remember the nights spent outside, tucked behind grocery stores, laundromats, and beside waste disposal units where the unknown sounds pressed in from all sides, heavy as a blanket I could never throw off. Out there loneliness was a vast, echoing symphony. Here in these rented rooms, it was noisy and crowded, yet safe.

Sharing space was somehow louder than solitude. Yet, within that din, I discovered something new—a restless belonging, tentative and unsure, stitched together by the apartment's peculiar orchestra. Each sound, whether jarring or gentle, marked my adjustment: a reminder that I was still moving forward, learning how to exist beside others, letting the noise teach me how to belong.

We talked little.

The girls were older—maybe seventeen or eighteen. They moved in and out like drifting shadows. Cheyenne left early, came back late, and always looked tired, her hoodie pulled up and her eyes soft with exhaustion. Once, as I fumbled with the microwave, she caught my glance and offered a brief, crooked smile—so quickly I wasn't sure if I'd imagined it, but it stayed with me longer than the taste of reheated noodles.

Talia wore three layers of eyeliner and used curse words like punctuation. The first night, as I struggled with my suitcase zipper, she leaned against the door frame, arms crossed, and said, "You know, it doesn't bite. Just yank it." There was a flash of humor in her eyes, sharp but not unkind, and I found myself almost smiling back.

They were not unkind; just uninterested—at least, that's what I told myself. I was the new girl, and the new girl just wasn't part of the group yet.

So, I learned the rules.

Touch nothing that's not yours.

Don't ask questions.

Label your food.

Keep your shoes by the door.

Take fast showers.

Don't cry where anyone can hear you.

My bedroom was small, but it was mine, with a bed and a locking door.. I pinned my list to the wall with a strip of tape, feeling an ache in my chest—the familiar twinge of being out of place. Sometimes as I lay on my back at night, staring at the unfamiliar ceiling, I wondered if I was invisible here, or if I was finally starting to exist. There was loneliness, yes, but also a strange quiet hope that maybe, with enough days, I'd earn my place in the pattern.

I kept my notebook under the pillow, lined up my folded shirts like soldiers in the drawer, and stashed my essay in a file folder beside the bed. The sheets smelled sharply of bleach and the floor creaked when I stepped too close to the wall. Still, I could sleep through the night, comforted by the solid click of the lock on my door, and the comfort of security.

On the third day, as I debated eating a spotted banana, Talia tossed me a protein bar.

"I hate peanut butter," she said. "Want it?"

I caught it and thanked her.

She replied, "Don't get used to it."

Talia rarely offered anything, so even her begrudging generosity felt like a rare weather event—unexpected and fleeting, leaving me wondering whether it had really happened at all. I tucked the bar in my pocket, holding onto the small comfort longer than I needed to.

Later as I unwrapped the bar, my eyes drifted to the rules taped above the sink—a reminder that kindness here had boundaries, just like everything else. The apartment's rules formed a strict perimeter around my life: curfew at 9 p.m., no guests, mandatory check-ins once a week, and dishes washed and dried immediately. If the staff knocked, you answered. If something broke, you fixed it or logged it in the maintenance binder.

There was a binder for everything—chores, meals, meds—a landscape mapped in lists and obligations. Sometimes I wondered if all these rules were meant to protect us, or simply to keep us from spilling too far into each other's lives.

It felt like living inside a contract. And maybe I needed that-something with walls and boundaries.

However, I continued to miss the comfortable setting of Mrs. Grant's couch, as well as her thoughtful approach—offering tea and creating a welcoming atmosphere without prying. Additionally, I regretted not having the opportunity to see Boots.

Here, no one handed you anything. You got it yourself. Or you went without.

School remained a constant and familiar place where I could breathe—a steady refuge from the tense rules and clipped exchanges at the apartment. The smell of old books and the hum of voices in the hallway felt familiar., a gentle background noise that steadied my thoughts. In class, I knew what to expect: lessons, bell schedules, the shuffling of feet beneath desks. There, I could slip into a routine where my troubles softened, if only for a few hours. Among classmates, I found a quiet sense of belonging, even when we didn't speak much. The classroom was a space untouched by the chaos at the group home, a place where I could let my guard down and—just for a little while—inhale fully and feel at ease.

Lila didn't ask about the apartment, but she gave me the rest of her sandwich every day at lunch, and we made small talk, but I could sense her desire to know more.

Mr. Danner asked how I was settling in. I told him the truth: "It's fine." He didn't push, just handed me a sketchbook and said, "New space and a new page."

That night, I stood in the kitchen brushing my teeth over the sink—because the bathroom was occupied and the tile out here didn't smell like mildew. Cheyenne walked past in a hoodie three sizes too big. She had a way of noticing things no one else did, even when she pretended not to care.

"You write in that notebook every night?" she asked.

I blinked as I swallowed.

"I see the light under your door," she added.

I nodded. "Yeah."

She tilted her head. "You like… writing a novel?"

"Something like that."

"Let me know when it's a movie," she said, walking away. "I'll stream it illegally."

I didn't laugh until she turned the corner and was out of sight.

On Friday, someone knocked on the door just before curfew. We all froze. Talia always took charge when things felt uncertain; she opened it with her shoulder like a weapon. It was the staff coordinator—Ms. Nina, always with her clipboard, messy bun, and a voice like she'd seen it all and didn't flinch anymore.

She gave us a quick update—apartment inspections that were coming next week and a reminder to update our emergency contact information. She also handed us a flyer for a job fair at the downtown library.

Then, she handed me an envelope.

"This came to the district office," she said. "Looked kind of important."

My name was typed on the front. No return address.

My hands shook as I turned it over, wondering if it would bring news or trouble. I didn't want anyone to see how much it mattered. The paper felt heavy, like it held all the air in the room. For a moment, I pressed my thumb against the seam, listening to the distant hum of the fridge, the shuffle of footsteps down the hall—trying to steady myself, trying not to hope too much.

Back in my room, I sat on the bed, envelope in my lap, afraid to open it.

I stared at the taped-up list on the wall.

#4,   Go to college.

#12.   Learn how to live as if you are staying.

#13   Keep going.

I ran my finger over those lines—paper smooth under my skin, the ink smudged in places where I'd traced it too often.

Then I tore the envelope open.

Inside was a letter, printed and neatly folded.

Dear Makenzie Rowe,

You have been selected as a recipient of the Southeast Youth Resilience Scholarship...

I did not read the rest right away.

I didn't cry or scream. I simply endured it.

My hands trembled, and for a moment, I couldn't breathe—caught between disbelief and hope. The corners of the letter pressed into my palms. My mind spun with questions: Was this real? Did I deserve it? What now?

I listened to the silence, expecting the world to rush in and take it back.

Later, I added a new line to the list:

#14   Believe it when the world says yes.

Sometimes it does.

And this time, the promise stayed—real and solid—anchoring me to a future I could finally imagine.

Chapter Twenty:

The Yes

I folded the letter back into the envelope as if it might break, my fingertips brushing the smooth paper—a fragile proof of a world I'd barely dared to imagine. I placed it gently in the drawer beside my bed, closed it with a soft click, and then sat there, hands still trembling, staring at the closed drawer for twenty straight minutes as if the letter could vanish the moment I blinked. I repeatedly opened the drawer to verify that it remained in place.

I had imagined this moment so many times: the long-awaited yes, the acceptance, the tangible sign that my story was worth more than enduring and surviving. But now, with the letter real and solid in my possession, joy felt strangely elusive. Instead, I was filled with something heavier—a wary awe, a voice whispering: Don't trust it; not yet. Wait for it to be taken away, and then you can finally allow yourself to grieve.

I didn't tell anyone, not that first day. Neither Lila, my fiercely loyal best friend who always saw possibility in me; nor Mr. Danner, my patient art teacher who saw my potential and believed in my talent long before I did; nor Cheyenne, my sharp-tongued but protective roommate; nor Talia or Ms. Nina, mentors at the youth center who had become like a patchwork family to me; not even Mrs. Grant, my caseworker and sometimes confidant, whose steady encouragement had carried me through more than one crisis. I wanted to call her most of all, just to hear her say, "Of course you got it"—as though the universe had always known.

Instead, I went through the motions. I showered, got dressed, drifted through the hallways of school as if underwater. I sat in classes I could not recall, ate lunch without tasting it. All the while, the letter pulsed in the back of my mind like a second heartbeat—one I wasn't yet convinced belonged to me.

After school, I lingered in the art room, the scent of turpentine and pencil shavings grounding me in the present. Most of the students had cleared out, leaving only the hum of the janitor's buffer and the hush of falling light. My sketchbook lay open in front of me, blank—a challenge and a refuge.

Mr. Danner was cleaning out a cabinet, moving quietly, not filling the silence with forced words. He glanced over now and then, waiting, his presence reassuring in its steadiness. He finally broke the silence and asked, "Did something happen?"

I nodded, unable to trust my voice. "Yeah."

He put the lid back on a jar of paint and leaned against the desk, his posture attentive but unintrusive. "You want to tell me?"

I reached for the envelope in my backpack, holding it like it was radioactive, afraid it would burn right through my hands. I handed it to him, unable to find the right words—not yet.

He unfolded the letter slowly, his eyes moving over the lines once, then again. Silence stretched between us, heavy but not uncomfortable.

When he looked up, his eyes were glassy. "Makenzie," he said, his voice steady and gentle. "You did it. I knew you could!"

A dozen conflicting memories surged up—foster homes and closed doors, the nights I slept with shoes on in case I had to run, the teachers who said I was too much or not enough, the caseworkers promising hope that never came. All that history knotted in my chest, making it hard to breathe.

I shook my head, words tumbling out. "I have done nothing yet."

"You applied," he said. "You told your story. You gave them a truth most people would've buried. That's everything."

His faith in me felt like a challenge to my yearlong self-doubt—could I let myself believe it, even for a moment?

My throat burned. "What if it disappears? What if they change their minds?"

"They won't."

"You don't know that."

He smiled gently. "I know you."

Something broke inside me—some old, brittle defense. I dropped my face into my hand, cried softly and just breathed, memories swirling: the fear of being let down, the ache of always waiting for the next disappointment, and the unfamiliar warmth of being seen and believed. Mr. Danner handed me a glass of tea, and we shared a peaceful silence until I felt prepared, the warmth of the tea soothing my nerves as I gathered my thoughts. In the hush, I noticed the faint clink of ice against the glass and the mellow glow of sunlight stretching across the worn table, each detail grounding me as I searched for the right words.

Later that night, back in the apartment—walls patched with posters, a single lamp casting soft shadows—I sat at the kitchen table with a pen in one hand and the scholarship paperwork in the other, the envelope now a little crumpled at the edges. There were forms to fill out, boxes to check, and I felt the weight of every signature as a step toward something real.

Cheyenne walked past, eyes lingering on the envelope. "Is that what I think it is?" she asked, arching an eyebrow, her tone more gentle than usual.

I blinked. " Maybe?"

She nodded, almost approving. "Knew you were one of those try-hard kids—the kind that turns pain into fuel."

A laugh escaped me, surprising us both. "Is that a compliment?"

She shrugged, opening the fridge. "Don't let it go to your head." She grinned sideways. "I saved the last taco. It's yours."

That was how I knew we were beginning to bond in some small way.

The next day, I finally told Lila. We sat on the front steps after school the sky pale blue. Lila, my only friend, my witness to everything, froze mid-sentence as I handed her the letter.

She scanned it quickly, lips moving, eyes growing wide. "Mak—"

"Holy crap. You got it!"

I nodded, tears building.

She screamed—not a full scream, but enough to make three first-year students jump. Then she hugged me, quickly and tight, anchoring me in the here and now.

"You deserve this," she whispered fiercely into my ear. "Every word."

For the first time, I wanted to believe her.

That afternoon, Janelle—the case manager who had seen me through endless placement applications and paperwork—came by for my weekly check-in. I handed her the letter.

She read it slowly, her usual calmness replaced by something deeper, raw, and proud. "You're the reason this program exists," she said, her voice firm and certain. "Congratulations Mackenzie!".

I hesitated. "I don't want another apartment," I told her. "I don't want more transitions."

She nodded. "You won't need them. This opens doors options for students include housing, stipends, long-term plans. You get to choose."

My voice shook. "You're sure?"

She pressed the letter back into my hands, conviction in her gaze. "And you earned every line of this."

Back in my room, I stared at my list that I taped to my wall.

#1   *Have a room with a door that locks*

#2   *Take a real shower*

#3   *Eat hot food I didn't have to steal*

#4   *Go to college*

#5   *Never cry again over people who left*

#6   *Forgive, not forget*

#7   *Make my life count*

#8   *Be seen*

#9   *Tell someone the truth*

#10   Don't hurt the people who try to help you

#11   Try again, even if it breaks you first

#12.   Learn how to live as if you are staying.

#13   Keep going.

#14   Believe it when the world says yes

I uncapped my pen and beneath it all, I added one more:

#15   Say yes back.

Chapter Twenty-One:

Lavender and Light

I hadn't called ahead. After months away at school, I wasn't sure Mrs. Grant would welcome me back, or if I even deserved to cross her threshold again. Each step up to the small red-brick apartment felt heavier than the last, my thoughts tangled between gratitude and guilt. The scholarship letter in my bag was proof of how far I'd come, but it also reminded me of every restless night spent wondering if I belonged anywhere.

I stood outside, breath quick and uncertain, remembering the day I first arrived—an awkward teenager lugging a box, desperate for safety. Mrs. Grant had given me that, no questions asked. Now, returning with something to show for it, I was terrified she wouldn't recognize the person I'd become.

Boots barked before I could knock, his tail thumping against the door in a rhythm that felt like hope. The door swung open, and there she was—Mrs. Grant, hair pinned up, hands dusted with flour, apron creased and familiar. Her eyes softened as she took me in, reading every line of worry etched across my face.

"Makenzie," she said, her voice wrapping around me like the softest shawl.

I hesitated in the doorway, the aroma of cinnamon and lavender drifting out to meet me. "Hi," I whispered, unsure if this was truly my home anymore.

She smiled, warmth radiating from the space behind her. "Come in, sweetheart, as she gave me a big hug."

Inside, everything was as I remembered: the faded rug, the hum of the kettle, the gentle clatter of Boots' nails on linoleum. I dropped my bag and was instantly swept into the routine we had always shared—her making tea, me settling into the chair where I'd learned how to relax.

As the kettle sang, I closed my eyes and let the sounds fill me. The clink of porcelain, the quiet hush between us, Boots' soft whine as he curled at my feet all reminded me why this place mattered. When she placed the cup in my hands, its warmth seeped into my fingers, grounding me in the present. Steam curled up, carrying hints of mint and honey, and I realized how I'd missed these simple comforts.

While she waited, I fumbled for the scholarship letter. Passing it to her, my hands trembled—not just with nerves, but with the weight of everything this achievement meant. Receiving the scholarship was more than financial relief; it was validation, proof that all my struggle had been seen. It meant doors would open. It meant I could stay.

She read the letter, tears gathering in the corners of her eyes. "Oh, Makenzie…" she breathed, voice thick with pride. "You did it. I'm so proud of you"

In that moment, I understood: Mrs. Grant hadn't just given me shelter. She had given me a foundation, a reason to believe I could build something lasting. Coming back wasn't just about revisiting the past—it was about honoring the journey, cherishing the rare warmth of belonging, and learning, finally, how to say thank you to her and yes to myself.

I smiled, tears pricking at the corners of my eyes. "We did it."

She looked up, her gaze gentle and steady. "No, honey, you did this. I just opened a door. You walked through it."

She reached for my hand across from the table, her fingers warm, still dusted with flour. "I saw a girl who had nothing but still held her head high. I didn't give you strength. I just gave you a place to rest."

For a moment, I was lost in the hush of the kitchen— the low hum of the refrigerator, the faint creak of the old house settling, sunlight streaming through the lace curtains and painting shifting patterns on the faded linoleum. What Mrs. Grant called 'rest' had been a sanctuary when the world felt jagged and unforgiving. In the quiet of this house, where the clock ticked steadily and the scent of cinnamon and lavender lingered in the air, I learned how to breathe again without fear.

My voice cracked. "It saved me."

We sat together in a silence that felt full, not empty—a silence filled with clinking cups, the soft thud of Boots' tail, and the reassurance of being seen.

"I was scared," I admitted, my thumb tracing the chipped edge of the teacup. "Every day I was here."

She nodded, eyes shining. "I know."

"I thought if I got used to it—this bed, this roof—I'd lose it again."

She said, "But you did not!. You are a scholarship recipient and a future college student. You are building a life."

I smiled softly, watching the dust motes swirl in the golden light. "It still feels… fragile."

"Everything does at the start. That's how you know it's new."

Before I left, I walked to the guest room—my old room. The door's brass handle was cool against my palm, and the wood grain felt smooth and familiar beneath my fingertips. Inside, the air was thick with sunlight, bedding crisp and lavender-scented, the faint whir of a box fan stirring the curtains. Someone else's duffel sat in the corner now; the desk's surface was clean except for tiny scratches I remembered making during late nights spent tracing dreams in my notebook.

I did not ask her name-Didn't need to know.

I left something behind on the desk, tucking it just under the lamp where the glow would catch it at dusk—a note:

It read "You do not know me yet, but I know you! And I believe in you because I now believe in myself" - *Makenzie*

Mrs. Grant hugged me again at the door—a long, tight, motherly hug, her apron still faintly warm from the oven. The murmur of the radio drifted from the kitchen; Boots' nails clicked on the floor as if echoing a heartbeat.

"You'll visit?" she asked, her voice soft as a well-worn quilt.

I nodded.

"Bring updates."

"And maybe laundry." I added"

She laughed, brushing a stray wisp of hair from my cheek. "You are always welcome."

As I walked down the street, with the envelope in my bag and a future blooming quietly ahead, I realized something: I had never truly been given a home. Instead, my life had been pieced together by a patchwork of gentle gestures—like the neighbor who once slipped a sandwich into my backpack when they thought I wasn't looking, or the librarian who let me hide among the stacks after school on rainy afternoons. Each kindness, small and fleeting, had become a brick in my foundation.

Now, as the city shifted around me, I understood that I longed to build friendships that would last past sunset, build memories I could tuck away like pressed flowers, perhaps even, at last, have a place to call my own, and now, I was ready to begin.

Chapter Twenty-Two:

The Knock

It happened on a Thursday.

I had just come back from the school office with a stack of paper course registration forms, housing details, and a checklist of everything I'd need before moving in. It was all like a fragile trophy—a future I once saw as unattainable now glimmering and almost within reach.

The apartment was quiet when I returned. Talia was out, Cheyenne slept with a textbook splayed over her chest, and the summer heat pressed through the window screen. The smell of sun-warmed dust hung in the air, mingling with the papery scent of new beginnings. Somewhere, a faint rustle of pages settled into the silence.

Then someone knocked.

Three soft taps, not urgent, unexpected.

My heart thudded against my ribs, each second stretching as I tried to guess who could possibly be on the other side. People didn't just visit here. There was always a reason. Visits were for appointments—caseworkers, deliveries—never surprises. And surprise, here, rarely meant anything good.

I opened the door slowly.

And the world stopped.

He looked smaller than I remembered. Thinner, tired in a way that seemed to seep into his bones. A faint beard shadowed his jaw as if routine had slipped away from him. He wore that old sweatshirt he always pulled first from the laundry, insisting it was lucky—some kind of magic stitched into its seams.

Though I hadn't seen him in years, the memory came back vivid yet fragmented.

And his eyes were mine.

My father.

"Makenzie," he said.

My hands trembled at my sides, and the scent of bitter coffee hung between us. My throat tightened, my feet rooted to the worn entryway rug.

I didn't move, didn't speak.

"I… I wasn't sure you'd be here," he said, awkwardly adjusting his grip on the paper cup, knuckles pale.

"How did you—?" My voice cracked in half.

"Your mom," he answered quietly. "She found out through the school district. Said they had an address."

I shifted, stepping into the doorway and blocking it behind me, the edge pressing against my shoulder.

Silence stretched, thick and overwhelming.

"You left," I whispered.

"I know."

"You both did." The memory of that empty house flashed behind my eyes, making it hard to breathe. I felt a noticeable tremor in my knees as I worked to regain composure. .

He looked down, then back up. "I wanted to say I'm sorry."

That wasn't enough-it was never going to be enough.

But it was something—a crack in the wall I'd built, even if I weren't ready to let anything through.

"I didn't come to fix things," he added quickly, his voice faltering. "I just… I needed you to know I never stopped thinking about you."

His words echoed in the quiet, stirring old ache and a stubborn hope I tried to ignore.

"Four years," I said. "You thought about me for four years?"

He shifted, jaw tense. "I was ashamed. I didn't think I had a right to find you."

"You didn't." The words hung between us, heavy with memories neither of us dared to voice.

He nodded, silence swelling. My thoughts raced with images of empty rooms, half-packed boxes, the silence after the shouting. Part of me wanted to yell, demand answers, but I stayed where I was.

But he didn't walk away.

"I'm getting out," he said. "Of everything. We're not together anymore. I'm sober. I'm in a program." His sentences tumbled out, raw and unfinished, hope stitched into each phrase.

I didn't ask for proof because I didn't believe it. But I didn't slam the door either.

He hesitated, fingers curling tightly around something in his pocket. Then, with a slow, uncertain movement, he pulled out a piece of paper—creased and softened at the edges, worn thin from being folded and unfolded too many times.

"I wrote you a letter," he said, voice hoarse. "A while ago. But I didn't know where to send it."

I stared, my throat suddenly dry, at the tremble of his hand. The paper looked fragile, as if it might dissolve in the August air between us.

"Can I give it to you?" he asked softly, his voice uncertain.

I managed a nod, unable to trust my voice.

He set the letter gently on the metal railing. His footsteps echoed as he stepped back, widening the silence between us. I caught the faint scent of rain on hot pavement, the cool brush of a breeze against my skin.

"I'm not expecting anything," he said. "Just… I'm proud of you."

"How would you know?" My arms tightened around myself, heart thudding.

He swallowed, lips pressed thin. "I asked about you. Heard you got a scholarship. That you're going to college."

"I did," I said, barely more than a whisper.

"I hope it's everything you want."

He hesitated, gaze flickering to the ground. "You deserve good things."

As he turned and walked away, I watched the letter, feeling its weight before I ever picked it up. I wondered what it had cost him to come here, to admit he'd been watching from afar. The silence carried both loss and a faint hope for renewal.

And just like that he was gone.

I didn't pick the letter up right away. The hallway smelled faintly of dust and old paint, the dim light pooling at my feet. I stood in the doorway, heart pounding, arms crossed tight over my chest, as if I could keep the world out just a little longer. The house was quiet and empty as I stood there, noticing the stillness and silence.

Finally, I stepped forward, the floor creaking beneath me. My fingers trembled as I touched the envelope, feeling the rough grain of the paper against my skin. Outside, a distant car door slammed, sharp and incongruous in the thick air, but here, inside, everything was quiet except for the shallow sound of my own breath and the faint ticking of a wall clock.

It was handwritten. Slanted. Familiar.

Makenzie,

I do not expect you to read this, nor do I anticipate your forgiveness. Nonetheless, it is important for me to express these thoughts.

Our actions were inappropriate; we did not simply leave a house but also left you behind. This is something I reflect on every day.

You were truly significant in our lives, and we did not uphold our responsibilities toward you. There are no justifications for our conduct. We struggled, and rather than support you, we withdrew.

I am uncertain whether reconciliation is possible or desired. Should that opportunity arise in the future, I will accept your decision and remain present as you progress.

It is now clear to me that you have always demonstrated greater resilience than we did.

–Dad

I folded the letter slowly, carefully, the paper crinkling beneath my fingers. I stared at the folded sheet in my hands, unsure if I wanted to keep it or throw it away. The words echoed in my mind, stirring something I wasn't ready to name.

I sat on the edge of my bed, the letter's weight a presence in my palm, my fingers pressing into the soft creases as if I could press answers out of old paper. My chest felt tight—like the words had taken up residence there, crowding out air, making every breath deliberate. I could almost hear Dad's voice in the silent room, those lines looping through my head, gentle and persistent.

I didn't cry. Not this time. But the ache lingered, subtle and deep, like a bruise you only notice when you touch it.

I haven't forgiven him yet—not after that winter night when he left without saying goodbye. The distance between us felt both narrow, like a hallway I could almost cross, and impossibly wide, like a frozen river I dared not step onto. I kept the letter anyway, even as memories tangled around my fingers: the warmth of his laughter at my tea parties with dolls, the ache that now came with remembering. Holding the letter felt both soothing, like a blanket pulled over old hurts, and sharp, as if the paper itself knew how to sting. I couldn't let go, but I wasn't ready to reach out, either.

That night, as I stared at what I hadn't thrown away, I realized forgiveness isn't a race—it's something I get to decide, in my own time, on my own terms.

So, I added a new line to my list:

#16   Forgive at your own pace. You get to choose when.

Chapter Twenty-Three:

Orientation

The letter stayed folded on the desk for days—its presence quietly demanding, quietly overwhelming. Every time I glanced at the envelope, my chest tightened with memories I wasn't ready to face. I wondered if I'd ever be ready. The words inside lingered: a gentle apology, a hope for understanding, a bridge not quite built. I didn't reread it, didn't confide in anyone. I just let it exist, pressing against my life like a bruise I kept hidden.

But I didn't let it stop me.

Between the silence of the letter and the uncertainty it carried, I found myself holding my breath—waiting for something to pull me forward. Then, Thursday morning, the email arrived.

Welcome to the Southeast Youth Scholars Program!

This was the program I'd dreamed about since freshman year—the one that felt out of reach until now. Attached was a checklist, a welcome packet, and an invitation to orientation weekend at the university.

Orientation! That word made me want to cry, or shout, or scream!

Not from fear, but from the sharp, sudden hope that replaced all those years of bracing for disappointment.

For the first time in my life, the future wasn't just something I hoped to survive, it was something I was choosing.

The ache of old memories would remain, quietly marking where I'd come from. But here, in this new moment, anticipation pulsed beneath my skin, eclipsing old doubts with possibility and belonging.

The sound of the pen scratching against the paper provided a sense of stability. On the page, everything appeared straightforward:

☐ Financial Aid ID

☐ Government-issued photo ID

☐ Health records

☐ Housing forms

☐ Course selections

☐ School supplies

☐ Linens, toiletries, dishes, clothes, laundry stuff

While reviewing the list, I realized I lacked both confidence and essentials. The familiar room seemed restricting, making me question if I was ready to move on.

Still, hope pressed close, nudging me to move. I thought of my mom's quiet goodbyes and the way my heart clenched at the idea of mornings without her familiar footsteps in the hallway. I'd imagined college as freedom, but now I saw the wide-open space of it—equal parts thrilling and terrifying.

Lila found out at lunch, nearly spilling her smoothie on my schedule.

"Wait, you're going to orientation?!"

I nodded, trying to contain the swirl inside me.

"Yes."

"Like, with a roommate and a dorm and a weird R.A. who does icebreakers?"

"That's the plan."

"Makenzie. This is major!"

She leaned in, eyes sparkling. "You'll need more than one Target run."

I laughed, my voice sounding lighter than I felt. "I don't have money for Target runs."

She grinned. "Lucky for you, I have a mom who works retail and an older cousin with storage bins full of dorm stuff she swears she doesn't need."

I raised a brow. "Are you serious?"

"Dead serious. We're going scavenger hunting."

Two days later, I was wedged among stacks of rumpled sheets—soft and a little scratchy from years in storage—in the back of her mom's van. The desk lamp shaped like a pineapple glittered in the sunlight, its base cool and smooth beneath my fingertips. Every turn sent the dishes clattering lightly, a jumble of ceramic and plastic stacking and unstacking with each bump in the road. Somewhere beneath a pile of towels, a gently used backpack gave off a faint vanilla scent, mingling with the clean, powdery aroma of fabric softener.

Surrounded by these odds and ends—each one with its own history—I felt a rush of nervous excitement, tangled with nostalgia. It was as if the past and the future were packed alongside me, shifting with every mile, and I wasn't sure whether I was ready to let go or leap forward.

"This is the fun part," Lila said, her chipped nail polish catching the light as she spun a pen between her fingers. "You're curating your new identity. new pens, new notebooks, and new chance to be whoever you want."

"I don't want to be anyone else."

She smiled, fiddling with a friendship bracelet half-unraveled on her wrist. "Good. Because the world's getting ready to meet the real you."

Back at the apartment, I spread everything out across my bed, the faded comforter catching the sunlight in a way that made every item look like a tiny artifact. Talia peeked her head in, her hair up in a messy bun, paint flecks still visible on her hands from an afternoon project.

"Nice haul," she said, nudging a stack of notebooks with her elbow.

"You think?"

"You're going to be one of those over-prepared kids."

I laughed. "Probably."

She lingered in the doorway with soft eyes. "Good. Don't show up with just a pillow and shame. Trust me." For a second, her gaze drifted to the watercolor taped above my desk—the one she made for my last birthday, all blue and gold and a crooked sun. "Remember when you tried to move in here with nothing but a plastic bag and a granola bar?"

I smiled at the memory, the granola bar stale and the bag already tearing. "You rescued me then, too."

She shrugged, but her grin was proud. "It's what roommates do." The way she said it, simple, and solid—made me feel anchored.

Packing became sacred. I ran my fingers along the smooth rim of each storage bin, the cold plastic grounding me. Each t-shirt folded was a silent promise. My checklist grew, lines blurring with excitement and worry: label, double-check, tape. I tucked my orientation invite into my closet, smoothing the paper flat so it wouldn't crease, heart thudding faster with each small act of preparation.

Ms. Nina popped in for a room check, jingling her keys like a pocket-sized wind chime. She caught me organizing highlighters by color and smiled, that rare, crooked smile. "You ready for the next step?" she asked, voice low and knowing.

I nodded, the feeling knotting in my chest—not fear, but the kind of nervousness that tastes like hope.

That evening, my phone buzzed, and Mrs. Grant's name appeared. I told her everything but not about Dad or the letter, voice tumbling out in uneven bursts. There was a long pause on the other end, then the soft rustling of papers—the comforting sound I'd come to associate with her presence. "Let me drive you to orientation," she said gently. I could almost see the way her eyes crinkled in the corners, the way she always set a hand on my shoulder when words weren't enough.

I said yes, not for the ride, but for the comfort of her steady presence beside me. The kind of steadiness that felt reassuring.

I didn't call my dad. He hadn't earned that yet. But I slid his letter between two pages in my notebook, the paper rough beneath my thumb—a secret, unfinished story I controlled now. Maybe someday I'd reply,. or maybe not. The choice felt clean, crisp, and entirely my own.

The night before orientation, the apartment was hushed, the familiar hum of the fridge and the muted city lights outside making the ordinary extraordinary. I stood by the wall glancing at the list that had started it all. Each line was an echo, faded but indelible: Go to college. Learn how to live like you're staying. Keep going anyway. Believe it when the world says yes. Say yes back. Forgive at your own pace.

#1   *Have a room with a door that locks*

#2   *Take a real shower*

#3   *Eat hot food I didn't have to steal*

#4   *Go to college*

#5   *Never cry again over people who left.*

#6   *Forgive, not forget*

#7   *Make my life count.*

#8   *Be seen.*

#9   *Tell someone the truth.*

#10   *Don't hurt the people who try to help you.*

#11   *Try again, even if it breaks you first.*

#12.   *Learn how to live as if you are staying.*

#13   *Keep going.*

#14   *Believe it when the world says yes.*

#15   *Say yes back.*

#16   *Forgive at your own pace. You get to choose when.*

Finally, I grabbed my favorite pen—deep blue ink, warm in my hand from being held too tight. I added a new line, right in the center.

#17   Unpack your life without apology.

The pen left a small indentation against the paper, a tangible sign that something had shifted. I looked around at my shadowed room, the quiet broken only by the soft rhythm of my breath. For the first time, I realized the hope I'd scribbled into old lists had become something real—a future I was finally ready to carry beginning in the morning.

Chapter Twenty-Four:

The Doorway Moment

The night before moving in, sleep barely came. Every sound from the apartment pressed in—Talia's quiet humming through the wall, Cheyenne's footsteps trailing past my door, the fridge's steady whir. I lingered in that noise, knowing these familiar voices and rhythms would soon become memories.

As I packed, my list kept me anchored. Backpack: zipped. Forms: stacked. Bedding: rolled. Notebook: tucked under my hoodie at the top. The bag felt heavier than its contents, a vessel for all the versions of me it had carried. I was ready to go but letting go of this chapter hurt more than I expected.

From the hallway, Talia's voice called out, soft and teasing. "Don't forget your charger this time, Makenzie." I grinned, promising, "I won't. Not leaving any part of me behind." Cheyenne, passing through with her hair tied up, winked. "Send us a postcard. Or just text us at 2 a.m.—I'll pretend to be wise."

Mrs. Grant arrived early. Boots rode shotgun, tail thumping in time with my heart. The car, scented with lavender and lemon the familiar felt welcoming. My box sat beside me, my stomach tight with anticipation.

"You nervous?" she asked, eyes meeting mine in the mirror.

"Kind of."

"You're allowed that."

"I feel like I'm walking out of one life and into another."

She smiled. "You are, but you're bringing the best parts of yourself."

The drive was quiet, but not empty—the kind of silence that lets meaning settle. Mrs. Grant didn't rush me. She let me hold on, even as everything changed.

When we reached the dorm, the scene was alive: bins ricocheting upstairs, laughter echoing from open doors, signs declaring WELCOME HOME. I clutched my list, the weight of goodbye and hello mingling.

Mrs. Grant parked and said, "It's okay to be nervous, but remember to be proud." She gave me a hand-painted frame with a photo: Boots asleep on her lap and me writing at the kitchen table. I looked safe and at home in the picture.

"You think I'll be okay?"

"I know you will. You already are."

The goodbye came swiftly—a lingering hug, a whispered "Don't be afraid to accept space," a kiss on my forehead. Boots barked, sensing the moment. Mrs.

Grant walked to her car without looking back, and I watched her, knowing this was her win too.

 I unfolded my list, reading each line, tracing the journey. In bold pen, I wrote:

#18   Say goodbye without losing where you came from.

#19   Say hello to who you're becoming.

Chapter Twenty-Five:

Two Beds, One Chance

The door swung open before I even reached for the knob, my pulse quickening in my chest.

A girl stood there, barefoot and clutching a leafy plant. Her gaze was direct, yet warm, and I felt the weight of my own uncertainty pressing into my shoulders.

" You Makenzie?" she asked, as if she already knew.

"Yeah. That's me."

She grinned; a flash of easy confidence that made me wonder if I could ever feel as at home here as she did. "I'm Riley. Sorry about the jungle—I brought too many plants and now we live in a greenhouse."

I glanced past her, taking in the scene. She wasn't exaggerating.

Vines trailed along the window, succulents lined the sill, and something leafy and purple spilled from her closet. The air smelled of basil and a sharp citrus tang, mingling with the faint sound of leaves brushing against the glass and the soft rhythm of Riley's humming, making the room feel alive and vibrant.

"I like it," I managed honestly, my voice thinner than I wanted. "It's… fresh."

She stepped aside, letting me in. "Come in. Your side's the one with less moss."

As I crossed the threshold, a surge of nerves tightened in my stomach. Riley spoke with the ease of someone who belonged everywhere: showing where she kept her books, pointing out the best outlets for charging, warning me not to touch the cactus named Kevin. Her mismatched socks peeked out from beneath a faded tote bag adorned with hand-drawn constellations. Her hair, piled into a messy bun, bounced as she unfurled a rug patterned with tiny yellow moons.

I unpacked slowly, careful not to let the nerves show. My hands trembled slightly as I placed my books on the shelf, hoping Riley wouldn't notice how uncertain I felt. Every tiny sound—a book thudding gently against wood, the crinkle of a plastic bag—seemed magnified in the newness of the space.

Every time I glanced at Riley, she was in motion— placing, folding, organizing with a focus I envied. Her easy confidence made me wonder if I could ever feel as at home here as she did. Beneath my quiet exterior, questions buzzed: Would I fit in here? Could I thrive, as Mrs. Grant suggested

I didn't know if I belonged yet.

But I was trying.

"So," she said finally, flopping onto her bed with a gentle thud, sending a cloud of dust swirling in the golden light. "What's your story?"

For a moment, I wondered how much to share—how much of myself I was ready to unpack in this new place, with this stranger who might become a friend. My heart fluttered, unsure if this room could hold all the pieces of me. The faint scent of new linens mixed with the tang of fresh paint as we moved boxes around, each item shifting the landscape of our shared space. Sunlight slanted through the blinds, casting striped patterns across Riley's unmade bed and painting the walls in warm, uneven bands. Somewhere outside, distant laughter and the thump of footsteps echoed down the hallway, blending with the soft hum of our kettle heating on the desk.

Riley must've sensed my hesitation because she added, "You don't have to tell me yet. I'm just one of those overly curious 'let's trauma-bond over iced coffee' types."

I laughed—a real one this time, surprised at how easy it felt. "I guess… my story's still being written." The words came out softer than I intended, tinged with nerves and hope.

She pointed a finger at me, eyes bright. "That's a great answer. Sounds mysterious. Also sounds like a poet. Are you a poet?"

"More like… a survivor with a notebook." I glanced at my battered journal atop a stack of textbooks, wondering if its pages were ready for a new chapter.

She gasped dramatically. "I knew you had layers," she said, pulling her faded tote bag closer and fishing out a handful of sparkly pens.

We spent the afternoon arranging our room, the faint scent of basil and citrus mingling with the sterile freshness of new paint. The kettle whistled softly, and I put my photo of her, I and Boots by the lamp, hung my list on the corkboard, and taped a small watercolor card from Mrs. Grant above my desk. It just said: "Shine quietly but never shrink." Each item found a place, shifting the room from blank canvas to shared story.

Riley watched me but didn't press, humming under her breath as she unboxed a pair of mugs and declared, "We're making dorm tea nights a thing, just so you know."

I smiled, my nerves starting to loosen. "Sounds like a plan."

Later, we went to the campus welcome mixer.

Bright lights flickered, darting across faces and walls, a kaleidoscope of color that danced in time with bass too heavy for the old tile floors. The air was thick with the scent of popcorn, cheap cologne, and something sweet—maybe someone's perfume, maybe spilled soda. Laughter bounced off the cinderblock walls, spilling out of open doors and echoing down the hallway like a chorus of possibility and nerves. My shoes squeaked on the linoleum as I tried to stay near

Riley, who breezed through the crowd with effortless charm, tossing compliments about shoes and squinting at potted succulents as if they were old friends.

I stood just behind her, hands tucked in my pockets, scanning the room for safe corners. The bass from the speakers rattled the old floorboards beneath my feet, while the air shimmered with the scents of spilled cider, sugary perfume, and buttery popcorn. Neon colors ricocheted off the cinderblock walls, casting strange moving shadows across clusters of laughing students. Every so often, Riley caught my eye and grinned, a silent invitation to join her lively orbit. "This is my roommate Makenzie. She's the best," she announced to someone over the thrum of music, and I felt a flicker of warmth spark in my chest. No one had ever introduced me like that before—like I belonged here by default, not by explanation. For a moment, I wondered if anyone else noticed how my shoulders relaxed, how I fit in. The thought hovered, delicate and hopeful, as the party spun on around us.

I wondered if anyone else felt as invisible as I did in crowds like these, or if Riley's confidence were something you could learn. Maybe there was a trick— a secret handshake, a password to unlock the part of you that asks questions and expects answers.

That night, the party faded to memory as we slipped back into our room. The dorm felt different somehow—still bathed in the sterile brightness of new paint but now layered with voices and laughter lingering in the air. I pressed my forehead to the cool glass of our window, letting the city sounds drift up through the screen: distant sirens, muffled music, the hum of campus life pulsing beneath us.

Dozens of new lives stacked floor by floor, each room a pocket of hope and uncertainty. I could have been anywhere. I almost wasn't anywhere. But here I stood. Alive. Exhausted. Hopeful.

Riley lobbed a granola bar at me from across the room. "Emergency dorm snacks," she declared, her eyes twinkling. "Rule one of survival: always share with your co-explorer."

I snorted and tossed her a crumpled bag of trail mix. "Rule two: only snack with people who laugh at your jokes."

She raised an eyebrow. "Trail mix? Living dangerously. Next thing you'll say is you write poetry about raisins."

"Only on Thursdays," I replied, the words lighter than I expected. We laughed and it stitched another thread into the fabric of our friendship.

As Riley burrowed under her covers, she called out, "Goodnight, mystery roommate."

"Goodnight, plant queen," I said, glancing at the succulent she'd perched on our windowsill.

Lying in my own bed, the mattress unfamiliar but somehow comforting, I traced the lines of light shifting over the ceiling. The room felt more like ours now scented with basil from Riley's plant, citrus from her lotion, and the faint echo of the party. I felt the beginnings of something soft and new, like the start of a poem or the first page of a story that might one day be mine.

Let this be the start, I thought, gripping my journal beneath the covers.

I scribbled in the margin:

#20   Make room—for new people, new chances, and a self who doesn't need to hide.

And somewhere quiet, I wondered if tomorrow would be easier, or if I would finally ask Riley for the secret handshake.

Chapter Twenty-Six:

Words Without Stamps

It started with an ache—dull, persistent, like the press of a stone lodged just beneath my ribs. I lay in bed after my first real college class—Intro to Social Psychology—feeling the room's hush settle around me, the faint hum of distant music leaking through the walls. The professor's words echoed in the silence: "formative wounds."

Resilience. Abandonment. The terms hung in the air long after the lecture ended, snagging on memories I was trying to suppress. I remembered the hush that filled our house after my mother's laughter disappeared, the way I used to trace the pattern on the hallway rug, waiting for footsteps that never came back. That kind of absence shapes you, even if you pretend it doesn't.

Lying there, I struggled to sort through the tangled thoughts pressing on me each one buzzing under my skin, intense and unrelenting.

So, I did what I always do when feelings become too tangled to sort out:

I reached for my notebook.

And started to write.

Dear Mom,

I'm not sure if I'm writing to the person you were or the person I needed you to be—or maybe just the idea of you that I've carried all this time.

There are days I hate you. Not just because you left, but because you stayed gone. I remember that Thursday in October—rain ticking against the window, the smell of coffee from the kitchen. I spent hours tracing the faded pattern on the hallway rug, glancing at the clock every few minutes, convinced I'd hear your keys in the door. I told myself you were just running late, or that you'd turn around when you remembered how much I needed you. But the clock kept moving, and you never shared.

I needed you to fight for me, just once. Even a little. Your absence carved a hollow in me I'm still learning how to fill.

But I also remember when you laughed in the kitchen after I dropped your favorite mug, spinning a story about how it must have been cursed. I remember the mornings when you braided my hair before school— your fingers gentle, the scent of your lavender and lemon lotion filling the air, your voice telling me that each braid was a kind of armor. The first time I had to braid my hair alone, I fumbled with the sections, my hands clumsy and cold, and I cried quietly all alone. I just wanted you there.

Now, years later, I'm in college. My dorm room smells like coffee and laundry detergent and green plants. Riley, my roommate, talks with a kind of fearless brightness. I'm learning slowly, how to stay, how to show up for myself, how to braid my own hair even when it's messy and uneven. You should've been here to see it. But you're not.

So, I'm writing it down for both of us. Because even though I don't owe you this, part of me still wants you to know I'm making it. I waited, I grew, I survived. Without you.

Maybe, someday, the truth of that will stop hurting. Maybe, one day, that will be enough.

–Makenzie

I sat with the letter in my lap for a long time, the paper soft and a little worn at the edges, cool against my fingertips. The room was soaked in the scent of brewing coffee drifting faintly from the hallway, and something sharp and clean—laundered sheets, ozone from a passing storm—floated through the open window that let the plants breathe.

Riley was asleep, one arm dangling off her bed, a podcast murmuring through her earbuds. Outside, the night was stitched together with the steady chorus of cicadas and the distant click of bicycle gears on the pavement below. I let the quiet settle into me, but a tightness pressed beneath my ribs, a small ache that radiated with every breath. For a second, I heard my mother's voice—soft, amused—reading a fairy tale to me under the kitchen table, the world safely suspended around us. The memory flickered and was gone, leaving me raw and awake.

I didn't cry.

I didn't rip the letter up.

I ran my thumb over the creased fold, noticing how it trembled just a little—like the wing of a moth caught between window and night. Then I folded the letter carefully and slid it into the back pocket of my notebook. A page meant for me, not her.

 Letters are like that.

Unsent but never wasted.

That night, before I fell asleep, I added one more line to my list:

#21   Speak your truth, even when no one's listening.

Because sometimes, saying it to yourself is what sets you free.

Chapter Twenty-Seven:

The Slip

It was the kind of day that started with spilled coffee and grew heavier with every misstep. My alarm failed, breakfast was a casualty of rushing, and by the time I crashed into my ethics seminar—late and disheveled— my confidence was already fraying. I dropped my notebook, and it landed open, exposing the list I'd scribbled for myself. A girl beside me glanced over, eyes lingering on my handwriting.

After class, she caught me at the stairs. "That list— some kind of journaling therapy?" Her tone was half-curious, half-mocking.

I blinked, not knowing how to answer.

She smirked. "You know, trauma-core stuff. Looking for attention or publication?"

I stiffened. The sting of her words scraped raw against the thought that maybe she was right. Maybe I didn't belong here—maybe I was just a story waiting to be picked apart.

She offered a hollow smile. "Good luck," she said before vanishing down the hallway.

I found myself alone on a bench near the student center, notebook in my lap, list splayed open: Go to college. Learn how to live like you're staying. Make room—for new people, new chances.

My hand hovered, mind circling back to that brutal doubt: What if I didn't belong here? I had one hoodie, three good pens, and a story I only half-believed I'd earned the right to tell.

Later, in the library, words on a psychology textbook blurred. Her accusation—attention-seeking—echoed in my head, making me wonder if everyone saw me that way. Was I just a pity scholarship? Had I weaponized my past to gain entrance to this world?

I shut the book, the question—What if I didn't belong here? —sharpening inside me. I wandered around campus without purpose, convinced I was an imposter among the confident, the prepared, the ones who fit.

Back in my room, Riley glanced up from her laptop. "You okay? You look like someone kicked your dreams down a flight of stairs."

"Just… a long day."

"You want tea or silence?"

"Silence," I said.

She nodded; volume dialed down and made me tea. Sometimes, the right kind of quiet is what sets you free and a friend who knows what you need.

That night, in the bathroom mirror, I stared at my reflection—same face, same doubts, unraveling inside.

I wanted, just for a moment, to go back to a version of me who didn't have to prove anything, who just stayed hidden and survived. Failure that felt expected—a part of the landscape, not a betrayal. Maybe that was an easier way.

I returned to my room and tore out a blank page. My hand shook as I wrote: Today, I wanted to leave. I wanted to shrink. I wanted to stop pretending this version of my life fits. But then I remembered—I didn't come here to blend in. I came here to build something new.

For the first time all day, I believed it—just enough to keep going.

I added to my list:

#22   You still belong—even on the hard days.

Because the hard days are when belonging matters most.

Chapter Twenty-Eight:

The Words I Needed

I sat back and stared at the words. In the hush of the evening, hope felt real—like a pulse in my chest. Becoming wasn't just surviving or enduring. It was the courage to step forward with everything I'd carried, to let the past become part of the foundation instead of a shadow. In that moment, becoming felt like daring to believe my own story could shape the world ahead, and letting myself claim it fully—even with the rain falling and the silence thick, even as something new unfolded inside me, bright and quiet as dawn.

It was raining.

The kind of slow, steady rain that settles over the day like a soft apology.

I was still shaken from yesterday. My confidence had cracked, and even sleep hadn't filled the gap. I walked to class with my hood up, my head down and my heart quieter than usual.

The lecture hall felt colder than I remembered. The sociology professor—Dr. Mayer—stood at the podium, her shoulders straight but her eyes soft. As she adjusted her glasses, she scanned the room, her gaze lingering on me for just a moment, as if she sensed I needed something more than the usual lesson.

I slipped into the back row, trying to go unnoticed. Most students murmured to each other, the rustle of notebooks and the tap of pens filling the air. A girl near the window chewed her pen, eyes darting nervously between the clock and the door. In the front row, a tall guy with curly hair balanced his chin on his fist, looking more awake than usual.

"We have a guest today," Dr. Mayer announced, her voice gentle but resolute. "Someone who speaks on youth resilience and systems that fail—and how we rise anyway."

A woman stepped forward. Late thirties, maybe. Braids, boots, a sharp posture softened by kind eyes. She looked like she knew things—real things. Her presence quieted the room, curiosity settling around us.

Her name was Dr. Elan Rhodes.

She didn't use slides or notes. She just stood in the center and began.

She spoke about aging out of foster care, sleeping on couches. Working two jobs in high school and lying to landlords about having parents.

"I wasn't a statistic," she said. "I was a warning. That's what the world told me."

She paused, eyes scanning the room. A student in the front row wiped away a tear, mirroring my own quiet relief. Even the professor, arms crossed, seemed to hold her breath.

"Now I know—I was a blueprint."

That word hit me like thunder: blueprint.

She wasn't ashamed of where she came from.

She used it, built on it, and rose because of it, not despite it.

My hands trembled in my lap.

She talked about teachers who overlooked her. Friends who didn't understand and systems that didn't expect her to go beyond survival.

"I was always 'at-risk,'" she said, air-quoting. "Never 'at-potential.' But here's what they didn't see—resilience is a muscle. And I'd been lifting heavy since I was thirteen."

Someone laughed—a small, emotional sound. I realized it was me.

Dr. Rhodes kept going. She shared how college terrified her, how roommates didn't know what it meant to budget down to nickels, how she wondered every day if she belonged.

"And I didn't," she admitted. "Not at first."

The class held its breath. For the first time since yesterday, I felt something loosen inside me—a belief that maybe I could build something new from everything I'd survived.

"But belonging isn't something you wait to be given. It's something you claim. You don't earn it by fitting in. You build it by standing exactly where you are and daring the world to make space for you."

I blinked hard. My notebook was open; pen pressed to the corner of the page. My heart, battered but still stubborn, beat a little stronger.

I started writing almost without thinking.

"You don't have to erase where you've been to grow. You must bring it with you."

When she finished, the applause was loud and honest. Students wiped their faces with jacket sleeves. Dr. Mayer smiled—proud, maybe, or simply grateful for the silence that followed.

I stayed still.

Because something had cracked open again inside me—and this time, it felt like light.

After class, the room emptied slowly, leaving behind a hush so thick it seemed to press against the windows. The last footsteps faded, and the door swung closed with a soft click. I sat for a moment, letting the silence settle over me. Dust motes hovered in the pale shaft of sunlight, and the faint, powdery scent of chalk hung in the air. My pen rolled across the desk, whispering against paper. I felt the cool plastic of my notebook beneath my palm, grounding me.

Dr. Rhodes was zipping her bag when I finally stood. The echo of her words lingered, gentle and undemanding. I hesitated, feeling the weight of everything I wanted to say.

"I just… I wanted to say thank you," I said, my voice quiet in the empty space.

She looked up, her gaze soft, unwavering and understanding. "You needed to hear it today?"

"Yeah." The air felt charged, as if every molecule were listening.

She nodded, her tone gentle and direct. "I did too. Every time I tell my story, I remember the girl who needed someone to tell it to her first."

She handed me card, and I noticed how it pressed into my palm—solid, textured, almost warm from her touch. On the back was a quote:

You are not too broken to begin.
You are brave enough to build.

I held it carefully, as if it might shatter. The silence stretched, but it felt safe—like a cocoon rather than a void.

"Keep going," she said softly.

"I'm trying," I replied, the vulnerability in my voice met with understanding in hers.

She smiled, earnest and kind. "Then you're doing it."

Back in my room, the world outside blurred by rain against the window, I taped her quote to the wall beside my growing list. The card's edges curled slightly, and I ran my finger along them, feeling their promise.

Then I added:

#23   *Don't shrink your story—someone else needs it.*

Chapter Twenty-Nine:

Still Here

I waited to reply—not out of anger or indecision, but because I wanted my words to be genuine. Now, ready at last, I took the worn letter, grabbed fresh paper, and wrote honestly.

Dear Dad,

I was uncertain about responding. The word Dad feels unfamiliar to me now. You left—both of you did. Those events carved deep marks, and no letter can smooth them away.

But—

You showed up. You stood at the door and looked me in the eye. You didn't ask to come in. You didn't expect a parade. You just stood there. That... mattered more than I wanted it to.

Grief doesn't always announce itself. Sometimes it's not tears, but the hush that follows. For years, you were silent. Birthdays passed quietly. Holidays felt incomplete. Each year made your absence both heavier and easier to carry.

I had to learn how to grow quietly. I filled the silence with questions, with anger, with moments where I almost forgot the sound of your voice. Seeing you again brought all of that rushing back—not as answers, but as reminders that healing is rarely simple.

I still don't know why you left. Not really.

And honestly? I don't need or want to know.

Not today.

This isn't about your explanation; it's about my own choices—about the agency I reclaimed for myself.

I'm choosing to write this letter, not because you've earned it, but because I am strong enough to give it. You were once a painful chapter in my story, but never the whole book.

While those days shaped me, my world now is filled with new people and possibilities. I've been building something different—a life with roots that reach beyond old wounds.

There's lavender on my desk, its gentle and calming scent; sunlight spills across my window in the early mornings, and sometimes I pause just to watch the dust shimmer. There's a girl across the room who believes in astrology and offers tea as medicine. When professors welcome me, they show genuine warmth, recognizing that I am more than just another student— I am a person who matters . I share laughter over late-night pizza with friends who know the shape of my hope and the weight of my history.

And there's me—still here. I'm no longer the girl who begged for answers. I'm the young woman who carries her own. The hum of the city outside reminds me that the world keeps moving, and so do I.

You wrote that you're trying, working your way out of the bad places and habits. I hope that's true. Not because I owe you another chance, but because I want you to become someone worth knowing again, for yourself.

Maybe, someday, I'll see you again. I might introduce you to your grandchildren, let you help hang curtains in a nursery, or even ask you to wash a dish on Thanksgiving. Each possibility feels distant, but not impossible.

This is my decision, and it will only happen if I see you've changed for yourself, not for me.

Until then, know this: I'm not angry anymore, I'm not waiting, either. Furthermore, I'm not bitter.

The weight I once carried has lifted, leaving space for something new to grow inside me.

It took time, reflection, and the steady presence of hope to reach this place, and now, looking ahead, I feel both lighter and more open to what the future may hold.

Bitterness rots the things I'm growing—tender shoots of trust, slow-blooming self-worth, the fragile petals of peace I coax from dark soil. Each day, I water hope and let sunlight warm forgiveness, careful not to

I stared at the letter after I wrote it.

It didn't feel triumphant.

It felt... whole, fulfilling, cleansing.

Like I'd built a bridge between my past and my future, and now I could decide who I allowed to cross it.

I chose not to mail it. For now, I kept it folded, placed it in my notebook, and put it beside his. There are two accounts of events. Two attempts to connect across difficulties.

Holding onto the letter is its own kind of closure—the space between what still aches and what is ready to heal. It doesn't mean the work is finished; it means I honor the time it takes to mend. The letter is a promise to myself: I can let go when I'm truly ready, not when anyone else asks it of me.

Later that night, I sat at my desk, looked at the wall, and wrote:

#24   *Healing isn't loud.*

Sometimes, it just looks like writing a letter you're strong enough to send—or to keep for now.

Chapter Thirty:

Showing Up

I didn't volunteer because I wanted to be a hero.

I volunteered because I remembered what it felt like to be invisible.

It was the memory of sitting at the back of my eighth-grade classroom, pressed against cold cinderblock, quietly hoping no one would call my name. I had once lingered after school, waiting for a ride that didn't come, watching teachers chat and laugh as if I was just another shadow on the wall. Sometimes, I wondered if anyone noticed how I always left last.

So, when I saw the flyer taped crookedly to the student union corkboard:

"Seeking Peer Mentors – Help Us Reach At-Risk Teens Before They Fall Through the Cracks."

—I stared at it, my heart thudding in my chest. The phrase "fall through the cracks" didn't just feel familiar, it carried the echo of those afternoons, the hush of being overlooked.

I took a photo of the flyer with trembling hands. That night, I lay awake, replaying moments from my own past—the times I wanted someone to see me, not rescue me, but just sit beside me in \ silence. How I would have given anything for one person who noticed me without pity. I kept imagining what it would mean to be that person for someone else.

The next morning, after a restless sleep and a slow walk across campus, I filled out the application. Each question felt like a small confession. When the youth center director, Tori—a calm-eyed woman whose presence seemed to steady the room—asked why I wanted to mentor, I hesitated before answering. "I used to be… one of them," I said softly.

She nodded, her gaze gentle. "Then you already know more than most of us."

The first time I walked into the youth center, my steps felt heavy with hope and uncertainty. The space was bright but worn—graffiti half-scrubbed from the entryway walls, posters that proclaimed You Are Not Alone and Breathe In, Breathe Out hung above sagging bulletin boards, their corners curling. The hum of ancient computers mixed with laughter from down the hallway, while the couch fabric pressed scratchy against my palms as I steadied myself. I paused, scanning the faces scattered across the room: a wiry boy in a threadbare hoodie who bounced his knee in restless rhythm and a girl with a buzz cut, her eyes sharp and distant, tapping chipped nails against a coffee-stained table. For a moment, I wondered if I would find belonging here, or if my story would blend into just another shadow in a place built for second chances. Some glanced up, their gazes wary; some looked away, retreating into silence. Each person seemed to carry history too heavy for their age, and I found myself hoping that by showing up, I could learn where I fit among them.

I took a breath, reminding myself why I was there. Not to fix, not to save—just to show up and notice what others might miss. Every day since, I've tried to be the person I once needed.

My responsibilities included listening, being present, assisting with homework, and facilitating small group discussions when required. Primarily, my role was to consistently attend, which was considered sufficient according to Tori.

The air in the center smelled faintly of stale coffee and disinfectants, underscored by the hum of old computers and laughter echoing from the hallway. I observed the young woman with the buzz cut and chipped black nails carefully assessing me, her expression notably discerning. "You're too clean to get it," she said, her voice edged with challenge. This is when I met Jordan.

I didn't argue. I just nodded, letting the weight of her words settle between us. "I was dirtier once." My voice was quiet, honest. She didn't respond, but she didn't look away either. That continued for some time; I was present but not trusted, and I understood earning trust would require patience.

By the third week, Theo—who rarely trusted adults and kept his hood pulled tight—started sitting beside me during group. He didn't speak at first, just hovered in my shadow, his presence as quiet as a held breath. Sometimes I'd catch the scent of rain on his jacket or hear the faint click of his bitten nails against the plastic chair.

After watching a documentary on kids aging out of the system, he finally whispered, so soft I barely heard it over the buzz of the heater, "That's going to be me."

I didn't offer any easy comfort, I just looked at him and replied, "Yea, I think you're right."

One afternoon, while sorting donations in the cramped storeroom, I found a worn gray hoodie in the bin—same brand I used to wear, same size. The fabric felt rough under my fingers, seams stiff where the lining had frayed. It smelled faintly of detergent and dust, mingling with the musty odor of old coats and cardboard boxes. The fluorescent lights flickered overhead as I stood holding it, lost in memory—late nights searching for warmth, the scratch of fabric against my skin.

Tori, the program coordinator noticed my hesitation. "Memory?" she asked softly, her tone inviting but never prying.

"Yeah," I said, the word coming out like a sigh. "It's strange what sticks."

She smiled, understanding passing between us. "Want to keep it?"

I shook my head, letting the hoodie slip back into the pile. "Someone else needs it more." The moment lingered, and Tori's nod felt like a small anchor in the noisy room.

The center became a rhythm in my life—a shelter for teens who'd seen too much, lost too early, or simply needed a place to land. I started going on Tuesdays and Thursdays, an hour after class. There were no real expectations, but the walls held stories and silences, and the air buzzed with a kind of cautious hope. Sometimes, just being there felt like an act of defiance against everything that had tried to grind me down.

Riley worked at the center part-time too, but she was more than a staff member—she was the steady presence who brewed "bad day" tea, the one who could listen without needing every gap filled. Jordan, with her buzzcut and wary eyes, was one of the first residents I met—always testing boundaries, always watching to see who would flinch. Over time, their presence, routines, and quirks helped anchor me, making the center less of a stopgap and more of a place I belonged.

I noticed the change in myself slowly. Each time I walked through the doors, something softened inside me, a gentle loosening of defenses I hadn't realized were so taut. I wasn't just surviving anymore; I was giving—my time, my attention, my willingness to sit in the quiet with someone else's pain. And somehow, that act of giving returned something to me, too, a feeling I'd lost touch with.

One night, Riley asked as we wiped down tables after group, "Doesn't it feel heavy sometimes, carrying all this?" She didn't ask to pry but because she understood—she'd carried it, too.

"Sometimes," I admitted. "But I think… maybe I do it because they need someone who won't flinch. Someone who isn't scared off by the mess."

She smiled a little, that knowing way of hers. "You're really good at that."

Later, it was Riley's quiet encouragement that helped me see Jordan differently. I started noticing the small ways she reached out—a flicker of a glance, a muttered joke she pretended I didn't hear.

So, when Jordan handed me a sketch one afternoon, her movements abrupt and awkward, I understood it wasn't just a drawing but a gesture—a test of trust. In ink, she'd captured me from the side, sitting cross-legged on the floor, notebook open, caught in a moment of focus.

"You looked real when you wrote," she muttered. "Like you weren't scared of the room."

The words landed hard, but I managed, "Thanks." My voice wobbled, but I meant it.

"You can keep it or whatever. I don't care." She walked off before I could say more, but I taped the drawing above my bed that night, letting it remind me that being seen—really seen—was its own kind of bravery.

Looking back, I realized that my sense of belonging here didn't come from blending in or pretending my edges were smooth. It came from standing up, from showing up, from letting myself be steady for others even when I wasn't sure I could be.

Walking home one Thursday, notebook tucked under my arm I found a bench under a huge Oak tree and found myself scribbling with a new entry:

#25   Sometimes healing means holding space for someone else, even if no one ever held it for you.

Giving someone hope doesn't drain you—it grows you.

And as I walked towards the dorm and passed under the yellow glow of the streetlights, I felt the truth of it rooting deep inside, quiet but unshakable.

Chapter Thirty-One:

The Kind of Brave That Whispers

It started with tea and a thunderstorm.

Rain drummed against the window in soft bursts, the rhythm almost hypnotic, as if the sky itself were trying to hush the knot of worry inside me. Riley brewed her usual "bad day" blend—chamomile, honey, and a curl of orange peel—letting the steam wrap the room in calm. She called it "Calm the Chaos," but today, the chaos felt anchored in my chest.

We sat in our dorm room, legs crossed, fairy lights spilling golden pools across the scattered papers. The scent of chamomile drifted between us, grounding me just enough to notice the tremble in my own hands as I cupped the mug. Its warmth barely seeped through the chill I couldn't shake, the one that had followed me since morning—since I saw the notice taped to my mailbox, since the teacher paused just a shade too long when reading out assignments, since the feeling of being out of place pressed in, louder than usual. I wasn't prepared to share my story again.

I hadn't planned to speak. My thoughts kept circling— about the drawing above my bed, about what it meant to be seen and whether I deserved it. There was a heaviness to the day, a stubborn ache that made every gentle thing—Riley's quiet presence, the comfort of the room—feel both a relief and a reminder of everything I lacked.

Riley didn't ask what happened, just handed me the steaming mug with a glance that said, if you need to talk, I'll listen. She leaned back in her chair, the soft music barely loud enough over the rain, letting the silence stretch between us. There was no need to fill it.

I traced the rim of the cup, feeling the heat seep into my fingertips. I wanted to believe that warmth could reach deeper, that it could loosen the grip of fear, anxiety, and that old familiar loneliness. The words pressed at the back of my throat—resentment for the day, uncertainty for tomorrow, a longing to belong somewhere that didn't keep shifting beneath my feet.

If I were going to say anything, it would be now, to Riley, in this room where the world felt gentle, even when I didn't.

So, I let the silence soften me and let myself imagine—for just a moment—that it was safe to let go.

"I used to live behind a laundromat," I said, the words tasting metallic in my mouth, voice barely rising above the hush of rain tapping the glass. My heart thudded hard enough to make my hands tremble against the mug. Thunder rolled in the distance, and I pressed the heel of my palm into my thigh to ground myself.

Riley stilled, her eyes tracking every shift in my expression. Her fingers curled tightly around her mug, knuckles whitening, and she leaned in as if bridging the gap between us with nothing but her presence. The glow from the fairy lights caught the worry furrowing her brow, but she didn't interrupt.

"I stayed in that house after my parents left, just me and the echo of their arguments. I counted the days until the lights flickered out and the fridge hummed its last." I paused, shoulders tense and aching, the room seeming to contract with the memory. "Then I slept in shelters—sometimes a warm cot, sometimes just cold tile. But mostly, behind buildings, anywhere the rain couldn't reach."

Outside, the storm shifted, the rain suddenly pounding harder, rattling the window. It felt like the sky was echoing the pulse in my chest.

"I never told anyone. Not really. I was afraid if I did, I'd just disappear into a system that didn't notice people like me. So, I vanished on my own terms."

Riley's jaw tightened, her lips parting as if to speak, but she stayed silent. Her foot tapped nervously against her chair, the only sound besides the rain. There was no pity in her gaze—just a kind of fierce, aching empathy.

"I had this rule," I admitted, voice rough. "No one could help me. If they tried, it meant I owed them. And I already owed the world too much."

Pieces of me tumbled out—unfolding in flashes of memory bright and raw. The taste of rainwater caught on the rim of a chipped cup, the rough scratch of wool on discarded couches, the hum of vending machines at midnight. I spoke of the cold ache that settled into my bones on tile floors, and the relief of sunlight warming my face through dirty glass. Of Mrs. Grant, her house smelling of cinnamon and must, the way old floorboards creaked with each cautious step. And Boots—the way his tail wag let me know he cared I told Riley how the crackle of static on her ancient radio made silence feel less lonely, and how lemon—sharp and bright—could, just for a moment, make me feel safe.

She said nothing, only nodding, her eyes never leaving mine. Every so often she set her mug down, the click gentle, a small reassurance that she was still there, comforting me in the storm.

"You must have been terrified," she finally said, her words falling into the hush between thunderclaps.

"I didn't have time to be terrified," I said, my voice rough with memory. "Survival doesn't leave room for fear. Just doing whatever comes next. Counting tiles, breaths, minutes until daylight."

My laugh was brittle, but real. "College scared me as much as the streets did-Not knowing where I fit, or if I ever would."

Riley's gaze held mine across the subtle light of a desk lamp. She broke the silence with just a few words: "Can you picture the future?."

I hesitated, feeling that future brush against me—
strange, unknown. It was like standing barefoot at the
edge of a lake, the water cold and full of possibility,
but also dark and deep. Hope flickered, tentative and
trembling, tangled with the old, well-worn uncertainty.
I'd spent so long bracing for the next storm that the
idea of reaching for something better felt reckless
necessary.

Slowly, I nodded, letting the quiet stretch and settle
between us, rich with things felt but not spoken.

I felt my chest loosen, as if the tension that had held
me tight for years was slowly unraveling, replaced by
a trembling breath—a fragile strand of new air. The
lamp cast a bright light over Riley's desk, catching the
rain streaks that mapped their way down the window.
The room felt wrapped in hush: thunder low and
distant, the soft patter of water against glass, the sigh
of old floorboards shifting beneath my feet.

"I don't want you to treat me differently," I said,
noticing how my hand clenched the blanket, knuckles
whitening before I let go. My voice threaded through
the silence, rough but steady.

"I won't," she replied. "Unless it's with more snacks
and permanent respect."

My laugh came again, softer now—like wind teasing
through half-open curtains. The warmth in my chest
flickered, a small sunrise cresting behind old clouds.

Riley grabbed a marker from her desk. The faint scent of dry-erase ink drifted between us as she clicked the cap off, her fingers stained with blue from earlier notes. The sound was sharp but gentle, anchoring me to the moment. I watched her hand move, veins visible, writing with quiet precision.

"Add this to your list," she said, her voice low, almost conspiratorial.

I raised an eyebrow, pulse fluttering—a bird waking in its nest.

She uncapped the pen and wrote:

#26   Tell your story to someone who makes space for all of it.

Then she drew a tiny star beside it.

"Because you're a galaxy, Mak. Not just a star. You hold constellations the world hasn't mapped yet."

For a moment, it felt as if my memories—fractured and sharp—were drifting into orbit, tethered by gravity to something warm and luminous. I realized I'd spent so long shrinking myself into wounds and shadows, I'd forgotten the sky inside me was vast.

I didn't sleep much that night,

Not because I was afraid.

But because something had shifted—like an eclipse giving way to light, darkness yielding to new constellations of hope.

Someone else knew now.

And instead of feeling exposed, with my old fear of
being judged or misunderstood gnawing at my edges,
relief crept in—a quiet, weightless sense that my story,
in all its chaos and brilliance, was not too much.
Letting Riley see the truth of me cost a sliver of my
old armor, but in its place, I felt seen—expansive,
infinite, and stitched together by more than pain.

Chapter Thirty-Two

Worth More Than Free

I checked my emails early in the morning before class.

Subject line read: "Job Offer."

I almost deleted it. My chest fluttered—an uneasy mix of nerves and hope sparking in my brain. I couldn't help but wonder if this was another automated message, or maybe a professor reminding me of some forgotten deadline. But then my eyes landed on the sender: Tori Greene – East Street Youth Center, Program Coordinator.

The center had changed my life once before—what could they want now? I hadn't heard from anyone since I'd volunteered there last summer.

My fingers hovered above the mouse, heart thumping louder with each second. I clicked, swallowing against the dryness in my throat. The computer lab seemed to hush around me, all background chatter fading into static. My palms grew damp as I opened the message, afraid it might disappear if I rushed—afraid, too, of what it might hold. Each word pulsed with possibility, and my mind raced ahead, piecing together every memory I had of those sunlit afternoons at the center, wondering where this could lead.

Hi Makenzie,

I was truly impressed by the way you showed up for the teens—with patience, consistency, and genuine empathy. You don't flinch or force things, and that's rare. Just last week, when you helped Jamie through a tough moment, it really highlighted your gift for connecting with youth.

We have a new grant-funded position for a part-time youth outreach assistant: 12 hours a week, paid. You'd be perfect for it.

If you're interested, just reply to this email or stop by my office any time this week—I'm happy to answer any questions you have about the position. No pressure, just proud of you.

–Tori

The email subject line glowed on my screen: "Job Offer."

I read it three times.

Then I stared at the screen, hardly breathing.

Twelve hours a week-Paid!.

Someone wanted to pay me for work I'd only ever done from the heart—work that I never thought counted, because it didn't fit neatly on a resume. Was this real? Did I deserve it?

An ache of disbelief and hope pressed in my stomach, the cursor on the screen flickering like it was daring me to trust this moment. I blinked rapidly, my hands trembling ever so slightly, as if the words might vanish if I moved too quickly.

When I got back to the dorm later after the day's classes., Riley was pampering her snake and ivy plants while balancing, a cup of yogurt in her palm with her neon highlighter wedged behind her ear. She looked up, eyes flicking over my face, searching for clues.

"You look like someone just got picked for a reality show," she said, lazily as she clipped another dead leaf.

"I got offered a job."

Her spoon froze, yogurt clinging to the edge; then she shrieked, launching herself backwards. The yogurt nearly toppled onto her comforter, but she caught it just in time, leaving a smear on her wrist. "Shut up. Where?"

"At the center."

Riley whooped, flinging her arms around me in a sudden hug, the highlighter tumbling from her ear and rolling under the desk. "Mak! That's huge! Like, worthy of confetti huge!" She pulled back, grinning, pink yogurt dotting her sleeve. "Wait, do we have confetti?" She was already half off the bed, rummaging through her desk drawer with one hand, still squeezing my shoulder with the other, as if she needed physical proof this moment was real.

"I know," I whispered, voice wavering. "It doesn't feel real."

Riley let out a shaky laugh. "That's how you know it's real." She grinned, her eyes shining in the soft lamplight, then reached over and squeezed my hand, her fingers warm and a little sticky from the yogurt. For a second, everything felt impossibly bright—like the small dorm room had become the center of the universe. I could hardly sleep that night.

I met with Tori the next afternoon in her tiny office tucked behind the community kitchen. The air smelled faintly of cinnamon tea and dry-erase markers, sunlight falling in rectangles across stacks of handouts. She wore a denim jacket with enamel pins on the collar—one read Empathy Is a Revolution—and she was smoothing the edges of a color-coded schedule when I stepped inside.

"I didn't think I'd qualify," I said, settling into the chair across from her desk. My hands were cold, fingertips buzzing with adrenaline as I traced the grain of the faux wood tabletop.

Tori looked up, eyes steady, her thumb still absently brushing over the "Empathy" pin as if drawing strength from it. "You more than qualify," she said. "You embody the job."

I hesitated, searching for her face. "You really think so?"

Tori's smile softened, her fingers still tracing the edge of her "Empathy" pin. "I know so, Makenzie. You've been putting your heart into this place long before there was a title to go with it."

I let out a quiet breath, the tension in my shoulders easing. "Guess it's official, then."

She gave a gentle nod. "Official and deserved. I'm glad we can finally recognize what you've already been doing."

She slid a folder across the desk—job description, schedule options, pay rate. It wasn't a fortune, but it was enough.

Enough to buy better groceries and, for once, feel a small rush of pride at the checkout when I chose the brand-name cereal instead of the plain bag. Enough to maybe take the bus back to the dorm—not hunched in the back, hoping nobody noticed me, but sitting by the window, ticket clenched in my fist, telling myself I'd earned this.

Enough to prove—mostly to myself—that I wasn't a charity case.

In that moment, the practical things felt almost miraculous: the idea of standing in a grocery aisle, adding fresh fruit to my basket without double-checking the price, or tapping my bus card with the quiet confidence that comes from knowing I belonged. These small victories mattered, each one an affirmation that I was valuable.

When I got back to the center for group session that evening, everything looked just as it always had. The same faded bulletin board with flyers curling at the edges. The vending machines hum hovered in the air, softer somehow, almost like it was greeting me. The familiar cracked tile by the sign-in sheet still caught my eye—a small imperfection in a place I'd come to know intimately.

But something inside me had shifted. I wasn't the same person who had first walked through those doors. It felt like I'd finally received a key to my own sense of belonging. For the first time, I carried a quiet certainty that I deserved to be here, that my presence meant something. My words and actions were meaningful; confidence, self-acceptance, and understanding of my worth made the difference.

Even the air seemed different—warmer, touched with the scent of cinnamon from the staff kitchen down the hall. The echo of laughter from the rec room didn't feel like something happening to other people anymore. It felt like something I was part of.

I stepped into the group circle feeling the weight of those small miracles—each detail familiar and yet made new by the knowledge that I belonged.

Jordan—the buzzcut girl—caught my eye from across the circle, her chair tipping back on two legs.

"Yo," she said, half-grinning. "You're late."

I shrugged, lowering myself into an empty seat. The circle of chairs creaked as I settled in, the vinyl cool against my legs.

"By, what, thirty seconds?" as I smiled back at her.

"Still counts," she said, letting the chair fall forward with a thump.

Sunlight slanted through dusty blinds, catching on the turtle-shaped beanbag—the talking piece—that Theo rolled across the linoleum toward me. Its faded green looked almost golden in the light, the seams worn soft from years of passing hands.

As I looked around at the group seated in a circle, I noticed a mix of unfamiliar and familiar faces. Theo leaned forward, placing his elbows on his knees. "Where have you been?" he asked. Smiling gently, I replied, "It's good to see you too."

The hum of quiet breathing filled the space as the faint scent of coffee lingered through the room..

This was home—strange, bright, and real!

"Yeah," I said.

And then I told them.

Not everything. But enough.

That I was once where they were. That I still carried not just the weight of old fears and loneliness, but also a quiet hope for belonging—a delicate thread tying my past to this present. And that, somewhere along the way, life had looped around and created space for me here—like the first time someone saved me a seat in this circle, or when laughter over coffee made the room feel less like a meeting and more like a gathering of friends.

Later, when most of them had left, Jordan handed me a folded paper from art class.

On it was a hand-drawn cartoon turtle with a speech bubble that read:

"Congrats. You're legit now."

The little turtle, grinning up at me in blue ink, felt like a secret handshake—proof that I was seen, not only for where I'd been but for how far I'd come. And that maybe I was in some small way helping someone else to hope.

My throat tightened unexpectedly. I realized I was holding more than a drawing; I was holding the quiet acceptance I'd searched for, tucked inside a simple gesture.

I smiled so hard it hurt.

When I returned to the dorm, it started to rain. My hands were unsteady as I began writing, each letter carefully formed. I wrote:

#27   You are not just surviving you're making a difference—and you are worth investing in.

Then, almost defiantly, I wrote it again in all caps, the
ink smudging just slightly beneath my fingertips.
Around me, the hum of distant laughter filtered
through the thin dorm room walls, mingling with the
soft glow of the desk lamp. I stared at the words,
letting their truth settle over me like a warm blanket—
layer after layer of hard-won acceptance. The quiet tap
of rain against the window reminded me I wasn't alone
in this moment. It needed to be shouted—even if only
on paper.

Chapter Thirty-Three:

Staff Badge, Same Heart

The badge felt heavier than it looked.

It wasn't metal—just plastic, laminated with my name typed in bold

Makenzie Rowe

Youth Outreach Assistant

But when Tori clipped it to my hoodie, the cool edge pressed against my collarbone, making my heart flutter with a cocktail of nerves and pride. The overhead fluorescent lights buzzed softly, casting pale stripes across the linoleum, while the faint scent of lemon cleaner lingered in the hallway—details I'd never noticed before, as if the world had shifted in small, perceptible ways.

For a breathless second, I remembered the countless afternoons I'd faded into the background: the time last winter when I waited for hours in the lobby, wondering if anyone would bother to learn my name. Now, my name gleamed in block letters for everyone to see— proof that I belonged, that I mattered.

"Ready?" Tori asked, her voice warm and soothing.

I nodded, feeling the badge tug gently at my hoodie— solid, undeniable. Maybe I'd still make mistakes.

Maybe no one would listen right away. But this time, I wasn't invisible, and the possibility of what I could become shimmered ahead, thrilling, and unknown.

"Ready," I whispered, letting the sound settle between us. Then again louder-"Ready!"

It wasn't that the center looked any different.

Same faded welcome mat, scratchy beneath my shoes. Same scuffed floor tiles, cool and hard underfoot, and chipped paint catching the static glare of the overhead lights. Same circle of folding chairs near the back, their metal frames creaking whenever someone shifted. The faint aroma of cleaner lingered, mixing with the musty scent of old carpet and rain-soaked coats by the door. Somewhere down the hall, a distant radio played tinny pop music, half-swallowed by the hum of fluorescent bulbs.

But I was different.

A nervous energy prickled beneath my skin. I wondered if anyone could tell how uncertain I felt, stepping into shoes that suddenly seemed too big. My badge was a small shield, but the weight of expectation pressed in from all sides, making my pulse thrum in my ears. Was I ready to be seen this way? Was I ready to be the one people turned to, not the one who vanished into the edges of the room?

I spent the first hour in the supply closet, where the air held the sharp tang of lemon and the earthy musk of old cardboard boxes. The overhead bulb buzzed softly, flickering every few seconds so the shadows danced on the shelves as I sorted through markers, journals, and hygiene kits. My fingertips brushed gritty dust, smooth plastic, crinkled wrapper textures that reminded me I was here, real, and responsible.

Theo poked his head in while I was labeling deodorant bins.

"You're official now," he said, trying to hide a grin.

"I guess I am."

"Does this mean we have to listen to you?"

"Not unless I have a clipboard and a whistle."

He laughed, his voice echoing in the small space, then asked, "Do you like it?"

"I do," I said. "I wasn't sure I would. But I do."

He nodded, his gaze lingering a moment longer, like he understood more than he let on, and the quiet stretched comfortably between us.

Then he disappeared, leaving the closet door ajar so the mingled scents and sounds of the center drifted in, and I realized—maybe for the first time—that I was part of it, woven into the patchwork of all these lives.

Around noon, a new girl appeared.

Ivy-Thirteen, with sharp collarbones under a faded hoodie and wary eyes darting back and forth.

She hugged a threadbare drawstring backpack close—knuckles white, like she was holding fast to the last piece of herself.

Tori brought her in, offering me a quick, questioning look: Can you manage this?

I nodded, but inside, my chest tightened. I remembered what it felt like to arrive with nothing but fear and a bag of clothes. That ache, raw and familiar, flickered through me as she hovered in the doorway.

Every movement was small—a shifting foot, a twitch at her sleeve—like she was trying not to assume space.

We sat together on pillows on the worn linoleum floor, a little apart from the noise—cards slapping, someone's laughter muffled through the wall.

"You don't have to talk," I said, keeping my voice low. My hands stayed busy with my notebook, pen scratching. Ivy didn't answer, but her backpack crinkled every time she shifted.

She watched me, silently. The fluorescent hum laid a thin edge to the quiet. I tried not to look at her too long, didn't want to make her flinch.

After a minute, she whispered, "Are you staff?"

I shook my head yes. " and someone who's been there."

She chewed her lips and eyes flicking between me and the chipped tiles. "You stayed here, too?"

"Yeah."

She nodded, just once. I could feel her unease in the space between us—how hard she worked to stay invisible.

We didn't say much after that. It wasn't awkward, just a hush that felt like understanding. For now, that was enough.

"Yeah."

She picked at her sleeve "My mother left me at a center, assuring me it was only temporary; but it's been over a year now."

I nodded slowly.

The room smelled faintly of disinfectant, and I could hear her breathing slowly and steady beside me, grounding us both in the moment.

I wondered what it took for her to speak—how many words she swallowed before letting through. She didn't cry. Neither did I.

We just… sat together.

Later, I was able to lead my first group circle, as the fluorescent lights buzzed, and the smell of dry-erase markers hung in the air. Chairs scraped softly against the waxed linoleum as everyone settled in, their sneakers tapping an uncertain rhythm. Somewhere in the hall, an intercom crackled, then fell silent.

Tori watched from the back, arms folded protectively, her gaze steady but gentle, as if measuring the space I accepted. We used the turtle again as the talking piece; its shell was smooth and familiar beneath my fingertips.

"I don't have a speech," I told them, voice low but clear. "Just this: you're not broken. You're not lost. You're just carrying a story that the world hasn't caught up to yet."

A boy in red sneakers—frayed laces trailing—shrugged his shoulders, his fingers drumming on the chair. "What if no one ever catches up?" he whispered, not quite meeting my eyes.

"Then we write the story anyway," I said, trying to catch his gaze and offer a half-smile. "For ourselves."

After group, Jordan elbowed me playfully, a smirk tugging at the corner of her mouth, eyes glinting with approval. Her laugh was low, almost musical, warm in the otherwise sterile room.

"Not bad, newbie."

"You've got high standards now?" I teased, nudging back with my knee.

"Always had them. You're just finally passing." Jordan winked, then disappeared into the crowd, leaving behind the faint scent of peppermint gum.

I grinned, feeling tension slip from my shoulders.

When I got home that night, I unclipped the badge and stared at it, the smooth plastic warming in my palm. The window was open just a crack, letting in the chilly hush of evening and the faint hum of distant traffic.

I wasn't just pretending anymore. This was me!

Maybe I didn't have degrees or credentials or polished shoes. But I had something just as valuable: Experience. Empathy. Endurance.

I opened my notebook, the pages crisp beneath my fingertips, and wrote:

#28   You're allowed to accept space in the room— even if you used to sleep in hallways.

Then I drew a tiny turtle in the corner, shading its shell carefully. Because showing up wasn't enough anymore.

Now, I am leading.

And somehow, I was ready.

Chapter Thirty-Four:

The Vanishing Point

A door closed with a sharp, reverberating sound that echoed down the hallway, causing the windowpanes to rattle. Then, nothing. The silence settled in, thick as fog, making the air feel heavy. The rec room felt empty except for the faint trace of Ivy's berry-scented shampoo still lingering where she'd been curled on the bean bag chair, graphic novel splayed open and pages fluttering in the draft.

Her absence filled the room—a space where her laughter should have been, now replaced by a hollow quiet that pressed in on my ears.

I didn't see her leave. None of us did.

It was the kind of careful vanishing we'd all learned too well. Shadows slipping through cracks in the routine. The whoosh of the door swinging closed. The static cling left behind on her favorite hoodie, now gone.

A cold knot formed in my stomach when I noticed her backpack was missing from its usual spot by the chair. Confusion first, then worry set in. Did I miss something? Was there something I should have said, or seen? Guilt crept in, prickling my skin, as if maybe I had failed to hold the pieces together.

And in that moment, the room felt too still, every
sound—every absence—too loud.

It hit me when my eyes landed on the empty patch of
floor where Ivy's backpack always sat—a jolt, sharp
and electric, running through my chest. My hands
started to tremble, and a cold sweat prickled across my
forehead. I felt the faint, bitter taste of panic. Had she
left already, slipped past us all? I called out, my voice
barely steady, "Ivy?" The word hovered, thin and
uncertain. "Hey, Ivy?" Still, the silence pressed back,
thick, and unyielding, and the room seemed to close in
around me.

I searched the hallways, bathrooms, kitchen, and
bunkroom.

No hoodie. No bag. No Ivy.

Panic settled—that old, familiar kind, living in my
chest like a fire alarm I couldn't mute. For a moment, I
stood frozen, heart hammering, unsure where to turn
next.

Then instinct took over. If anyone knew what to do, it
was Tori.

I found her by the intake desk.

"She's gone," I murmured, the words barely more than
breath, swallowed up by the hush of the hallway. My
fingers curled tight against my jeans, and for a second,
I let myself lean into the cold plaster wall, eyes
flicking to the faded photograph of last summer's

picnics, caught mid-laughter, a flash of sunlight across Ivy's cheek. The silence pressed in, broken only by the distant hum of fluorescent lights overhead and the faint shuffle of papers behind the desk. I wondered if Tori could hear how my voice trembled, how the air seemed suddenly heavier, thick with the memory of footsteps that would not return.

Tori's eyes narrowed, sharp and focused. "When?"

"Maybe ten minutes, maybe an hour. I'm not sure."

Tension crackled in the quiet corridor as they scanned the deserted street outside, the weight of possibility pressing down. After hearing a distant shout echo from somewhere beyond the lobby, Tori's hands trembled as she dialed her phone. "Check the alley and the bus stop," she said, voice clipped but tight with worry.

I hesitated for a split second, a cold rush of adrenaline sparking through me, before heading toward the alley. "I'm going."

My demeanor was composed yet marked by determination and strength.

I knew what this was and what it meant for a kid who understood too well how to vanish into a city's edges—how to slip away, invisible, without a sound. I knew how her hands shook as she walked, knuckles pale, clutching the strap of her bag so tightly her fingers tingled. I knew she would keep her eyes fixed on the sidewalk, careful not to meet anyone's gaze, wary of what they might see reflected there.

The sun was starting to dip when I reached the bus stop three blocks down. The distant hum of cars echoed as I skidded to a stop, breathing sharply in my chest and sweat cooling on my forehead. The coolness of the evening air wrapped around me, tinged with the faint scent of wet pavement and exhaust. My legs trembled from the run, pulse thrumming in my ears.

And there she was!

Hood up, bag clutched, shoulders hunched—sitting on the bench like she'd aged ten years in one day.Seeing her like that made my heart clench—I'd never seen her look so small, so lost.

I stopped a few feet away.

Didn't call out.

Didn't chase.

Just… waited and gave her space.

She saw me. Her shoulders tense. But she didn't move.

I stepped closer, slowly, and carefully.

The air was thick with anticipation, heavy between us.

"Hey," I said, voice barely above a whisper. "You don't have to run."

She glanced over her shoulder. Her breath came in quick bursts, shoulders drawn tight.

She didn't answer.

I sat at the other end of the bench, the wood damp and cool beneath my palms.

She nodded, her fingers curling into the fabric of her sleeve. The tension in her jaw eased, and for a moment, the silence between us was not empty, but full—each of us anchored by the presence of the other, our breaths visible in the golden dusk.

A cold draft brushed against our ankles as dusk deepened. Then her voice dropped to a whisper. Her hands trembled as she spoke.

"I don't want to go back."

"I know," I said. "That's why I came." We sat briefly before I spoke. "Ivy, you're safe there; people care about you, including me. Ultimately, it's your decision.

She didn't say she was ready, but the way her fingers unfurled from her sleeve and her shoulders pulled back told me enough.

I rose beside her, careful not to disturb the hush that had settled between us. As we stepped out, gravel crunched softly under our feet, each step carrying the hum of mutual understanding. The air was cool and damp, clinging to our skin like a quiet reminder of everything unresolved. I glanced at her, noticing the way she shivered slightly, her arms drawn close against the chill. My own hand brushed the sleeve of my jacket, the fabric cool and slick from the lingering mist. Our shadows stretched long across the path back to the center, silent witnesses to everything left unsaid. I wondered if she felt it—the weight of all we hadn't spoken—or if she was simply grateful, as I was, not to be alone in this moment.

When we reached the center, Tori was waiting at the door, arms crossed—but not angry.

She just nodded when she saw us. "Thank you," she said to me.

Ivy brushed past her, straight into the lounge.

I turned to go, but Tori stopped me.

"You okay?"

I did not respond immediately. I reviewed the events that had occurred. Did I really want to talk about it now? The words caught in my throat, heavy and uncertain. Guilt, relief, exhaustion—all tangled together, crowding out any easy response. I wanted to say I was fine, to sidestep the question, but the truth pressed at the edges of my silence.

Because no, I wasn't.

But I was *trying.*

"I felt responsible," I admitted. "Like if she didn't come back, it would've been my fault."

Tori shook her head. "It wouldn't have been. But I get it."

I stared at my shoes. "What if I'm not strong enough to hold other people's stories?"

I searched for Tori's face, unsure if she truly understood, but grateful she didn't turn away. The silence between us settled, not awkward, but tentative—an invitation to speak or just breathe. I stared at my shoes. My chest tightened with the weight of her words, and I wondered if I'd ever feel ready. There was comfort in her presence, though, a quiet assurance that I didn't have to carry this alone.

Tori spoke again, her tone softer still. "You know, you're not the only one who worries like that. I do, too. All the time." She hesitated, glancing toward the lounge where Ivy had disappeared. "Sometimes it feels like if I let go even for a second, everything will fall apart."

I let out a shaky breath, the words tumbling out before I could stop them. "But what if it does? What if I'm not enough? What if it falls apart?"

She shook her head, a gentle smile playing at the corners of her mouth. "Then we pick up the pieces together."

A small laugh escaped me—part relief, part disbelief. "That sounds… terrifying."

"It is," Tori agreed, "but it's less terrifying when you're not alone."

I nodded, sensing a tension I hadn't noticed before slowly relax within me. Maybe I wasn't fine, not yet. But in that moment, I believed I could be.

"You don't have to hold them," she said softly. "You just have to stand next to them. And that's what you did."

That night, with the hush of the dorm settling around me, I sat at my desk and wrote until my fingers ached.

#29   You can't save everyone. But sometimes, you can remind them they're worth coming back for.

Beside those words, I sketched a small backpack—not just Ivy's, but mine too. It wasn't made of canvas or leather, but of layered memories: the heavy ache of secrets I'd never told, the weight of responsibility for kids I wouldn't be able to fix, the silent guilt I would carry in moments I failed to show up. Each zipper and pocket held something—lost chances, old fears, wishes I'd tucked away for safekeeping.

Sometimes, it felt too heavy to bear, its straps digging into my shoulders, reminding me of every burden I'd claimed as my own. But tonight, tracing the outline with a pen, I realized I didn't have to shoulder it alone. Setting it down wasn't surrender—it was relief. My heart thudded in my chest, lighter for the first time in years. For Ivy, for myself, I was learning that letting go could mean making space for something better: hope, trust, the possibility of a future brighter than today, for me and for them.

Chapter Thirty-Five:

Her Voice, My Echo

The room held its breath waiting for Ivy to speak.

Not the dull, background hush of waiting—this was a stillness that rippled through the air, settling into skin and bone. Every shuffle ceased. Even the fluorescent lights seemed to buzz softer, as if the walls themselves were listening. It was the kind of quiet that arrives when someone cracks something open—a secret, a memory, or a truth too heavy to ignore. Like the sudden hush after a glass that shatters on tile, everyone braced for the sharp edges that might follow.

Across the circle, heads turned, eyes flickered—some wide and fearful, others soft with understanding. Shoulders stiffened, hands stilled mid-fidget. What Ivy had broken wasn't just the silence, but the fragile line between what was shared and what was hidden. This was different. In that moment, it felt as if something invisible had shifted. Trust passed through the room, tentative and raw, changing everyone just a little, whether they wanted it or not.

It had been three weeks since Ivy ran.

Three weeks since the bus stop, where her hands trembled as she clutched her backpack, knuckles white, afraid to let go; Since the slow walk back, every step heavy with unsaid words and the weight of things neither of us could fix. Since the moment she looked at me—not for answers, but for proof that someone else understood what it meant to wait for something that might never come.

Since then, Ivy had stayed close, not clingy, but just close- like a shadow that lingered at the edge of lamplight.

She sat next to me during groups, her shoulder barely brushing mine, her gaze fixed on the floor, fingers worrying about a frayed bracelet until the threads threatened to snap. She helped pass out snack bags, moving quietly, her laughter rare but real—soft as a breeze through half-open windows. But her silence hung between us, thick and careful, a border searching for trust and certainty.

She hadn't shared anything until tonight.

The circle was only half full the empty chairs making the room feel even larger, the hush even heavier. From the hallway came the faint hum of voices and the shuffle of someone's shoes on linoleum—a soft counterpoint to our collective stillness.

Tori had asked everyone to share a word that scared them.

People chose "alone," "jail," "lost," murmured into the quiet until the turtle found its way to Ivy letting her know it was her turn. Her fingers curled protectively around its smooth shell, pulse flickering at her wrist.

She kept her head down, a lock of hair shielding her eyes, breath shallow as if afraid to disturb the air.

She sat there, silent, for a moment that stretched thin as glass.

When she spoke, her voice faltered on the word, which was so quiet it was almost inaudible.

"Left."

A ripple passed through the group—a chair creaked, someone's pen stilled mid-doodle. None of us dared to break the moment, as if her word might shatter if we moved too quickly. Ivy's grip on the turtle tightened, knuckles pale, but she didn't let go.

No one moved, no one pushed her.

She stayed there, fingers seeking security, confirmation from the turtle-smooth, cool, digging gently into her palm. Her voice drifted out, thin and tentative.

"My mom said she'd come back in an hour. That was over a year ago.."

A pause. The fluorescent lights hummed overhead, casting pale shadows on the circle.

"I waited on the stoop all night." She swallowed. "The air was cold. My skin prickled, but I didn't go inside."

Her grip tightened, knuckles white.

"She took my charger, too." A dry, breathless laugh. "Left me with 10%."

I suddenly noticed I wasn't breathing because I remembered what that felt like.

That weird, stupid detail you cling to.

Not the leaving.

The charger, the partially consumed sandwich, and the door that remained closed.

For Ivy, every forgotten item was a marker—a silent witness to what was lost or left unresolved. She wondered if leaving those things behind meant she was leaving behind more than just objects.

Ivy looked up. "It's dumb, right? The stuff I remember."

"No," I said firmly. "It's not dumb."

"It's just… what sticks," she said, her voice barely above a whisper. "Sometimes I wish I could forget it, but I can't. It's like the small things burrow in deeper than the big ones—the cold step, the charger, the way the door stayed shut. They're what come back at night, when it's quiet, and everything else has gone to bed."

And that was the moment, the shift.

The proof she was still here—not just physically, emotionally too. She took a deep breath and let it out slowly..

She relished the warmth on her skin, a sensation absent for weeks. For once, she breathed deeply in the calm after group, not rushing to leave..

After the session ended, only Ivy stayed.

She stayed close as I stacked chairs, the faint scent of floor polish lingering in the quiet room.

She didn't speak—just drummed her fingers on her knee, a silent question.

After a pause, she asked, "Did you feel any different after your first time speaking in front of the group?""

I paused, letting the hush settle between us. "Not really different," I said, keeping my voice low. "But less alone."

She nodded. Her fingers twisted nervously in her lap.

"I kept thinking if I said it out loud, it would make it more real," she said, voice barely above a whisper.

"Did it?"

"Yeah." A small smile flickered across her face. "But in a way that made it feel like it didn't own me anymore."

I wanted to reach out and hug her.

But instead, I slid my hand into my bag and found an index card worn and soft at the corners from being carried through so many meetings. It was the very first thing I wrote for myself when I began to heal.

Without a word, I offered it to her.

She took it, unfolding the faded lines with care.

You are not the thing they forgot.
You are everything you choose to remember.

She looked up, her eyes searching mine—a question she didn't voice hanging in the quiet. I saw her hands, delicate and unsteady, trembling just slightly as she folded the card along the faded crease. For a moment, she didn't speak, her gaze lingering on the words as if weighing their truth against old memories.

"Did you write this?" she finally asked, her voice a thread between us.

I nodded. "A long time ago. "

She tucked the card carefully into her jacket pocket, pausing to press it flat with her palm. "I think maybe I'm beginning to believe that now," she said, her voice steadier, the tiniest curve of hope at the corner of her mouth.

We sat there quietly together for some time, her thumb tracing the edge of her jacket pocket where the index card rested. I saw it in her face: a hush of fear, but also something new—a fragile anticipation and the first light of possibility. Maybe, for both of us, this moment was a beginning, a bond forming, an understanding that hadn't been there

That night, I didn't just write a new line for my list.

I read over the old ones, every faded memory and promise I'd scribbled in the margins. Each entry was more than ink on paper—it was evidence that I'd survived, that I'd imagined a future beyond what hurt.

My notebook was more than a journal.

It served as a framework and a clear direction, guiding me as I proceeded to compose my latest entry with assurance.

#30   When someone else finds their voice, listen with your whole heart. It will teach you something about yourself.

I understood that leaving the light on symbolized my openness to new voices'. I sketched a porch light, its glow inviting, always shining, and waiting to welcome.

Chapter Thirty-Six:

The Edge of the Map

The question, though gentle, pressed against me like a cold wind through the open window. My heart stumbled, fluttering in my chest, and for a moment I lost track of Riley's words, caught in a tangle of thoughts that scattered like loose pages in a draft. The room was quiet except for the occasional rustle of wrappers and the distant hum of a car passing outside, headlights briefly painting gold stripes across the walls. The air held the faint sweetness of blooming trees and soy sauce from our forgotten takeout. Riley's voice hung in the space between us, soft and careful as she tucked her hair behind her ear, the granola bar still cradled in her palm.

"What are you doing after graduation?" she asked.

I stared at the faded pattern on Riley's rug, feeling both exposed and far away, as if I'd stepped right up to the edge of something unseen. I hadn't let myself consider the future, not really, and now, with the simple weight of her question, I felt the world tilt—possibility and fear swirling together in the spring-lit room.

We sat cross-legged on the floor, the faded carpet prickling beneath my bare feet, surrounded by cartons of takeout and textbooks whose pages felt papery and sharp beneath my fingertips. The windows stood open to the city's pulse—distant laughter, the murmur of traffic, a siren rising and fading somewhere down the street. Spring air drifted in, carrying the sweet, unfamiliar scent of something blooming, mingling with the salt and soy of our half-eaten dinner.

We were supposed to be studying for finals, but instead, it felt like we were peering into an unknown future neither of us was ready to name. It was as if we'd come to the edge of an old map, where the careful lines gave way to blank parchment and the warning Here Be Dragons lingered like a breath of uncertainty. In that hush of possibility, the world outside pressed in—alive, restless, and full of questions we hadn't learned how to answer yet.

"I don't know," I said honestly, my voice rising above the soft patter of rain against the window.

Riley paused to glance outside, watching raindrops race down the glass, the city lights blurring at their edges. "You've thought about it though, right?"

"Not really." I shifted, the faded carpet rough beneath my legs, feeling its prickly texture anchoring me to the present. The room was shadowed, the dim light from the hallway barely reaching our corner and casting soft shapes across piled textbooks. The gentle patter of rain against the window mixed with the distant hum of traffic outside, while spring air, cool and damp, drifted in and brushed against my skin. I'd been so focused on staying… here. Showing up. Surviving. I never made room for what comes next. I could tell Riley was worrying about something, but I couldn't seem to put my finger on it,

She was quiet for a minute. The scent of wet pavement drifted through the cracked window. Then: "Do you want to stay at the center?"

"Maybe," I said, tracing a finger along the rim of a plastic container. "It feels safe. Familiar. But I don't know if that's enough of a reason."

Riley nodded, her gaze flickering between me and the streaked glass. "Sometimes comfort can look like purpose."

I paused, attentive to the sound of rain against the window ledge, while concealing my awareness that something was troubling her.

Then I said what I hadn't dared say aloud.

"Riley, I know you're hiding something. What's going on?"

Riley's fingers twisted the edge of her sleeve, her eyes darting to the rain-streaked window. Then she finally looked at me, her voice shaky and soft. "Mak, I… I think I might be pregnant." The words landed between us, fragile and unsteady, like a glass teetering on a table's edge.

My heart thudded so loud I could barely hear anything else. I pressed my cold hands to the plastic container, trying to keep myself steady. "Wait—are you sure? Maybe it's just stress. I mean, these last few weeks have been…" I couldn't finish. The worry was thick in my throat.

She shook her head; lips pressed tightly like she was still getting used to the taste of the truth. "I don't know for sure," she said, voice barely above a whisper. "But it feels… different. Like something's shifted inside me, and I can't quite find my footing." She let out a nervous, breathless laugh. "But you… you always make me feel safe, no matter where we are. It's like you bring home with you."

I couldn't answer right away. The room felt smaller, shadows curling in the corners. I wanted to say the right thing, but I worried that sharing my true feelings might hurt our friendship beyond repair. Who was I to tell her what to do when it was her life, her body? The lines between comfort and advice felt razor thin.

So, I took a breath and found my words gentle and real. "Home's always been something I lost, not something I carried. But maybe this—right here, right now—is your place, your moment. And whatever you choose, I'm with you. I've got your back, no matter what."

A small, persistent part of me said, "You can do this."

Riley knew it, too. She always did.

Sometimes, that voice interrupts me in the quiet moments—when I try to picture building something new, it inserts doubt mid-thought, flashing images of empty rooms and unanswered texts. Its persistence has shaped the way I hold onto routine, the way I hesitate before stepping forward. Even now, I feel it somewhere at the back of my mind, waiting to speak.

"I'm thinking of applying to grad school," she said suddenly.

I blinked. "You are?"

She nodded, her eyes shining with a mix of fear and resolve. "Social work. Trauma-informed care. Maybe even youth outreach. I've seen how many kids struggle without support, and that's why youth outreach matters to me. I figure I should walk the walk—and if I'm pregnant, my baby will be going with me. I want to make a difference, especially now. If I am a parent, I want my child to see me fighting for something that matters. It's scary, but it also feels like the right thing. I want them to see strength, hope, and the real work of helping others."

"That's amazing," I said, moved by the honesty in her voice and the weight of her dreams.

She smiled. "It's also terrifying."

We both laughed.

Then she added, "And it might be in another state."

The words dropped like a pebble in a pond—small, but enough to ripple everything. My chest tightened as I tried to picture her somewhere far away, the room suddenly feeling colder. I forced a smile, but my mind was already racing with questions I wasn't sure I wanted answered. The air between us felt charged, as if it might hum with everything unsaid.

After she mentioned leaving, I just sat there. The plans, the distance, all of it tangled in the air between us.

I didn't say anything.

Not right away.

Because this is how it always went, right?

Build something beautiful.

Watch it as it scatters.

"I don't want us to drift," I said quietly.

"We won't," Riley said, her voice steady but soft. "We'll shift. That's different."

Her words landed somewhere deep inside me, sending a tremor through my chest—like a sudden gust bending the branch of a new-leafed tree. My heartbeat louder, a quiet drum of hope and fear tangled together. For a moment, I was twelve again, remembering the sting of a friend slipping away, the way distance crept in quietly, a tide you only notice once you're ankle-deep.

I studied Riley's face in the half-light, searching for assurance that this time the current would carry us somewhere new, not just apart. Around us, the world felt poised on the edge of petals unfurling, seasons shifting, all of it fragile and fiercely alive.

"Feels the same from where I sit." I felt my own uncertainty swelling—heavy as the dusk pressing against the windows. A feeling of warmth moved up my arm, providing stability while other things seemed uncertain.

"I assure you—when the time comes to leave, we will accompany each other. It just might not be in the same location."

I tried to smile, but my chest tightened with the weight of everything unsaid—the fear that, after all our plans and promises, we might still be undone by miles and change. My eyes traced the dust motes floating in the narrow beams of light, searching for answers where there were none.

I swallowed hard. "I don't know where I'll go."

"You don't have to," she said, her voice threading carefully through the quiet.

I hesitated, half-turning toward the window as dusk deepened in the glass. "But what if I choose wrong?"

She glanced at the closed door before answering, her fingers twisting nervously in her lap. "Then you choose again."

That night, I wandered the campus alone, the world stretched wide and unfamiliar. My sneakers scuffed against the rough pavement, each step echoing in the hush between distant bursts of laughter. Somewhere across the lawn, music drifted out from an open dorm window—muffled, half-recognizable, a reminder that life continued in a thousand small rooms.

A cool breeze tangled through the branches overhead, carrying the scent of fresh-cut grass and the faint, sweet hint of spring blossoms. I breathed it in, sharp and clean, grounding me in the present even as my thoughts spiraled into what-ifs. The chill brushed against my skin, raising goosebumps along my arms, and I welcomed the sensation—proof that I was here, alive, and uncertain.

Every sense felt heightened: the scrape of gravel beneath my feet, the gentle rustle of leaves, the way my heart thudded of hope and fear. I was suspended between every possibility, longing to believe that choosing—just choosing—was enough to move forward, even if I didn't know what waited around the next bend.

I lingered in that tension, vulnerable but awake, each breath a quiet act of faith in the road ahead.

When I got back to my dorm, I pulled out my notebook—its cover worn soft from years of scribbles, half-forgotten lists, and late-night confessions.

Before the ink even touched the page, I found myself replaying the conversation from earlier, the way her words had landed—gentle, but electric. The memory of all the plans I'd made and abandoned, the roads I'd feared to take, pressed against me in the quiet.

I wrote:

#31   You can't always see the road ahead., but the fact that you get to choose it? That's the miracle.

As I circled the word choose—once, then again, and again —I remembered last week, standing at the crossroads between two majors, turning down one internship, saying yes to another. Each decision had felt like a risk, but now, the act of circling was a small rebellion against the years I'd spent feeling powerless. The motion steadied me, tracing possibility into the paper.

For the first time, I really could. The sense of freedom didn't come all at once, but now, with every loop of my pen, it gathered—unexpected yet real.

Chapter Thirty-Seven:
Return Address Unknown

It came in the mail.

Not an email. Not a message. Not a call.

Just an envelope slipped into my campus mailbox, its corners softened by the journey, the paper a muted cream with faint impressions where it had been overseen. No writing on the front, just my name in steady print.

No return address.

My hands trembled as I turned it over, memories pressing at the edges of my mind—the scent of old letters, the echo of voices I hadn't heard since I was thirteen, the ache of questions I still carried.

The handwriting was unmistakably my mother's. The careful slant, the open loops on the R's, the way she always crossed her Ts like she was fencing with the page—each stroke was vivid and familiar. The paper itself felt soft beneath my fingers, its edges slightly worn, and as I leaned in, I caught a hint of her favorite lavender hand cream mingling with old ink. Seeing those familiar marks sent a rush of apprehension through me, as if she were standing right beside me again.

I stared at it for a long moment, the world narrowing to the weight in my hand. My hands trembled as I held up the torn envelope, its edges stained and familiar, heart pounding in my chest.

Riley passed by on her way to the elevator.

"You okay?"

I nodded, unable to look away from the envelope.

She froze. "Is that from…?"

I nodded again, a lump swelling in my throat.

She walked me straight to our room, sat me down, and didn't say a word while I opened it. The chair beneath me was cold and unyielding, its edges pressing against the backs of my legs—a steady anchor as the rest of me seemed to vibrate with nerves. My heart thudded, quick and uneven, as anxious thoughts tangled in my chest—was this the moment everything would change? A portion of me considered discarding the letter or simply setting it aside, choosing to stay unaware for a while longer..

The paper was folded three times—a single sheet, cream-colored, and a little smudged. As I slid my thumb along the crease, I caught the soft scrape of paper, the hush of Riley settling on her bed, holding her breath for me. I unfolded it slowly, half-expecting it to vanish the second it hit air.

Dear Makenzie,

We realize this letter might come as a shock. Please know that we've thought about reaching out for years, unsure if we even deserved the chance to approach you.

There's no excuse for what we did. We were overwhelmed, scared, and selfish—and we left. No version of this absorbs us of responsibility, and we carry that weight every day.

We still remember your laughter echoing through the house on Saturday mornings, your feet padding down the hallway in search of cartoons. You always insisted on helping with dinner—especially stirring the sauce, your small hands determined and careful, your proud smile when you set the table just so. These moments live in us. We wish we'd held onto them better, instead of letting fear break our family apart.

Your Dad and I have chosen to make another attempt at our marriage, and we are currently back together residing in Kansas.. We work at the food bank and volunteer where we can, trying to rebuild some goodness in our lives. But there's a part of us that will always be missing, because we broke something precious in you first.

If you ever want to talk—whether it's a phone call, a letter, or just sharing a coffee—we're here for whatever feels right to you. There's no pressure, no expectations. Just hope, and a wish that you know you are loved and remembered for who you are, and who you're becoming.

Love,

Mom and Dad

I read the document twice, the paper soft and unfamiliar beneath my fingers. The room was silent except for the ticking clock on the wall, each second stretching longer than the last. Folding the letter with slow, deliberate care, I set it aside; my hands trembled just slightly as I released it onto the bedspread.

Riley watched, her eyes steady but gentle.

"You don't have to say anything," she said, her voice barely more than a whisper.

I pressed my palms to my knees, grounding myself against the cold edge of the chair.

"I don't even know what I feel if anything," I murmured.

She nodded, the hush between us settled deeper.

"That's allowed."

How can you process that?

You grow up believing the people who were supposed to love you most simply left.

You learn to piece together a new existence from the remnants they abandoned—quiet mornings spent with only your breath for company, laughter that never quite fills a room, relationships-built brick by cautious brick. With time, you convince yourself you're solid again, even if the foundation sometimes shifts beneath you. Trust is earned slowly, in small, fragile increments.

And then—years later—they send a letter, a thin envelope slipped through the mail slot like a ghost from another life, reawakening aches you thought you'd buried. The paper is cool and unfamiliar, but the ache in your chest is not. What do they expect?

"I thought they forgot me," I said.

Riley stayed quiet, letting the silence settle between us.

At one point, I let out a weary laugh—surprised that even now, I could find something to amuse me in the emptiness, as if my heart were evaluating the edges of its own resilience.

My fingers trembled as I picked the letter back up, its edges crisp against my skin—a fragile anchor to this impossible reality. "And now they want to meet?" My voice was barely a whisper, the words dissolving into the hush of the room.

Riley's gaze lingered, gentle but searching. "Do you want to?" she asked, each syllable balancing on the edge of concern.

A tightness settled in my throat, and I realized I was holding my breath. "I don't know," I admitted, my nails tracing anxious patterns atop the envelope. Part of me wanted to scream, to let grief and anger spill out unfiltered. Another part yearned to ask why, desperate for answers that might mend the old fractures. Yet, somewhere deep within—hidden and perilous—a tiny spark ached for something softer. I wanted, almost despite myself, to let them hold my hand, just to see if connection could quiet the ache.

The silence pressed in, thick as dusk, and I felt my heart stumbling over memories and invisible hopes, uncertain which to trust.

Riley placed the letter back in my lap.

"You don't owe them anything," she said. "Not forgiveness. Not a reply. Not your peace. That belongs to you."

My fingers curled around the edge of the paper, knuckles white, as I tried to steady my breath. A thousand unspoken questions flickered behind my eyes, but the weight of Riley's words pressed a fragile calm into my chest.

I nodded slowly, swallowing hard.

"I just… never imagined this."

Riley watched me for a long moment, her gaze searching and gentle. "Most people don't imagine their ghosts writing back."

A faint, uncertain warmth stirred somewhere in the tangle of my confusion and longing, as if part of me believed—just for a second—that maybe ghosts could carry hope as well as sorrow.

That night, I lay awake, tracing the faint light shifting across my ceiling, unable to surrender to sleep. It wasn't fear that kept me tethered to the darkness, but something subtler, more surprising—a gentle pulse of possibility.

It started with the echo of Riley's words in my mind, looping softly: You don't owe them anything. Yet, beneath her certainty, I remembered another moment—a summer afternoon years ago, laughter spilling across the kitchen table before everything cracked. I remembered how connection, once, felt as natural as breathing. The memory flickered, stubborn but tender, and in its glow, I felt the longing soften just a fraction.

Perhaps my pain isn't a barrier but an opening. Sharing my letter with Riley and showing my vulnerability was a first step—not closure or forgiveness, but a move toward healing.

Though the ache remained, I realized that opening, allowing myself honest words and honest silence, made room for something new. Possibility seeped in— not with a crash, but like the first thread of dawn beneath a closed door. And for now, that was enough.

In my notebook, I wrote:

#32   Healing is not forgetting. It's remembering without letting it poison you.

And beneath that, in small, determined script:

I'm still here.

I'm still whole.

I get to decide.

I get to forgive on my own time.

I remember the sound of laughter echoing in empty rooms, but now it no longer stings. The memories—sharp or gentle—pass through me without claim. Each time I choose to stay soft, to stay open, I remind myself: I am the one who writes the ending.

Chapter Thirty-Eight:

The Letter Back

It took three days before I picked up a pen.

I'd stared at my parents' letter for hours.

Folded, unfolded—the paper kept its stubborn creases soft at the edges where my thumb worked the same spot repeatedly.

They left.

They knew.

My friends in the dorm watched from a distance, their voices echoing faintly when I passed closed doors.

The ink bled through in places, smudging my fingertips.

The silence between paragraphs felt heavier than the words themselves.

And now, after everything, they wanted a meeting?

After years of silence, their request felt like an echo from another life—a knock that rattled doors I'd long ago bolted shut.

A part of me said: No! You don't get to come back. The urge to armor myself, to keep my heart locked tight, pulsed strong. But another part—the one I rarely fed—whispered: Maybe answering is for you, not them. Maybe letting myself speak is its own kind of survival.

So, I sat down at my desk, took a deep breath, and began to write.

Dear Mom and Dad,

I don't even know what to call you anymore.

It's been a long time since I said "Mom" or "Dad" and felt those words meant anything safe. When you walked out that morning, I waited for footsteps on the stairs that never came. After you left without saying goodbye, every photo in the house felt like a lie—proof of a family that no longer existed except in framed memories. But I'm writing back because I need to say things. Things I never got to say when you left. Things I carried in silence because there was no one left to say them to..

You left me when I was thirteen. You didn't just disappear—you made me invisible, a shadow searching for light in every dim-lit room. There were nights I curled up on the cold linoleum of a shelter hallway, or behind the dryers in a laundromat the hum of distant vending machines and quiet voices pressing against the dark, each sound a reminder of how far I'd fallen from home. Hunger became familiar, and I grew skilled at weaving stories—convincing teachers, counselors, even myself—that everything was fine.

But in the quiet, I started to see something else: endurance. Those nights taught me how to listen for hope in unlikely places, how to find comfort in sunlight streaming through dirty windows or in the kindness of a stranger's gesture. Pain did not break me; it sharpened my senses, forced me to notice the details of survival, and, in time, offered a clarity I carried forward.

I remember the last fall we spent together—the quiet dinners, the games of cards on the rug, the way you used to look at me as if nothing could break us apart. All those nights I pressed my forehead to the cold window, searching the empty street for your silhouette, refusing to believe that you'd really leave. I waited, night after night, watching headlights drift past, praying one would stop and you'd come home. After enough mornings waking to silence, I finally accepted you were gone.

You knew how I needed you, how terrified I was to be alone. I reached out in every way I knew—the questions I asked that you answered with silence. All I wanted was for you to see me, to care enough to come back.

Now you write, that feels cruel—a kind of distant mercy. Like watching me drown from the shore and waiting until I've learned to swim before tossing me a life preserver. You could have been the rescue. Instead, you became the reason I learned to survive.

But despite everything, I'm not writing back in anger.

I'm writing because I am strong.

Not because of you—because of who I had to become without you.

I found my voice in the silence you left behind, the first time I stood up in class and told the truth, hands shaking but heart broken.

There were days I built myself up from nothing— learning to cook a simple meal in the shelter's kitchen, laughing for the first time with someone who knew what it meant to start over.

I realized that hope could be quiet and steady, like the light that crept through the window even after the darkest nights.

Each small victory became a brick in the foundation of who I am now: resilient, aware, and no longer defined by the spaces you left empty.

During school, there were weeks when I ate lunch alone in the library, pretending to study so no one would see how isolated I felt. Still, I pushed through and graduated with honors—proof that solitude didn't define my future, only my resolve. Now, in college, I work at the youth center, mentoring lost teenagers who battle the same loneliness I once knew. Just last month, one of them confided in me for the first time; in her hesitant smile, I saw my own reflection and realized how far I've come. Each time I encourage a nervous kid to share their story, I'm reminded that my scars have become steppingstones, guiding me toward empathy and purpose. My ability to connect stems directly from the nights I spent searching for belonging, and each small triumph—mine and theirs—reaffirms that healing is ongoing, but never solitary.

And that self is no longer the thirteen-year-old girl sitting on a porch with the light off and nowhere to go.

I don't know what, meeting you would be like.

I don't know if I'm ready to find out. But maybe it's time I face what I've been avoiding. The questions, the history, the ache I kept boxed away—maybe speaking is the only path forward.

I'm willing to talk.

Not for your sake, for mine.

If we proceed, it will be on my terms—I'll choose when and how. And if I decide to walk away, you'll let me. Because that's what I deserve.

After years of silence between us, this is what I need to move forward. The weight of your absence shaped me in ways I'm still trying to understand. After everything that has happened, I need to protect myself from further hurt. That's why these boundaries aren't just lines—they're shields, built from all the fear, confusion, and hope I carried alone.

I don't forgive you, but I'm willing to hear your side of the story- One day. Maybe.

–Makenzie

I didn't cry or feel relief after writing; instead, a quiet steadiness settled through my chest, as if the air were finally easier to breathe. My hands, always fidgeting, lay still on the table. The usual knot of tension in my stomach loosened a little—I felt present, anchored, maybe even strong enough to look up at the world again. For the first time in a long while, the story I carried felt like it belonged to me, not just to my past.

Riley read the letter in silence, eyes flicking between lines. When she finished, she folded it slowly, hands careful, then slid it across the table with tears in her eyes.

"You're brave," she whispered.

"Not brave," I said, meeting her gaze. "Just tired of letting silence win."

She smiled—a small, understanding thing—and squeezed my hand.

That night, I opened my notebook and added:

#33   Speaking your truth isn't about getting answers.

It's about claiming the right to ask.

Beside it, I drew a small mailbox, this time with the flag raised—an open signal, a quiet hope, a way of telling the world I was ready for my words to be noticed, and maybe, just maybe, my questions answered.

Chapter Thirty-Nine:

The Envelope That Opened the World

Some envelopes carry weight before you even open them.

The whispering scrape as it slid beneath my dorm room door set my nerves tingling, each inch of movement amplified in the morning hush. The paper—smooth and cool to the touch—felt heavier than its size suggested, corners sharp, edges crisp against my fingertips.

My name was printed in bold ink, letters standing out as if they'd been pressed with intention. I could almost hear the low hum of promise coming from within the sealed flap, the faint scent of fresh paper mingling with anticipation.

Return address: The Artemis Foundation for Young Women in Social Change.

My heart stuttered—I'd been waiting for weeks, hoping for news that could change everything.

I stared at it, heart thudding, mouth dry.

Because this wasn't just a letter—it was a portal.

Months earlier, Riley had nudged me to apply, insisting it would change everything. Now, holding the letter, I wondered if they were right.

"It's you, Mak. It's made for someone like you."

I wasn't so sure.

The scholarship was prestigious and competitive, for students who faced real obstacles and were actively trying to reshape their worlds.

It felt… too hopeful, too shiny, too much.

But I drafted the essay anyway. I wrote about the nights I spent huddling under my thin blanket, the dim flashlight flickering while the rest of the house disappeared into darkness. Sometimes, the silence pressed so closely it felt suffocating, and each sentence I scribbled onto the page carried the fear that I wouldn't be able to keep going. I remember the cold ache in my chest, wondering if anyone would ever truly understand how impossible hope seemed—yet I forced myself to believe in something better, even as doubt gnawed at me. I tried to capture those moments honestly, letting my uncertainty and stubborn drive spill through my words, unsure if they could ever be enough.

And then I let it go.

Until now.

Now it was here. The answer.

Riley was still in class, and I didn't want to open it alone.

But I also couldn't wait.

The mattress creaked beneath me as I leaned forward, my hands trembling slightly. The pale sunlight spilled across the covers, dust motes swirling in the quiet room. Every sound—the distant hum of traffic, the tick of the wall clock—seemed amplified yet suspended.

I pressed my thumbs against the seal, feeling the faint texture of embossed paper, catching the subtle scent of ink and envelope glue. I whispered, "Whatever this says, I'm still me." But what if it changed everything? What if Riley saw me differently? My heart pounded with a mix of hope and dread, tangled together until I couldn't tell one from the other.

Then I broke the seal, held my breath, and opened the letter.

Sitting alone on my bed, I opened the envelope with trembling fingers. My hands shook as I tried to focus on the words, but they danced away from me, blurred by the sudden surge of emotion.

Dear Ms. Rowe,

It is our great pleasure to inform you…

I stopped reading.

Because I already knew.

The words pulsed behind the tightness in my chest.

I got it.

The scholarship. A full ride to graduate school. Tuition. Housing. A stipend!

For two full years.

My hands trembled as I reread the letter, the edge of the paper catching lightly against my fingertips. My breath was shallow—each inhale sharp, as if my chest was too small for the swelling inside. The words seemed to throb on the page, anchoring me in this new reality: "Congratulations." That single word glowed, luminous, promising a life I'd only dared to imagine.

I pressed my palm to my chest, feeling the frantic flutter of my heart, the electric warmth spreading through my body. The tension that had knotted my shoulders slowly unraveled, replaced by a bright, startled hope. The road ahead didn't look so bleak—it glittered with possibility, steady and real. Stability, options, and freedom beckoned from just beyond the horizon, and I let myself begin to believe.

Riley burst into the room twenty minutes later, still breathless from her psych class.

I didn't say anything. I just held up the letter.

Her eyes widened. "Is that It?"

"No."

Riley's hands trembled at her sides, her gaze flickering between the letter and my face, searching for the answer in the silent space between us.

Then I nodded, tears gathering.

"Yes."

She let out a full shriek and tackled me onto the bed. We clung to each other, laughter spilling over into tears, both of us struck silent by the magnitude of what had just happened. When the room settled, we lay side by side staring at the ceiling, as if the stars themselves had shifted in our favor.

Later that night, I hesitated before calling Tori. My thumb hovered over her number, the weight of the news pressing into me. The Artemis wasn't just any scholarship—it was the kind that changed everything: tuition, research opportunities, mentorship, a door opening onto a future I hadn't dared to picture. For me, and for Tori, it was the promise that the struggles and sacrifices hadn't been for nothing.

She answered on the second ring. "Everything okay?" There was a softness in her voice, touched by concern and familiarity.

"I got the Artemis." The words hung in the air, trembling with all hope and fear behind them.

Silence. My heart thudded in my chest, each second stretching longer—a fragile moment where everything felt possible and impossible at once. I imagined Tori gripping her phone, searching for words. When she finally spoke, her voice was thick, edged with awe.

I clutched the acceptance letter in my hand, barely able to believe my luck—my whole future contained in a single page waiting for Tori's response. "Makenzie.

You what?" Tori's voice wavered between disbelief and rising joy.

"I got it," I said, breathless, voice frayed with awe. "All of it."

A stunned inhale came through the line. Tori's silence was edged with something fragile and bright, a shaky laugh, as if she were holding back tears. "Oh my God, Makenzie…" Tori's words trembled, but her relief and pride wrapped around me like an embrace, closing the distance between us.

There was a pause—and then a sound I'd never heard from Tori before. A full, delighted squeal. It was as if all her excitement burst out at once, and I realized just how much this meant to her—not just for me, but for everything we'd hoped for together. The joy in her voice swept through me, dissolving the weight of doubt and letting something bright and fierce settle in its place.

"Congratulations, you're going to change the world, Makenzie Rowe."

I let out a short laugh, raising an eyebrow as if weighing the compliment. "Change the world? I'm just trying to keep up with it" I replied. "Honestly, if I can make it through the week without tripping over my own ambitions, I'll call it a win."

But somewhere inside, I knew.

This wasn't just about school. It was about confidence and power. It was the realization that possibility could feel both terrifying and electric, pressing at the edges of everything I thought I wanted.

The confidence to walk into a sunlit morning without glancing back at shadows behind me.

The confidence and power to choose my path.

The power to choose.

And that, that was everything.

In my notebook that night, I wrote:

#34   Sometimes the universe answers softly—then suddenly, all at once it shouts!.

Underneath, I sketched a door opening, its edges glowing with a golden light. The brightness spilled outward, warm as sunlight against my skin, the kind that chases away morning chill and brings everything into clearer focus. That light wasn't just illumination— it was possibility, hope, and the promise of something uncharted waiting beyond the threshold.

For months, I had lingered at the edge of decision, my thoughts shadowed by uncertainty. But somewhere between the acceptance letter and Tori's laughter, a quiet courage had settled in me. I realized I was no longer afraid of what lay beyond—I was ready to step forward, drawn toward the warmth and clarity on the other side.

Because maybe, just maybe… I was finally walking
through it and into the light.

Chapter Forty:

The Things I Choose to Carry

The suitcase was half full.

Which felt like a lie—because my life had never felt so full.

I hovered over the open case, hands shifting through a stack of t-shirts. Each one was a memory—some faded, some stretched thin—reminders of moments when I tried to shrink myself to fit others' expectations. These shirts were relics from times I'd celebrated quietly or hidden my hopes in the seams, relics of a girl who used to live in corners and speak in half-sentences. She still existed inside me, but she didn't own me anymore.

Now, as I packed for graduate school, I realized how far I'd come. Every folded shirt, every chosen item, was proof of the courage that had quietly filled the empty spaces in me. This suitcase wasn't just carrying my clothes—it was carrying all the ways I'd grown, all the ways I'd learned to make room for my own voice.

I paused, a bittersweet ache blooming in my chest, and let myself feel the enormity of it. Change was no longer something that happened to me; it was something I chose, step by trembling step.

The words "you can do it" always seemed to belong in other people's mouths—girls with safety nets, kids who took first chances for granted, students whose parents dropped them off with care packages and good luck kisses. But here I was, folding my own sweatshirts, zipping my own bag, and packing not just clothes—but proof.

Every folded shirt was a silent argument against doubt, every zipped pocket a promise to myself that I belonged here. All those years spent shrinking myself to fit in, every uncertain step, had led to this moment where my courage finally took up space. The proof wasn't just in what I packed, but in how I carried it: with trembling hands, yes, but also with a steady pride I'd earned on my own. I didn't need permission to grow—only the willingness to claim it.

Riley entered, the door swinging softly behind her, the faint scent of rain clinging to her jacket. She balanced two sweating iced coffees in one hand and a plastic container of leftover lo Mein in the other, her keys jingling with every step.

"You know you'll be back to visit, right?" Riley set the coffees down, the ice cubes chiming as she slid one toward me.

My fingers curled around the cup, the cold pressing against my skin. "Absolutely," I said, my voice quiet but steady, though a knot had formed in my chest.

Riley grinned, a gentle warmth in her eyes. "But still. It feels big."

I nodded; the word caught somewhere between my ribs. "It is big," I whispered.

She perched beside me on the edge of the bed and picked at the frayed hem of one of my shirts, her thumb tracing the faded design. "Remember this?" she asked, holding it up so the old blueprint caught the afternoon light. "You wore it the day you got the job at the center. You looked so nervous, I thought you might run right out the door."

I laughed softly, the sound surprising me. "I needed a little luck that day."

Riley nudged my knee with hers, her voice gentle but firm. "You made your own luck, you know. All that courage—it was always yours."

The hum of the mini fridge and the soft patter of rain against the window filled the silence between us, and for a moment, I let myself lean into the comfort of her presence—the easy way she made the world feel less daunting, more possible. We held each other in silence for some time, our embrace saying everything that needed to be said.

That afternoon, I did a goodbye walk.

Past the campus bookstore, its windows fogged with the breath of rain-soaked students and the sharp scent of new paper and ink. Through the quad, where damp blades of grass brushed against my ankles and the breeze carried the distant laughter of friends sheltering beneath umbrellas. Each step pressed the cool earth, grounding me in a place that once felt foreign.

Into the coffee shop where we would meet after class- the air thick with the warmth of roasted beans and vanilla syrup, the whir of the espresso machine threading through the gentle murmur of voices and the soft clink of ceramic cups. I remembered how the barista always wore a crooked smile, and how Riley's jacket steamed in the light above our table, the air fragrant and safe.

By the alley where I once cried behind a dumpster, the world uncaring and hushed except for the steady drip of rainwater and the faint metallic tang of wet concrete. The chill there had wrapped around my arms and mixed with the lonely echo of my sobs—painful, but honest.

Each place was layered—a memory inside a memory, a scar that had turned into skin, and a silent invitation to remember not just who I had been, but every small way I'd changed.

I ended up at the youth center, heart open, ready to step into whatever waited next.

The late afternoon sun warmed our backs as Riley and I sat on the rough stone steps, their surfaces flecked with tiny pebbles pressing through the fabric of our jeans. Laughter from inside the youth center drifted out in bursts, mingling with the distant clatter of a basketball bouncing on concrete and the sweet, yeasty scent of fresh cupcakes.

Tori handed me the little box, the frosting squished and imperfect but so full of intent. "You're not allowed to cry," I warned, my voice catching on a tremor I couldn't quite hide.

"I already did," she admitted, brushing at a dry spot on her cheek. "Maybe twice."

The three of us broke the cupcakes in half, eating way too many with our fingers—crumbs sticking to our skin, the sugar melting on our tongues. We talked and laughed and remembered and for a moment, the world felt both achingly present and impossibly far away.

"You were our quietest voice when you arrived," Tori said, her tone gentle but threaded with admiration. "Now you're the reason other kids speak."

Her words made my chest tighten with pride and disbelief, memories of my first timid days rushing back—how the silence had once felt safer than trying.

I blinked fast, swallowing the lump in my throat. "You gave me that first key."

"No," she said softly, her eyes shining with certainty. "You were always holding it. You just stopped hiding it."

A breeze lifted the sounds of the center, carrying their laughter and promise into the golden afternoon, and I realized she was right.

I stepped inside one last time.

Ivy was there—taller now, standing with a confidence she once lacked. Her eyes brighter, her laugh echoing through the quiet room—a sound that seemed to fill the space and ripple outward, proof of how far she'd come.

She handed me a folded piece of paper.

A drawing of a turtle, and a note underneath – "Thank you for helping me feel seen."

I hugged her, tight and long. Her shoulders trembled against me, and for a moment, the world felt safe and small held together by the warmth between us and all we couldn't say.

Back in my dorm that night, I finished packing.

One more sweatshirt.

My sketchbook, my sketchbook, my notebook, especially my notebook!

I paused with it in my hands, feeling the softened, creased cover—a patchwork of old stickers and smudged thumbprints. The spine, battered and pliant, fit perfectly in my palms. As I thumbed through the pages, they whispered and fluttered, releasing the faint, reassuring scent of ink and paper.

I stopped at a jagged entry—my handwriting messy and hurried from that night I couldn't sleep, when the world felt impossibly heavy. I remembered how, in the quiet, scribbling lines across those pages had helped me breathe again. Each word was a promise to myself: That I could keep going. It carried every memory, every hope, every small discovery I'd, made along the way/

#1   *Have a room with a door that locks* ✅

#2   *Take a real shower* ✅

#3   *Eat hot food I didn't have to steal* ✅

#4   *Go to college* ✅

#5   *Never cry again over people who left*

#6   *Forgive, not forget*

#7   *Make my life count*

#8   *Be seen*

#9   *Tell someone the truth*

#10   *Don't hurt the people who try to help you*

#11   *Try again, even if it breaks you first*

#12.   *Learn how to live as if you are staying.*

#13   *Keep going.*

#14   *Believe it when the world says yes*

#15   *Say yes back.*

#16   *Forgive at your own pace. You get to choose when.*

#17   Unpack your life without apology.

#18   Say goodbye without losing where you came from.

#19   Say hello to who you're becoming.

#20   Make room—for new people, new chances, and a self who doesn't need to hide.

#21   Speak your truth, even when no one's listening.

#22   You still belong—even on the hard days.

#23   Don't shrink your story—someone else needs it.

#24   Healing isn't loud.

#25   Sometimes healing means holding space for someone else, even if no one ever held it for you.

Giving someone hope doesn't drain you—it grows you.

#26   Tell your story to someone who makes space for all of it.

#27   You are not just surviving you're making a difference—and you are worth investing in.

#28   You're allowed to accept space in the room— even if you used to sleep in hallways.

#29   You can't save everyone. But sometimes, you can remind them they're worth coming back for.

#30   When someone else finds their voice, listen with your whole heart. It will teach you something about yourself

#31   You can't always see the road ahead., but the fact that you get to choose it? That's the miracle.

#32   Healing is not forgetting. It's remembering without letting it poison you

#33   Speaking your truth isn't about getting answers

#34   Sometimes the universe answers softly—then suddenly, all at once it shouts!

.

I turned to the following empty page and began writing with my pen across the blank surface.

#35   Leaving doesn't mean forgetting.

It means trusting that the deep roots you've grown will keep you steady—wherever you bloom.

Beneath the words, I sketched a battered blue suitcase—its fabric faded, corners threadbare from being dragged across unfamiliar floors. The handle was soft and a little sticky from the time a leaky bottle of shampoo spilled inside; it fit perfectly in my grip, worn into the shape of journeys past. On the side, a heart-shaped sticker—bright and crooked and green smiling turtle about to speak, clinging bravely & stubbornly near a faded baggage tag.

I tucked my favorite scarf inside, pausing to breathe in the lingering scent of lavender sachets and old paper. The zipper rasped as I pulled it closed, teeth catching for a breath before sliding home with a gentle snap. My hand lingered on the handle—cool, textured, grounding—reminding me that this suitcase was more than fabric and zippers. It was a vessel for memories, hopes, and all the hidden pieces of myself I was finally ready to carry forward.

And I smiled—because the weight I felt wasn't holding me back. It was carrying me onward.

I wasn't running from anything.

I was running toward everything.

Chapter Forty-One:
Room for Me

The State University campus was quiet in a different way. Not the warm hum of undergraduate campuses with pizza boxes stacked in the corners, the distant thump of music, and the sugary tang of spilled soda lingering in the air. This quiet was sharper. Tighter. Here, the only sounds were the echo of my own footsteps and the faint smell of fresh cut grass, as if the buildings themselves were holding their breath. Back then, the noise meant belonging; now, the silence only made me feel more out of place. Like everyone already had somewhere to be. And I didn't.

My fingers traced the stitched spine of the new leather-bound notebook—a graduation gift from Riley, who always believed I could handle anything. Maybe that's why they chose this notebook, sturdy and unmarked, like a promise I wasn't sure I could keep. The cool leather pressed against my palm as distant voices echoed down the hallway, mingling with the sharp tap of shoes on linoleum and the faint hum of fluorescent lights overhead. The air was heavy with the smell of new books, grass, and a thread of old paper dust, grounding me even as nerves fluttered in my chest.

I scanned my schedule again: Social Work 610—Foundations of Trauma Response. It wasn't just an academic challenge. For me, it was a chance to learn how to piece together stories like my own, to understand the fractures that linger after upheaval and, maybe, to help others find steadiness amid the chaos.

A memory surfaced: Riley, pressing the notebook into my hands on graduation day, her smile confident and unwavering. "You'll fill this with answers," she'd said, "even if you have to invent some along the way."

But deep down, uncertainty gnawed at me. Was I smart enough? Was I ready for the weight of other people's stories? What if 'falling apart' meant letting someone down, or discovering that my own roots weren't as strong as I hoped? Each step down the hallway felt like a question, and every evasive answer seemed to matter more than ever.

Inside the lecture hall, students clustered in islands—backpacks slumped over chair backs, laptops bright, and quiet conversations weaving around me like small rivers, flowing toward unknown destinies. The low hum of fluorescent lights mingled with the faint aroma of coffee drifting from a forgotten cup on a nearby desk, deepening the hush that wrapped the room.

I chose a seat near the back. Not hidden but not exposed. My favorite kind of quiet in the middle. It was a place where I could observe without being observed, where I felt both present and invisible—a comfortable vantage point to notice everything and risk nothing, the gentle current of belonging just within reach.

The lecture hall buzzed with nervous energy as students shuffled in, clutching notebooks and coffee cups. The clatter of chair legs scraping tile, the scent of damp wool and espresso, and the soft static of whispered introductions filled the air, knitting all of us together in a fragile, anticipatory hush.

A girl slid into the seat beside me, the fabric of her blazer brushing against my sleeve. Her outfit was business casual, but her sneakers were scuffed in a way that suggested stories—places she'd been or maybe places she hoped to go.

She offered a warm smile. "First semester?"

"Yeah."

"Me too. I'm Harper."

"Makenzie."

"Nice," she said. "You look calm."

I wondered if she could see the way my hands trembled under the desk, or if everyone here was just pretending too. I tucked a stray hair behind my ear, steadying my breath.

I laughed softly. "I'm just good at faking it."

She grinned, shifting in her seat and tapping her pen against her notebook. "Same."

For a moment, I let myself believe we weren't so different—two strangers trying to look unbreakable in a room full of uncertainty.

The professor walked in, mid-conversation with himself, balancing a paper coffee cup and a stack of handouts that immediately toppled. The slap of paper against linoleum broke the hush, and the scramble began—the rustle of papers and hurried footsteps filled the air as a few students sprang up to help.

I didn't move.

I stayed in my seat, watching, focusing on the steady rhythm of my breath.

Years ago, I would have leapt from my seat without thinking, swept up by the urge to help. But after too many moments spent regretting hasty choices, I learned to pause and observe before acting. It wasn't indifference, but discipline—a lesson hard-won, shaped by experience and quiet reflection.

I'd learned the difference between reacting and responding. It had taken years.

He introduced himself as Dr. Greene, a psychological trauma specialist with twenty years in the field, and the lecture began—steady, deliberate, like the tide coming in. He used terms I knew and concepts I'd lived; words that once felt sharp now seemed… manageable. As he spoke about the difference between surviving and healing, his words settled somewhere deep inside me, winding through old fears and resting in places I'd kept hidden. Not everyone, he said, reaches true healing. He reminded us, we have a responsibility—to lift while they climb. In that moment, it didn't feel theoretical. It felt like an invitation.

And suddenly, something inside me shifted.

No doubt. No fear.

But a level of certainty began to settle.

It was as if a weight I hadn't realized I was carrying suddenly got lighter replaced by a quiet, steady resolve. The world didn't change, but my place in it felt new the familiar tension in my shoulders easing for the first.

Harper was friendly, her easy smile making the unfamiliar feel less daunting. At the end of class, she turned to me. "Want to grab coffee? I'm still pretending I know where everything is."

I hesitated. Then smiled.

"I've got the map app down. Let's go."

At the student center, conversation drifted easily between us, warm and unhurried.

Her brother's recovery, my time at the youth center, the essay I wrote for Artemis, and the attractive boy sitting in the third row during our recent trauma class.

She traced the rim of her coffee cup, eyes searching mine for something unspoken—a flicker of understanding passing between us.

"You wrote about your own story?" she asked, voice low but clear.

"Some of it."

She smiled, soft and genuine, and for a moment I felt exposed in a way that didn't hurt.

"That's brave."

I shrugged, glancing down at my hands. "That's survival."

A hush settled, comfortable and a little fragile, as if the room itself were listening in, giving us permission to just be in the present.

We had coffee for over an hour, started a comfortable friendship, and left with the intent to meet again.

Despite my exhaustion, the kind that settles deep and heavy—I unlocked my apartment and let the quiet envelop me. I dropped my bag in its designated spot, flicked on the lamp, and sat at the edge of my bed for a moment, listening to the faint buzz of streetlights outside. Still, I reached for my notebook, determined to capture not just the details of the day, but the ache and hope stitched through it.

Because today felt like more than just another day. There was something fragile and new in the way conversation had unfolded at the Student Center, in the trust exchanged over coffee in the beginnings of a new friendship. It was as if the world had given me permission, again, to speak without armor.

On the first page, I wrote:

#36   The first step into the unknown is the loudest—go boldly!.

Then, I let my pen hover, searching for an image that might hold the weight of what I felt. I sketched two chairs side by side. No name tags. No barriers.

To me, those chairs meant possibility—an invitation to sit with another person, or with myself, in the blank space between what is spoken and what is kept silent. Maybe tomorrow, she will find a seat beside me. Maybe I'll have the courage to fill the emptiness with more of my story. The empty space was a promise: room for understanding, room for healing.

I looked at the drawing and imagined the warmth of shared presence, the solace of having someone listen without judgment. The apartment was quiet, but the echo of the day lingered—a reminder that even the smallest act of openness could reshape the room around me.

And so, I wrote: There is always room for two. There is always space to begin again. I slept all night-a deep and peaceful sleep and dreamed of a bright future full of possibilities.

Chapter Forty-Two:

The Root System

The assignment was printed in crisp, stark black letters, the kind that seem to press extra weight into the paper. It slid across my desk like a challenge disguised as homework.

Assignment #1 – Reflective Paper:

"What is the root of your resilience?"

1,000 words. Due in two weeks.

No citations. No APA formatting. Just… truth.

I felt my stomach tighten, as if something had pressed unexpectedly against a bruise. I read the prompt again, each word burrowing inside. It was the word root that unsettled me—made me feel exposed, as though I'd been asked to dig into the dark, tangled places I usually kept hidden.

After class, the usual shuffle of feet and rustle of bags filled the hallway. Students voiced reservations about the personal aspects of the assignment, while others responded with lighthearted remarks or displayed noticeable hesitancy. Harper shook her head: "Geez. He's not going easy on us, huh?"

But I barely heard her. My mind spun with memories—the ones that live close to the heart.

Roots grow unseen, twisting through old pain and hope, anchoring us to the past. I remember sitting under a maple tree at dusk, touching its exposed roots and rough bark, finding comfort in its persistent presence even when I felt lost.

That night, I learned I could get through tough times by relying on support—friends, laughter, and simple gestures. These imperfect connections are my roots: messy but vital.

So, when the assignment landed in front of me, I felt gutted—not just by its honesty, but by the knowledge that writing would mean letting those tangled, private roots see daylight and be seen by someone else. It meant admitting how much I owed to the unseen things that had kept me upright.

And that, I think, is the truest kind of vulnerability: not just telling the world that you're strong but showing where the strength comes from—and all that you've clung to, deep underground, when the storms hit.

I went home and pulled out my notebook.

Not the new leather-bound one from Riley.

The old one—the cover soft at the edges, corners bent, its spine creased from years of being opened in hope and in fear. My thumb found the groove where I'd traced the title so many times it nearly disappeared. I could smell ink and a faint whiff of maybe rain, maybe dust from a dozen places I'd carried it.

I flipped through the pages, their edges worn and uneven, listening to the gentle whisper as they turned. And I cried.

Not because I was broken.

But because I'd come so far—and hadn't let myself feel the weight of it in a long time.

There, on the margin of a page halfway through, I found a note I'd written to myself at fifteen: "You've survived every night so far. You'll survive this one too." I remembered huddling on a mattress in a homeless shelter, the ache of loneliness pressing around me, and how writing those words gave me something steady to hold. That lesson—my own handwriting reminded me that even in the darkest moments, I could create my own reassurance—and become my own north star. It taught me that hope wasn't something given, but something built, word by word.

That night, as I closed the notebook, I realized I was ready to put my journey into words. The act of revisiting those old pages—of touching the scars and the small victories—had transformed what once felt like fragments into a story I was finally willing to share.

The next morning, I woke to pale sunlight filtering through the blinds, the notebook still resting on my desk. I opened a blank doc on my laptop, heart thundering. The cursor blinked—a heartbeat daring me to begin.

And so, I wrote:

The Root of My Resilience

I used to think resilience looked like strength.

Standing tall, keeping your head up, and being tough.

But now I know it's not that clean.

Resilience is crying in a public bathroom, then walking out like you didn't.

Resilience is eating lunch alone and then going to class.

Resilience is saying "I'm fine "even when you're not and hoping someone will ask again.

I didn't choose to be resilient. I had to be.

My parents left when I was thirteen. No explanation. No plan. Just gone. I waited on the porch until the sun came up, the wood cold beneath me, my breath fogging in the early air. From that morning on, survival became my new normal.

That night, I became a different person. Someone who made a bed out of gym mats—the vinyl so stiff it left lines on my cheek, the faint echo of basketballs bouncing somewhere beyond the doors. I memorized emergency exits. I walked through cities like a shadow, blending in so I wouldn't be seen. I knew every laundromat where I could sleep, every alleyway with a sheltered corner safe from the rain.

And still—I went to school. I read books in stairwells, where the hum of fluorescent lights and the muffled shuffle of feet above reminded me I wasn't completely alone. I found shelters, centers, and eventually—people.

One afternoon, when I was running on nothing but hope and vending machine crackers, a teacher named Mr. Danner found me hunched over a battered copy of "Jane Eyre" in the stairwell. She sat down beside me without asking for my story. She simply listened, offering a granola bar and a steady presence. That small act of kindness cracked something open in me— a belief that I was worth noticing.

I struggled my way through high school, feeling isolated and uncertain, carrying the weight of being completely on my own. Each day was a test of my perseverance—finding places to sleep, pushing through classes, and trying to hold onto hope even in the loneliest moments. Making it to college felt like stepping into a new world: both a relief from what I'd endured and the start of another challenge. And now, here I here, standing at the edge of new beginnings, both anxious and hopeful, ready to discover where I belong and what comes next.

My resilience didn't come from strength. It came from grit. From memory. From the people who gave me one more chance than I gave myself.

Support came from Tori, who saw past my silence and offered understanding when words failed me. Comfort came from Riley, who never needed the whole story before inviting me to join her, making me feel included even when I felt invisible. Purpose came from Ivy, who reminded me why this fight matters and inspired me to keep pushing forward. Their gestures didn't just help me survive the day—they helped me believe that I wasn't alone anymore, shaping the way I showed up for myself and others moving forward..

It came from me! From the part of me that still believed in light, even when the porch bulb was off.

The root of my resilience isn't a person or place.

It's a decision—to keep showing up, even when no one noticed. To believe that I was more than the girl my parents left behind when they disappeared without warning—that I wasn't defined by their absence, but by my own strength to keep going. And to build a life so full—with laughter in bustling kitchens, love that shows up in unexpected places, and purpose found in the warmth of friendship—that even the quietest moments feel complete, untouched by loneliness.

Breath shaky, hands damp, heart pounding—I hadn't just turned in a paper; I had turned over a piece of my soul.

The days that followed felt endless, each one heavy with anticipation until finally, Dr. Greene returned our assignments with quiet nods and the kind of reverence that told me he knew what he'd asked of us. He slid my paper across the table with one note written in blue ink at the bottom: "The most powerful roots are the ones no one sees. You're growing a forest."

That night, I opened my notebook and added:

#37   *Your truth is not too heavy to hold—especially when it becomes someone else's light.*

Then I drew roots beneath a tree, messy and tangled, but strong, holding everything up.

Chapter Forty-Three:

A Mirror Named Betty

Betty didn't say much at first, even after three meetings. She'd show up, arms crossed, hoodie drawn tight—a fortress. Her sneakers bore the names of bands in faded marker, and she always doodled in the margins of her notebook—tiny stars, crooked hearts, jagged lightning bolts. Sometimes she'd tap a rhythm on her knee, lost in thought. Mostly, she just sat in silence, her gaze darting from the clock to the floor, as if measuring how long she could hold out.

But I didn't give up. I remembered what that silence felt like when it was my own—heavy, protective, but lonely.

At our fourth session, Betty arrived early. No explanation. She dropped into her usual chair, pulling out her battered notebook. The cover was bent, corners stained with coffee, pages bursting with scribbles and lists. She ran her thumb along the edge absentmindedly.

"Your story?" I asked.

She shrugged, not meeting my eye. "Kinda."

When the silence stretched, she glanced up, almost daring me to be the first to speak. Then, softer: "It's where I write stuff. Dumb poems. Thoughts. Whatever." Her words lingered in the air.

I smiled, lifting my own notebook from my bag. "I've got one of those, too."

She looked up, eyebrows raised. "You write poems?"

"Mostly thoughts. Lists. Sentences I want to believe."

She snorted—a half-laugh, half-defense. "Like what?"

I flipped to a page, letting her see my scrawl: Lesson #19: *Say hello to who you're becoming.*

She read it, her fingers tracing the words. A muscle in her jaw twitched, and she leaned back, considering. "That's pretty good."

The silence that followed felt different—less guarded, more curious. Betty's foot stopped tapping. She turned her notebook over, fingers fidgeting with the elastic band, then looked up. Her voice was quiet, edged with vulnerability. "I used to think I was just 'trouble.'"

"Why?"

She squeezed her notebook and turned her knuckles white. "Because everyone said I was. Teachers. Social workers. My mom."

Her eyes flickered, the old label echoing in her mind. I leaned forward, gentle: "Were you?"

She frowned, lips pressed tight in thought. "I don't know, maybe" Her shoulders tensed, like she was bracing for judgment.

"Or were you just loud in a world that wanted you quiet?"

She blinked. A slow, uncertain inhale. Her gaze shifted—first confusion, then something softer. A realization settling in, like sunlight peeking through a window. That moment hung between us, suspended.

From that day, Betty brought offerings—a poem, a question, a memory. She never handed it all at once, just fragments: a line about her dad leaving, a familiar story of sleeping in a laundromat, a habit of counting ceiling tiles to calm her nerves. Sometimes she'd draw little constellations beside her words, connecting stars nobody else could see.

One afternoon, she tapped her pencil against her notebook. "Do you think people like us ever feel normal?"

I paused, catching her searching glance. "I don't think we're supposed to feel normal."

Her brow furrowed. "Why not?"

"Because we were built for more than normal. We were built for survival, for change. That's not normal. That's powerful."

She didn't smile, but her lips parted. The room felt lighter, her posture less defensive.

The next week, she handed me a folded page—her poem, Paper People. It was raw, jagged, beautiful. Betty watched my reaction, eyes flitting between hope and fear. The poem described how people fold themselves into shapes to survive, and how hard it is to ever unfold.

I read it twice, then met her gaze. "This is more than a poem. It's a map."

She stared at her shoes. "It's stupid."

"No," I whispered. "It's sacred."

Later that night, I opened my notebook and wrote:

#38   The broken ones build the strongest bridges— because they know where people fall.

And beneath it, I drew two girls sitting back-to-back. One with a notebook. One with a heart cracked open just enough to let light in.

Betty wasn't healed. She still had days she shut down, nights when staff called to say she wouldn't speak, moments she fought the urge to run. But she wasn't alone anymore, and she knew that, and that—was everything.

Chapter Forty-Four:

The Man in the Second Row

The event was held in a renovated library auditorium—red brick walls, arched windows, and rows of chairs filled with people I didn't know but who had come to hear stories like mine. The faint scent of old paper and polished wood drifted through the space, mingling with the nervous hush before a performance. I stood backstage, gripping a small card with bullet points I probably wouldn't use, my palms slightly damp against the cool, textured cardstock.

"Just speak your truth," Tori had told me.

And so, I would.

Riley helped me pick out my outfit during our regular Sunday night phone call. These weekly calls had become cherished rituals. Sometimes we'd laugh over recent memories, other times we would talk about her sweet baby boy Mac.. Even though we were miles apart, those Sunday evenings always made me feel close to Riley, as if distance didn't matter when our voices filled the space between us. "Professional, but powerful," she'd said, remembering my soft blazer in a dusty rose color. "Something that says, 'I know where I've been. And I know where I'm going.'" The fabric felt gentle and comfortable against my skin, a calming as I tried to slow my breathing. I didn't feel that confident yet. Sometimes, that was enough.

The moderator's voice echoed off the high rafters: "Makenzie Rowe—student, mentor, survivor, and advocate."

A ripple of applause as I stepped up to the podium, the warmth of the stage lights brushing my cheeks and casting gentle shadows on the worn floorboards. I paused, letting the silence settle, and met the sea of unfamiliar faces. One stood out. Second row third seat from the left. Tall, sharp features, calm, steady eyes. A man in a navy sweater who didn't look away when I scanned the crowd. Instead, he gave the slightest nod—like he saw me.

My voice trembled, just for a moment, before gaining rhythm. I spoke of being left behind, of loneliness, of empty pockets filled with scars, of shelters and silence. The words tasted metallic in my mouth, but I kept going—about the day I decided survival wasn't enough. I wanted impact. I wanted to make a difference.

By the time I finished, my throat was dry, the air thick with stories too heavy to name. The audience was silent in the best way—the kind that means people are holding breath, not judgment. Then applause, rising and warm. I let myself smile, feeling the heat of the moment settle in my bones.

During the reception, jazz played softly, glasses clinked, and the sweet, citrusy scent of punch curled through the air. I held a paper cup, the rim faintly sticky against my fingers, and tried to slip out early. But I didn't make it to the door.

"Makenzie?"

I turned and it was him from the second row, navy sweater. Up close, he looked even…better. Soft brown eyes-a presence that felt both new and familiar. My pulse quickened as our eyes met, a strange comfort settling over me despite the unfamiliarity, as if recognition had bloomed in a place I hadn't known was waiting.

"I just wanted to say thank you," he said.

"For what?" I answered

"For being honest. That kind of honesty changes rooms, changes lives."

I blinked, the compliment settled over me like a gentle weight. "That's… kind of you."

"I'm Steve," he said, offering a hand.

"Makenzie."

"I know."

We both smiled.

He asked if I'd ever considered turning my story into policy work.

"I've thought about it," I said. "But mostly, I just want to be where the kids are. The ones still on the edge."

He nodded. "I wasn't one of those kids, but my best friend was. He grew up in group homes until my aunt took him in. The foster system nearly broke him, but he was saved by a social worker who refused to give up. Now, he works in nonprofit development, helping fund programs for youth in crisis."

Steve explained that he volunteers for his best friend's nonprofit organization, helping support the programs to give back to kids who face similar challenges

Mackenzie leaned forward, curiosity sparkling in her eyes. "So, what do you do?" she asked.

Steve offered a modest smile, pausing for a moment before replying. "I've spent the last few years working. I'm a veterinarian. It's not always glamorous— sometimes it's late-night emergencies and muddy boots. Just last week, I got a call at 2 AM to help a client's dog that was hit by a car. I sat with her in the clinic until sunrise, patching her up and hoping she'd pull through. Moments like that remind me why I do this, even when it's exhausting."

He hesitated before adding, "Long hours and night calls leave me very little time for a social life." His voice carried both weariness and quiet pride, making it easy to see how much he cared for the animals—and the people—who counted on him.

Mackenzie found herself drawn to the earnestness in his answer. It wasn't just about the work; it was about giving back, about showing up for those who relied on him—four-legged or otherwise.

As he spoke, a tightness I hadn't realized I was carrying began to loosen. Surprise flickered through me—at how quickly this stranger became familiar. Relief bloomed quietly. It mingled with a new kinship. Here, at last, was someone who understood the terrain I'd crossed. I felt seen—not just for my scars, but for what I'd built despite them. Our stories, though different, overlapped in the places that mattered most. We were both in the business of helping others-be it kids or dogs.

"I sometimes speak at these programs," he stated, "but tonight I just wanted to listen."

"Looks like we traded roles," I said, a smile tugging at the edge of my voice.

He grinned.

We stood near the coffee table longer than necessary, jazz notes curling in the background. Not flirting. Just… unfolding. The punch was sweet and cold on my tongue, grounding me in the moment. It felt safe, like a conversation between two people who knew the shape of heavy stories, and how rare it was to find someone who didn't flinch at their weight. It was easy and flowed naturally.

Before he left, Steve handed me a small card. Not a business card—just a blank card that he'd written a message on. I could tell it was written in haste. "Would love to grab coffee sometime. No pressure. Just thanks—for being you." And then a phone number.

I folded it gently, savoring the smoothness of the paper and the warmth of the gesture. Not because I was nervous, but because I already knew I'd say yes.

That night, I opened my notebook and wrote:

#39   *Sometimes, the heart doesn't need fireworks— just recognition. The kind that whispers, "I see you."*

And I drew two chairs again. This time… a little closer together.

Chapter Forty-Five:
Coffee, Soft and Slow

The coffee ship wasn't fancy. Old wood floors creaked softly under each step, and the air pulsed with the low hum of conversation, punctuated by the hiss and drip of the espresso machine. The place smelled of warm vanilla, toasted pecans, and something sweet—like hope rising with the steam. Mismatched chairs, one often wobbly, hugged each small table. When I sat, the seat pressed comfortingly into the back of my thighs, hoping to calm my nerves of anticipation. A jazz tune—soft, almost apologetic—threaded through the clink of cups and the scratch of chalk on the menu board.

I arrived ten minutes early. Typical—always early to things that mattered, as if time itself could be coaxed into easing my nerves. I fiddled with the sugar jar, counted the flecks on the tabletop, and pressed my palm to my chest, feeling my heart's steady, anxious beat.

This meeting might have been more important than I realized. Steve had a way about him—something gentle, something lingering from our conversation. It left me hoping for a new beginning, even as I feared a quiet, ordinary ending.

Memories kept nudging at me. I pictured our first encounter at the library event: the two of us laughing over a shared anecdote, the easy understanding in his eyes that made me feel understood, as if I might finally stop explaining myself. That easy understanding still echoed between us, and today, I wanted that possibility to survive the daylight.

My heart raced with every minute that passed, torn between anticipation and dread, as I imagined all the way this meeting could change—or disappointment. I caught myself tracing the seam in my coffee mug, remembering the way Steve had grinned.

When I looked up, twenty minutes passed. I began to wonder was his life too busy to let someone in. And could I manage the fear of rejection?

When the bell above the door chimed, I looked up. Steve stepped in, shoulders tense but scanning the room as if he was in a hurry and searching for something. He wore the same navy sweater from before, sleeves slightly rumpled. His gaze caught mine and he smiled—a little uncertain, maybe, but hopeful, like he knew what it meant for us to be here.

He crossed the room, footsteps steady on the old wood. "Hey," he said, his voice warm and a little shy.

"Hi," I replied, fingers curling around my mug's warmth, letting the scent of coffee and the nearness of him settle my nerves.

He dropped into the seat opposite me and placed two lattes on the table with dramatic flair. "Voilà! A perfectly sourced coffee, delivered just for you. I'd rather not mention how many loyalty cards I burned through." Internally, I wondered, is there really no apology for being late?

I stifled a laugh. "You're on a first-name basis with the barista now, aren't you?"

Steve grinned. "I'm their unofficial taste-tester—got to watch the cinnamon. You've already got your coffee I see, so I hope the caffeine won't keep you up." He then said "Sorry I'm late, I had a last-minute patient show up that needed his ear's scratched.

The smell of roasted beans and warm vanilla curled through the air, mingling with the sharper sweetness of chai in my own mug. The cushion on the chair located to the right appears to show signs of wear.. Behind us, a spoon chimed against porcelain; a burst of laughter from the counter mingled with the steady, reassuring hiss of the espresso machine—each sound familiar and comforting.

Steve didn't rush the conversation on our first visit. Instead, he tapped a finger against the table, glancing out at the sunlit window before returning his gaze to me. "I meant what I said at that library event," he went on, his tone light but earnest. "You changed the temperature of that whole room. If you ever get bored, you could moonlight as a thermostat."

My cheeks warmed. "I was shaking so hard I thought my blazer would rattle off."

He leaned in conspiratorially. "Well, next time, try eating a muffin first. Sugar works wonders for nerves."

I shook my head, smiling. "I'll keep that in mind."

We spoke about the event for a while. Steve, ever the storyteller, spun tales about his work at the nonprofit and the vet clinic, how he'd once accidentally scheduled two pancake breakfasts on the same day, and the ensuing syrup disaster that somehow raised more money than any fundraiser before. His sentences overflowed with asides, a little self-deprecating, peppered with the occasional, "No kidding!" or "Would you believe it?"

"Nonprofits—they're like some of my cat patients. One minute, cuddly. The next, chaotic and claws out" he said, grinning.

I let my fingers circle the rim of my mug, as the cardamom in my chai tickled my nose. He continued "I used to think I wanted to work behind the scenes. Now I realize some people need to see us. See the living proof that survival isn't the end of the story."

As Steve's mischievous grin faded, a hush seemed to settle between us. The previous warmth in his eyes shifted to something more vulnerable, and I felt a surge of admiration for his honesty. His words lingered in the air, making me reflect on my own role in all of this— the gentle weight of responsibility settled in my chest. I know I am just a volunteer at this point, but I take my role seriously. Maybe that's why his openness struck such a chord; being present, even in small ways, suddenly felt monumental. The faint clatter of cups and the aroma of coffee seemed to recede, replaced by a quiet awareness that we were both, in our own ways, choosing to show up.

We drifted into lighter conversation—favorite books, worst school lunches, and the time Steve wiped out on a skateboard trying to impress a girl in middle school. "Scar shaped like New Jersey," he declared, pointing to his chin. "I offered to show it at parties, but there wasn't much demand."

I laughed, real and unguarded—the kind that bubbles up and lingers.

The café's background hum seemed to recede, settling into a gentle rhythm with our words.

Then, mid-sip of his latte—he always took exactly two sips before speaking again—Steve grew quiet. "Serious question, and you don't have to answer," he said, playing with his mug's handle. "When did you start trusting people again?"

I looked down at the swirling steam, feeling its gentle warmth rise. "I'm not sure I have completely," I admitted. "But I stopped expecting everyone to leave. That was a start."

He leaned back, fiddling with a sugar packet. "I spent years treating exits like fire drills. Hard to shake the habit."

"Same," I said. "This right now? Staying seated, making eye contact, laughing? It still surprises me."

He grinned crookedly. "Hey, it's progress. Next thing you know, we'll be swapping muffin recipes."

I nodded. "It really does feel okay."

We let silence bloom—just the clink of cups, the sigh of the espresso machine, the distant scrape of a chair. The café's warmth wrapped around us, a soft haven from the outside world.

Steve drummed his fingers, then asked, "You write in that notebook every day?"

"Almost."

He whistled softly. "Discipline. I'm lucky if I remember to buy milk."

"What kind of stuff?" he prompted.

"Whatever I don't want to forget-Lessons, Observations, Things I survived, Things I want to."

He leaned forward, voice dropping conspiratorially again. "Ever thought about publishing it? The world could use more of your kind of wisdom—less self-help, more self-honesty."

I raised an eyebrow. "You mean, like a book?"

"Exactly. If you need an official taste-tester for stories, I'm available. Reasonable rates."

My heart skipped. "No one's ever said that to me before."

Steve smiled, a little softer this time. "First time for everything."

The café lights dimmed as dusk settled, painting the windows lavender. Another burst of laughter rose from the kitchen, then faded. I hadn't even noticed the time slipping by.

"I should let you get home," Steve said finally, standing with a flourish. "But only if you promise this isn't the last expert latte I fetch for you. Next time I'll be on time, I promise…maybe"

"Yeah," I laughed, not wanting to leave. "I'd like that."

He held the door open for me, bowing with exaggerated formality. "Until next time, then."

Outside, the breeze tugged at my sleeves and the night smelled faintly of rain and roasted beans.

We paused at the corner.

"I don't want to rush anything," Steve said. "But I'd really like to see you again. No expectations. Just... more."

"I'd like that," I replied, surprised by my own certainty.

His grin was quick and lopsided. "Well, look at us. Progress."

He didn't ask for a hug or lean in for a kiss. He just let the moment linger, the air between us stretched with possibility.

And somehow, it was perfect.

That night, I opened my notebook and wrote:

#40   *Not all love arrives loudly.*

Some of it just pulls up a chair, listens without fixing,

and reminds you that soft is still strong.

I drew two mugs on a table again.

Steam curling into heartbeats.

Space between them—but less than before.

Chapter Forty-Six:

The Breakthrough

Betty was already sitting in the room when I arrived. The faint hum of the radiator filled the silence, steady and low. The sharp scent of ink lingered in the air, mingling with the musty smell of old paper stacked on the shelf. Her notebook rested in her lap, the cover worn and soft beneath her fingertips.

Hood down. Eyes on the window, not the door. Still. Like she was holding her breath.

"Hey," I said gently, easing the door closed behind me. The click echoed between us.

"Hey", she responded. That was new. Usually, it was just a nod.

I took the seat across from her, feeling the rigid cushion beneath me, and waited, letting the silence settle without pressure. My heart thudded as I watched her—the way her hands gripped the notebook, knuckles pale. She glanced at me, then back at the window, lips pressed tight. I sensed a change.

"Can I read you something?" Her voice was soft, barely above the hum.

This was very new.

I sat up straighter, pulse quickening. "Of course."

She unfolded a sheet of paper—not her usual notebook, but an actual typed page. Her fingers trembled on the edge, hesitating for a moment, then she cleared her throat.

Her voice shook slightly, but she didn't stop.

"I'm tired of pretending like I don't care." Betty's voice trembled, but she pressed on. "I used to think silence was safety. But it's just another mask."

Her eyes flicked toward me and then went away as she unfolded the page further. Her fingers tightened, knuckles paling again.

"When I was seven, I watched my mom get arrested. I remember the way her hands shook, how small she looked even though she tried to be so strong. When I was ten, I slept in a car with no heater in February, and I pretended I was camping to make it less scary. When I was thirteen, a teacher told me I was too angry to help, so I stopped asking. I stopped believing people meant it when they said, 'I'm here.'"

She drew in a shaky breath, words tumbling out now, urgent as if the act of speaking might hold her together. "But then I met someone who didn't try to fix me. She just stayed. And somehow, that made me want to fix a little piece of myself."

Her gaze lingered on me, searching for something—a sign I was still with her.

I let the silence settle, not wanting to break the honesty that hovered between us. For a moment, I remembered all the times I'd hidden behind my own masks, how exhausting it was to pretend. The truth in her words echoed in places I'd tried hard to forget.

"That's the bravest thing I've ever heard," I said softly, letting the admiration I felt steady my voice. I leaned forward, elbows on my knees, trying to bridge the space between us not just with words but with presence. "You say it's just something you wrote, but it's everything you've survived. That matters."

Betty gave a half-shrug, but the wall between us was thinner now, her eyes less guarded.

The air in the room shifted—not with the tension of secrets held, but with the gentle weight of truth spoken aloud. For a moment, honesty made our old masks seem lighter and allowed us to breathe. In that shared quiet, we were two people—unhidden now and seen— finding the courage to keep showing up.

It felt sacred.

The fluorescent lights hummed softly overhead, and the faint scent of old books lingered from the library next door. Outside, footsteps echoed down the hallway, distant enough to feel like their world was sealed off for this moment.

We'd been meeting for several weeks like this— shoulder to shoulder, piecing ourselves together one quiet conversation at a time—but today felt different.

Betty folded the paper once, then again, her fingers trembling slightly as she pressed the edges flat. She glanced at me, almost as if seeking permission, before handing it over.

"I wanted to give it to you," she said, voice barely above a whisper.

I reached out, letting the edge of the page brush my palm before I took it. She hesitated, then smiled faintly—a smile I'd come to recognize since our first meeting after school, when she'd begun to look for reassurance from me.

"It's not perfect."

"Neither are we," I said. "But we're still worth showing up for."

She crossed her arms, pulling herself into a gentle hug, but it didn't feel defensive this time. More like she was holding something precious inside.

"Do you think I could ever... I don't know... speak? Like at something? Like you do?"

"Absolutely."

She snorted, twisting the edge of her sleeve. "I panic just raising my hand in class."

I leaned forward, letting the chair creak beneath me. The hush settled again, as steady as our heartbeat.

"So, did I. Until the first time someone needed to hear what I had to say, and I needed to say it"

Her eyes found mine, searching for the truth in my words.

And something clicked.

I told her about my first panel—the way the stage lights stung my eyes, the wooden podium's edge biting into my palms as I clung to it. How my nerves made the paper tremble in my grip, how the sharp scent of marker ink cut through the auditorium's thick, recycled air. "I stumbled over the word resilience," I admitted, my voice soft. "My hands were slick with sweat. I thought I'd wreck the whole speech."

"But I didn't," I said, glancing at the window where the hum of distant traffic drifted through the glass, constant and low. "I stopped trying to sound like someone else. I just told the truth."

Betty nodded, her eyes fixed on the table's scratched surface, tracing invisible patterns with her fingertip. The faint scent of old paper from my notebook mingled with the warmth of her hesitant smile.

"I could do that," she murmured, her voice nearly lost beneath the quiet.

"Yes you could, and you will," I replied, "When you're ready."

 Betty was silent for a moment, the quiet punctuated only by the distant clatter of chairs in another room. "I think I like you," she whispered, her cheeks coloring as she said it.

My laughter broke the tension, light and real—the first in what felt like days. Betty's answering smile was crooked and shy, a flash of her fourteen-year-old self-unguarded and bright. For a moment, everything felt possible.

Afterward, as voices echoed faintly from down the hall, Bett asked, "You'll still be here next week?"

"Next week, and every week after, as long as you want me," I promised, my words steady as the solid, worn desk between us.

She nodded, clutching her sleeve. In the softest voice, she said, "Thanks for not giving up."

"You make it easy to stay," I answered, letting the truth settle in the space between us.

That night, as rain pattered gently against my window, I turned to a fresh page in my notebook. The smell of paper, comforting and familiar, reminded me of our afternoon. This time, I didn't write another note—I left the space blank, open for Betty.

Breakthroughs don't come from force. They come from stillness, trust, and the moment someone realizes they're allowed to be seen.

And with careful hands, I tucked Betty's poem into the fold. Held like something rare and protected it like treasure.

Chapter Forty-Seven:

Her Turn to Speak

Betty agreed to speak at the youth center's "Voices Rising" event, but her bravado looked stretched thin, like fabric pulled too tight. She rocked on her heels; notebook clenched and flicked a glance at the scuffed linoleum. "I mean, I'll do it," she tossed out, the words bouncing off a shaky exhale. "But if I freeze or throw up, that's on you."

I grinned, trying to meet her with the same teasing bravado. "Deal. I'll bring a bucket just in case."

Inside, I felt a knot of nerves that mirrored hers. Two weeks wasn't much time to prepare—for her, it was a heartbeat and an eternity all at once.

For Betty, speaking at "Voices Rising" wasn't just about reading words—it was about proving to herself that she could be heard.

I watched her mouth press into a line, her thumb tracing the spiral binding of her notebook. She kept glancing at the door, as if escape might still be an option. "I keep thinking what if my voice shakes, or I forget everything," she whispered, breath barely stirring the air.

"I've seen you weather bigger storms," I said gently. "You think you'll be alone up there, but you're not."

She gave a short, nervous laugh, cheeks flushing. "I just… I want it to matter. If I can do this, maybe they'll finally hear me."

Her determination flickered behind her eyes—wary but bright, stubborn as spring crocus breaking through frozen earth. She nodded, jaw set with a kind of fragile resolve. The event still loomed two weeks away, but for a fourteen-year-old who had once let silence fill whole rooms, the simple act of standing beneath those lights would be revolution.

I if anyone could do it, if anyone could step into that trembling moment and claim it as their own—it was Betty.

The next day, Betty slipped into the rec room, her footsteps soft against the faded linoleum. Fluorescent lights flickered overhead, casting thin shadows that stretched along the walls. She hugged her notebook to her chest as if it were a shield, the corners of its worn cover pressed into her palms.

"Wrote something," she murmured, voice so quiet it nearly dissolved into the hum of the vending machine by the door.

I watched her shoulders rise and fall, the little hitch in her breath as she found her spot across from me. The room smelled faintly of dust and coffee, a backdrop for moments like these.

"You want to read it?" I asked, keeping my own voice gentle, not wanting to scare the fragile courage she'd gathered.

"No," she replied, eyes flicking to the window, then back to me. After a pause, she added softly, "Yeah."

She settled into the plastic chair, her fingers trembling slightly as she flipped open the notebook. The soft scratch of paper seemed louder than her first words, as if the room were holding its breath for her.

"They say I have attitude-They don't ask why.

They say I'm angry-They don't ask why.

But someone finally did. She didn't fix it, didn't promise she could.

She just sat with me until the storm passed.

Now I know—maybe I'm not the storm.

Maybe I'm the calm after the storm.

Maybe I'm the survivor."

Her voice was quiet but steady, each syllable a small act of defiance against the silence that used to fill up rooms around her. As she read, I caught a fleeting shimmer in her eyes, the way her lips pressed together to keep from cracking.

Listening to her words, I felt a quiet pride blooming inside me—a hope that maybe she was beginning to see herself as I did. The poem lingered in the air, heavier than applause, and for a moment, neither of us moved.

I clapped, just once, softly. Not loud. Not performative. Just enough to fill the space between us, to let her know I heard her.

"That's beautiful," I said, and in the hush that followed, something unseen shifted—a brief, hesitant smile tugged at her mouth, and trust settled between us like dust in a beam of light.

"It's not done."

"It's never finished," I replied, "but it's real, and your story goes on."

During the days before the event, we regrouped several times. Betty rehearsed her lines quietly in a corner, either with me or by herself when the youth centre was silent and empty.

"I'm going to pass out, aren't I?" Betty whispered, her words barely above a tremor, on the morning of the performance.

"No," I told her. "You're going to rise."

The youth center's common room had been transformed for the occasion. Fairy lights glimmered overhead, their glow mingling with the late afternoon sun that slanted through the windows. Folding chairs were clustered together, the scrape of metal against linoleum punctuating bursts of nervous chatter. The air was warm, crowded with the scent of coffee, anticipation, and a flicker of something electric. The podium—a makeshift construction from a recycled art table—stood at the heart of it all.

Parents, teachers, volunteers, even Steve from the third row, filled the seats. But for me, the world narrowed to Betty's silhouette framed by the edge of the curtain.

She fidgeted with her sleeves, knuckles pale, breath shallow and quick. Her eyes darted to the floor, the ceiling, anywhere but forward.

"I can't," she whispered.

"Yes," I said softly, laying a reassuring hand on her shoulder, "You can."

She took a shaky inhale. "What if they look at me and only see the bad stuff?"

"Then they're not looking closely enough. But trust me—they'll see you."

Betty nodded—a small, serious gesture. She squared her shoulders, feeling the weight and warmth of my hand. For a moment she closed her eyes, and the noise of the room faded to a low thrum. In that brief stillness, memories flickered behind her eyelids: the times she'd wished herself invisible, the moments her voice had caught in her throat, the sting of being called "broken." But now, a different kind of heat pulsed in her chest—a hope, fragile but persistent, that maybe she could be more than the sum of past wounds. Maybe she could be seen.

As Betty stepped forward, the hum of scattered conversations and shuffling programs pressed around her, the fairy lights above soft and golden, warming the room. She remembered every time she'd wanted to disappear. But now, something inside her burned brighter than her fear.

Her name was called.

Betty stepped out into the light. The room quieted, saved for the faint hum of the overhead vent and the distant clatter of someone setting down a coffee mug. As she approached the podium, the warmth of the stage lights prickled her skin, making everything feel both surreal and immediate. She unfolded the paper— its scent of ink and old notebooks rising as it crinkled softly in her hands.

Her hands trembled, but her voice didn't.

"They called me broken. And sometimes, I believed them.

I remember the day I stopped raising my hand in class—convinced my voice didn't matter, that speaking would only draw eyes I didn't want. I thought it was easier not to be seen, easier to let silence swallow me whole.

But broken things can hold light too.

I used to think silence was strength. But now I know— it was fear dressed up in a costume.

I'm done being invisible. I'm done pretending I don't care. I'm ready to let my light be seen.

I care too much.

And I'm still here."

The applause started as a polite ripple, punctuated by the shuffle of programs and the hush of hopeful breath. Then it grew—real and rising, hands coming together in a rhythm that filled the room. Some people stood, the scrape of chairs adding its own music to the moment. Betty blinked against the bright glare overhead, her eyes searching for something solid in the flood of praise. She looked over at me—just for a second.

I didn't smile. I simply pressed a hand to my heart.

She understood.

Afterward, people approached her—parents, teachers, even Steve from the third row. They asked quiet, sincere questions; complimented her bravery with words that felt gentle, not overwhelming. Betty smiled, sometimes awkwardly, but she held her ground, her fingers curled around the folded speech like a talisman.

Later, she found me in the hallway, where the air was cooler, the buzz of the gathering fading behind closed doors.

"Did I really do it?" she asked, voice barely a whisper.

"You really did."

"I don't think I've ever felt... big before."

"You weren't just big," I said. "You were huge, and your light was Brillant."

We stood in silence, broken only by the distant echo of conversation and in that moment, I realized how much I'd learned from her courage. The exchange was subtle—a shared realization that growth isn't one-sided.

That night, sitting at my desk beneath a lamp's golden glow, I opened my notebook. This time, I didn't write a lesson. I simply copied Betty's words: "Broken things can hold light."

Underneath, I added:

Sometimes, those we mentor end up teaching us valuable lessons and helping us find unexpected answers together.

Chapter Forty-Eight:

A Different Kind of Question

The night after Betty's speech, sleep slipped further away with every passing hour. Not because something was wrong—but because something felt right. The glow of her words lingered like the soft shimmer from the lamp on my desk, looping in my mind—a melody both familiar and new. I kept replaying her steady voice, the way her shoulders squared under the spotlight, and the gentle hush as the audience listened. There was a warmth in me, a ripple that stretched beyond that single moment on stage.

The following afternoon, Steve phoned me—no text or message. His quiet, hesitant voice signaled he had something on his mind.

"Got time for a walk?" he asked.

"Always," I said, and I meant it.

Steve arrived a little late, just as I'd come to expect from him—not out of disregard, but because time always seemed to bend around his gentle distractions. I'd learned that his lateness was never intentional; it was simply part of his rhythm, one I'd grown to recognize and, somehow, cherish. He stood at the entrance, carrying two freshly prepared hot lattes—the same way he had after every big moment since we first met. The sight was instantly reassuring; his smile, soft and a little crooked, radiated the same warmth I'd felt a year ago, when he appeared after my first presentation with that same gentle grin. That smile had gotten me through anxious nights and uncertain mornings, always promising that I wasn't alone.

The sweet aroma of the latte unfurled in the crisp autumn air, mingling with the faint scent of fallen leaves. As I climbed into the passenger seat, the paper cup warmed my chilled fingers, and the familiar creak of the car seat pressed against my back—a comfort that settled deep into my bones. Outside, the wind rustled across the pavement, sending golden leaves skittering in restless patterns, their dry edges whispering beneath our feet before we closed the car doors. Steve's presence felt calming, the kind of calm assurance that reminded me of a memory: the time he waited for me under a lamplit awning after a rainstorm, his smile cutting through the gloom with a certainty that made the world seem less daunting.

Now, as the car filled with the gentle sounds of our breath and the muted percussion of leaves tapping against the windshield, I glanced at Steve. His eyes carried the unspoken promise of understanding—the kind that comes from shared stories, late-night confessions, and moments when words fall away but comfort remains. The day had shifted, subtle yet profound, and as the warmth of the latte seeped into my hands, I knew that maybe, just maybe, things were changing in ways neither of us had ever dared to hope.

As we drove toward campus, the city's golden leaves whirled past the window. I noticed the way Steve's fingers curled around the steering wheel, how he glanced at me with the same quiet certainty that had carried us through both triumphs and heartbreaks. The hope in the day felt tangible—a thread winding through the silence, tying us together, anchoring me in the delicate possibility that change could be gentle and good.

We walked along the university garden trail, leaves just starting to turn, and the air was cool enough to see our breath mingling above us. Each step crunched softly on the gravel, a subtle percussion to our time together. The faint scent of damp earth and dry leaves lingered, and I felt a calmness in the moment that felt both familiar and impossibly new.

He didn't say much at first, which was so like him— quiet, observant, steady as a stone in a stream. Yet there was something different in the way he held my hand, fingers curled and tight, as if the connection were an anchor for whatever he needed to say.

When we reached the small pond near the benches, he paused. Water rippled with the wind, a hush of gold and silver across its surface. We stopped walking, when we got to our usual bench overlooking the pond where the geese mingle

"I wanted to ask you something," he said.

I froze, not from fear, but out of instinct—every "ask"
I'd ever known came with expectations. Pressure.
Risk. I remembered the last time someone said those
words—how my heart raced, how I braced for
disappointment. But this felt different. There was a
gentleness in the way the light caught his profile, a
calm in the space he left for my answer.

He didn't reach for me, didn't rush. He just sat on the
bench and waited, letting the afternoon breathe around
us, letting autumn settle in with the promise of change.
The crisp scent of fallen leaves mingled with the cool
air, joining us in the moment. He seemed content in the
silence, his eyes reflecting something unspoken, while
I felt a gentle warmth growing between us—a silent
acknowledgment of trust. I joined him, and we just sat
there listening softly to the leaves, each one a quiet act
of trust..

Steve broke the silence, his voice soft and steady. "I've
been thinking," he said, tracing his thumb across the
side of my hand "People like us—we're not used to
being chosen, are we? Not in ways that feel like they'll
stick."

I felt the comfort of his hand and the warmth of his
presence that mingled with the sharp scent of fallen
leaves and the sound of geese curling ripples on the
pond. The day seemed to good to be true.

He glanced over, his expression open and unhurried,
eyes shimmering with hope. His hand moved slowly,
fingertips brushing softly against mine, anchoring us in

the quiet certainty of the moment. "I see you, I hear you, and I know you. I want to spend the rest of my life with you if you'll have me."

I pulled my knees up onto the bench, watching the light flicker across the pond's surface. My heart thudded loud enough to feel in my fingertips.

"Makenzie," he continued, gentle as ever, "I'm here. I'm not going anywhere. I want us to move forward with a future that we shape together."

His promise stirred something fragile in me, echoing the loneliness I once felt waiting on that dark porch. The words fell into the quiet space between us, soft but weighted, pressing against a part of me still wary of tenderness. The chill of the autumn air seemed sharper as the memory surfaced—an eighth-grade evening, backpack digging into my shoulders, footsteps echoing on empty sidewalks. The sky above had been bruised with evening, its colors fading into indigo. Each step home rang hollow, the porch light never coming on, and I waited on the front porch, invisible, swallowed by the cold and the hush, believing I was easy to forget. The faint scent of damp leaves and the brittle crunch beneath my feet made the solitude feel even deeper. In this moment, his words wrapped around me, stirring old aches and new hope, pulling me gently back to now.

Now, in the hush of autumn, I realized I was no longer that abandoned kid. The realization made me shift, shoulders relaxing as the warmth returned to my chest.

I swallowed, voice small but steady. "No one's ever said that to me before."

Steve gave me a crooked smile, careful and reassuring. "That's exactly why I'm saying it—to you, now."

A nervous laugh fluttered out of me, startling a pair of ducks from the reeds. My fingers brushed a loose strand of hair behind my ear.

"You're proposing?" I paused, carefully observing his expression for confirmation as the moment extended between us."

He chuckled, eyes crinkling with warmth, the sincerity in his gaze grounding me as he got down on one knee in front of the bench "Yes will you marry me?" No white doves. Just a promise—I'm in this, for as long as you'll have me." His words lingered in the air, steady and sure, and I felt my heart skip several beats, hope blooming quietly in the hush."

For a second, I hesitated. The old ache of loneliness flickered and faded, replaced by something gentler— hope, fragile and bright.

I let out a long breath, feeling the cool air settle on my skin. And for once, I didn't feel the need to run. I let myself lean in, letting the moment hold me.

"I do," I said quietly. "Want you in it. All of it.". I felt the warmth of his hand, the gentle pressure of his thumb tracing slow circles over my knuckle—a silent promise as real as words. He gently placed a dazzling two-carat, princess-cut diamond engagement ring on my left hand. The cool metal sent a shiver up my arm, grounding me in the moment. When I looked up, his eyes were shining with hope, steady and full of longing, and I knew I would remember this feeling— the weight of the ring, the certainty in his gaze—for the rest of my life..

The air grew cooler as shadows stretched across our knees, and the gentle rustle of leaves filled the quiet between us. Somewhere nearby, a bird called once and fell silent. I noticed the faint scent of woodsmoke drifting from a distant chimney, the earth underneath us soft and cold and the geese seemed to gather and circle around us.

"Someday can I meet the girl you were. The one who walked to school even when no one noticed she was gone. The one who didn't give up."

A memory flickered—the ache in my legs on that long sidewalk, the slap of loose shoelaces against my ankles, the thrill of finding wildflowers sprouting from cracks in the curb—small, defiant victories that kept me moving forward. I turned those images over, felt their weight and warmth.

"She's still here," I said, voice thick with old longing and new hope.

"I know. And I want to know her just as much as I know you now."

We sat there, his arm around me pulling me close letting the dusk enfold us, until the sun was only a golden smear behind the trees and the world went soft and blue. Nothing more needed to be said.

This wasn't a fairytale, I realized. It was something better tender and true.

That night, I took out my notebook and wrote:

#41   Love doesn't rescue you it just shows up and you let it in.

It joins you where you are and walks beside you toward what you can become.

And underneath, I drew two paths winding together— twisting through thickets and over stones, always side by side—our paths tangled but unbroken, carrying us forward into the unknown as our two paths became one.

Chapter Forty-Nine:

"I Do"

The morning of the wedding bloomed with promise—the sky was wide open and blue, so pure it felt like a quiet blessing. Light unfurled across the windowpane, gilding the edges of my quiet morning. The air was brisk, carrying the sharp freshness of new beginnings—and somewhere outside, the soft trill of doves beckoned the day forward. I slipped into a white dress that skimmed my skin, its fabric cool and smooth, embracing me with every breath. Beneath my fingertips, the delicate weaves reminded me of the strength it took to reach this moment; inside, hope and uncertainty tangled, a gentle ache blooming in my chest.

Each minute passing became a quiet promise, my heart attuned to the hush of possibility, the expectation humming beneath my skin. The soft rasp of the zipper echoed in the stillness, mingling with the scent of fresh linen and the gentle warmth of sunlight on my back. Riley stood behind me, her fingers deft and sure, their touch steady, familiar—a comfort rooted in years of friendship and unspoken support. I could feel her breath, quiet and close, and the subtle trace of her favorite lavender lotion in the air—a reminder of late-night talks, shared secrets, and the way she always found the right words when I could not. Her eyes shimmered with pride and memory, a silent acknowledgment of how far we'd come together.

"You look like hope," she whispered, voice fragile as spun sugar.

I smiled, but my hands trembled—not from nerves, but from the weight that pressed softly on my heart. The weight of crossing a threshold I'd once thought impossible.

As a girl, I rarely let myself dream of moments like this. My childhood was shadowed by uncertainty, by doors closed and voices telling me to be smaller, quieter, something other than myself. Weddings belonged to other people—people with perfect families and easy laughter. My own dreams felt too expensive, too delicate to risk in the world I knew.

Now, as I stood in that place, I realized this moment carried far more significance than a simple ceremony—it represented the result of all my efforts to overcome fear, as well as countless nights spent questioning whether love would ever come to me. The flutter of my dress, the sunlight warming my shoulders, Riley's gentle touch—all of it felt like proof that I had arrived at a place I'd built for myself, brick by uncertain brick.

I closed my eyes and let the air fill me, thick with the scent of jasmine from the courtyard below. In that quiet, I promised myself to remember hope can be fragile, but it is real. And today, I would let it carry me forward.

Steve and I chose to marry in the garden courtyard of the same community center where we first met. It was symbolic—intentional. The place where I first stood in front of strangers and told the truth was now the place I would vow my future.

Chairs lined the stone path. Soft music hummed in the air. Lanterns hung from tree branches, dancing in the gentle wind. The sweet fragrance of jasmine drifted through the courtyard, mingling with the crisp evening air. Cool stone pressed against the soles of my shoes, grounding me each time I shifted my weight. Everything was light. Everything was love.

People began to arrive.

Tori hugged me so tightly I nearly cried. "You did it," she whispered. "Not just this. All of it." Her words settled into my chest, heavier than I expected— reminding me how far I'd come, how impossible this day once seemed.

Betty arrived in a pale blue dress and her signature combat boots. She grinned wide and whispered, "I brought tissues. For you, and me."

Mr. Danner and Mrs. Grant stood in the back, hands clasped like proud guardians of the past that shaped this day.

Ivy showed up with a hopeful look in her eyes, clearly envisioning her own possibilities. When she saw me standing there, I could sense that my journey had inspired her; she knew that if I could achieve my goals, she could too. The quiet confidence in her expression spoke of dreams she was beginning to believe were possible for herself.

Even Lila, my only high school friend who was my rock through the bad years and who once told me I had "too much edge," showed up with a smile and a silk scarf around her neck.

And as I was getting ready to walk, I saw Riley rush down to join her husband and her two-year-old son Mac in the second row.

Everyone who mattered was there. As I scanned the crowd, my heart tightened, searching for faces I knew not be there. Their absence pressed at the edges of the moment—a quiet ache within joy, a reminder that some goodbyes are not meant for witnesses.

Yes, my parents were invited but I didn't send the invite at the last minute.

Not because I hated them. Not anymore.

But healing doesn't always come with a front-row seat. Sometimes, it's a quiet decision made behind a closed door: Not yet. I'm not ready. And that was okay.

The faint scent of roses mingled with the crisp air as I moved into the courtyard. The archway was textured beneath my fingertips, rough vines woven through soft petals, all trembling in the breeze. Lanterns cast scattered pools of golden light onto the stone path, and along the side the geese were just beginning to show up and find their places as the honked their approval.

With each step toward Steve, I felt the weight of old wounds shift—no longer anchors, but lessons carried forward. Steve stood beneath the arch, his suit simple, his posture steady, his eyes holding the whole story: not just the woman I'd become, but the girl I once was. And he loved both.

As I walked down the uneven stone pressed against my feet, the path showed me the way forward. Every step felt like an opening chapter—an unspoken punctuation between pain and possibility. Not an erasure of the past, but a turning of the page. I wasn't erasing where I came from; I was choosing where I was going.

Our vows were handwritten. Just truth—nothing fancy or rehearsed, only what mattered between us.

"I used to think survival was the end of the story," I said, voice steady but soft. "But loving you has shown me that survival is just the beginning."

Steve's voice caught on to the words. "You taught me that courage doesn't always roar—sometimes it just gets up, day after day, and keeps on trying. You are my courage."

When our lips met, there was a rush of warmth and sound—Riley, who'd stood by me through every storm, whistled so loudly I saw her grin split wide across the crowd. Tori cried—happy tears this time, her hands pressed to her cheeks, her eyes shining with the kind of pride that only comes from watching someone you love find peace.

We danced beneath strings of lights and laughter. The air smelled like roses and cake. People toasted us—some in English, some in jokes I'd only half remember. Every embrace, every smile, stitched me further into the fabric of this new life. The old stories didn't vanish, but they loosened their grip.

As the music faded and guests drifted away, I slipped outside for a breath of night air. The garden was quiet, lanterns flickering gentle shadows across the grass. I found the swing behind the venue, kicked off my shoes, and let my feet sway above the ground. The hush was a relief—just me and the night.

Steve found me out there, shoes in one hand, his tie pulled loose. "Too much dancing?" he teased, settling beside me.

"Too much everything," I said—honest, tired, content.

He held my hand and moved his thumb in a circular motion.

"You okay?"

"I'm just... letting it sink in."

He nodded, understanding without needing more words.

"Think they'll ever come back?" His voice was gentle.

"My parents?"

"Yeah."

"I think they will. Someday." I didn't have to explain.

He squeezed my fingers. "When they do, they'll be walking into something beautiful."

"And something mine," I said.

"Exactly."

Later, alone, I wrote in my notebook:

#42   Not every part of your past must make it to the altar. Healing is choosing who stands beside you in the light.

I drew a swing, two pairs of shoes underneath, and a ribbon tied to the branch overhead.

Because even on the biggest day of your life, sometimes it's the quietest moments—the ones you share with the people who know your whole story—that stay with you forever.

Chapter Fifty:

Settling In

We didn't have a honeymoon in the Maldives or Paris or even the mountains.

We had a little rental on the edge of the lake—brick, one story, a creaky screen door that groaned with every arrival, and a garden tangled with weeds and wild tomatoes. When the breeze blew through the open windows, it carried the earthy tang of damp soil and the faint promise of basil from a pot by the sill.

It was perfect. Not because of how it looked, but because of how it felt: like something we built, something that belonged to us.

The first night back at our new home, I forgot how to turn on the heat, and Steve dropped a box labeled "fragile" down the front steps. Inside was a cracked photo frame and three mismatched mugs. I laughed so hard I cried. In that moment, surrounded by imperfection, I realized happiness wasn't about flawless beginnings but about finding joy in our shared chaos. There, among half-unpacked boxes and chipped ceramic, I knew we were building something resilient enough to weather any accident, any stumble.

Our mornings were a study in contrast when he didn't have veterinary appointments, Steve liked slow starts—the gentle gurgle of the coffeemaker, strong and fragrant, the newspaper rustling as sunlight crept across the kitchen tiles, and a quiet ten-minute staring into space. I liked to move—wake up, write, shower, plan—my mind already racing ahead while he lingered in the soft edges of dawn.

We learned to dance around each other in the kitchen—him at the toaster, me with the kettle, both of us elbowing and apologizing until our laughter echoed off the cabinets. "Marriage is a full-contact sport," he joked one morning after I elbowed him trying to reach the honey. "I'm just practicing for real life," I said. He kissed my temple and added, "Then I want to be on your team forever."

Learning to navigate our differences taught us patience and appreciation for each other's rhythms—skills that would become the foundation of our partnership. In the scent of fresh coffee, the warmth of his hand on my back, and the simple comfort of laughter shared before the day began, we discovered that love was built quietly, moment by moment, in all the ordinary spaces we made our own.

We started making little traditions, almost without realizing it at first—each one a gentle attempt to stitch together the frayed edges of my past and make something new, something just ours. Every Friday night became frozen-pizza-and-documentary night, the living room aglow with the flicker of the television and the smell of cheese bubbling in the oven. On Sundays, sunlight would spill across the cluttered countertop as we fumbled through recipe books, each of us determined to master a new dish, even as flour dusted the floor and laughter tumbled between us.

I can still hear the sizzle and pop from the burnt French toast incident, the alarm's shrill insistence punctuating our panicked giggles, four fans whirring at full speed and the taste of slightly charred bread lingering long after we'd opened every window. Our kitchen disasters became legends, retold with a kind of pride—proof that we were living, trying, failing succeding together.

But there were quieter gestures, too—small rituals of care that felt like private codes. One morning, I woke to find Steve's sticky note trail winding through the house, each one scribbled with a reason he loved me. The notes led to a mug of tea, still steaming, and the final message: "Because you stayed." My fingers lingered on that last piece of paper; the simple weight of belonging settled in my chest.

Not every night was light and laughter. Some evenings, when the world was quiet old shadows crept in, uninvited. I'd bolt upright in bed, heart hammering against my ribs, throat tight with a panic I couldn't name. As Steve turned on the lamp, the soft amber glow pressed back the darkness at the edges of the room, but inside, my mind replayed memories that refused to fade—echoes of doors slamming, the chill of an empty hallway, words I'd never unhear.

He never rushed me. He'd wait in that hush, hands folded or reaching for mine, his presence steady as the tick of the clock. Sometimes the only sound was our breathing, slow and even. In those moments, I wondered if he felt my fear as his own, or if he was just quietly offering a safety I'd never known before.

Eventually, I'd find my voice, the words coming haltingly—confessions of old dreams and wounds, stories from before we were us. He never tried to smooth them away. He'd listen, eyes soft with understanding, as if each truth only made our bond more real. Sometimes, he'd squeeze my hand, and in that warmth, I felt the tremors in my chest begin to ease—not because the past was gone, but because I was no longer facing it alone.

We held on to these ordinary rituals and extraordinary attempts at comfort, building a life out of small moments: the smell of burnt sugar, the sound of laughter echoing off kitchen tiles, the hush of reassurance in the night, and the quiet, daily promise that, no matter what haunted us, we would face it— together.

We discovered that love wasn't just stolen kisses in the rain or the sweetness of dessert shared by candlelight. It lived in the scent of freshly brewed coffee, in the sound of socks sliding across the kitchen floor, in remembering to buy the honey oat cereal even it was left off the grocery list.. It was pausing in the heat of an argument to murmur, "I'm upset, but I still love you," voice trembling, eyes soft. It was the gentle celebration of small victories: the warm tumble of laundry finally folded, the relief of a finished essay, the satisfying click of a bill paid without stress, and the silent gratitude for peace.

With time, I noticed these moments accumulating— soft as sunlight on our kitchen tiles, fleeting yet persistent. So, I began to record these moments, scribbling them in a new kind of notebook I kept tucked beside the coffeemaker, its cover worn by morning hands.

Some of the entries:

- The way he says "home," his voice lingering on the word as if it's a place shaped by both of us.
- When his thumb traces slow circles over my back while I type, quiet reassurance blooming beneath my skin.
- How our fingers find each other even when we're angry, the warmth of his palm grounding me in the middle of an argument.
- The time he wiped away tears during Up, laughter tangled with emotion as he promised he wouldn't cry.
- The steady certainty in his eyes when he tells me, "You're safe," and I believe it, the words settling over me like a blanket.

In these understated moments—ordinary yet extraordinary—I began to recognize the shape of love:

not in grand gestures, but in the gentle, daily acts that knit our lives together, making us a "we."

Steve, in his quiet, unwavering way, carved out space for me to grow—not because I needed saving, but because with him, I finally had room to bloom. I was drawn to his steadiness from the start; the way he'd listen more than he spoke, how he believed in fixing what could be mended and letting go of what couldn't. He loved old radios, patching their static hearts back to life on Saturday mornings while blues crackled softly through the speakers.

What first caught me was the silence he brought—not an emptiness, but a calm that settled the air. I remember an early evening, curled on the faded sofa after a frayed day, beginning to believe that peace wasn't just the pause between storms. I asked him, "What if the other shoe drops?" He handed me a mug of tea, earthy and comforting, and said, "Then we'll pick it up together."

At first, I distrusted normalcy—looked for shadows behind every gentle thing. I'd flinch when the house got too quiet, half-expecting chaos to slip out from behind the curtains. But as the months unfurled, I found myself letting go. The shift was gradual: one morning, sunlight pooled across the kitchen floor while Steve whistled and portioned out honey oat cereal, and I realized I'd stopped bracing for disappointment. The scent of coffee, the sting of soy sauce from takeout dumplings, and the way our laughter chased away the hush—these became anchors.

Steve started coming to my workshops for teens aging out of foster care. He'd sit in the back with a thermos of strong coffee, never speaking unless I asked, but always present. Afterward, he'd squeeze my hand and say, "I'm proud of you." Once, I caught him saying the same to a shy kid, his tone steady and sure, and I saw how his belief could become a kind of shelter.

We didn't need fireworks. We had quiet mornings, jokes inside, takeout on the floor that tasted of ginger and garlic, and honest conversations that left us raw and warm. The walls of our tiny house glowed with sunlight in late afternoon, and the calendar was dotted with scribbled hearts, meal plans, and Steve's reminders to "buy more soy sauce."

I wasn't used to peace, but I was learning to trust it— slowly, then all at once. One-night, folding laundry, I said, "You know what's weird? I never thought I could be this... normal." He smiled. He just handed me a clean sock, gentle as always. "Normal's overrated," he said with a crooked smile. "But being loved? That's even better. Do you have the matching sock it's missing?"

That night, I wrote in my notebook:

#43   Sometimes the happiest thing you can do is to live quietly, fully, in the sunlight you once thought you'd never see.

And beneath it, I drew a little brick house—a yellow door, sunlight spilling over the mailbox labeled: The Bennetts. Because yes—I had taken his last name. A decision, like so many others, made together. With love, with light, and with forever in mind.

Chapter Fifty-One:

The Possibility of More

It started with a single sock.

A tiny, pink-striped baby sock, soft as a whisper, tangled amid towels in the community center's laundry basket. I plucked it out, holding it between my thumb and forefinger, its warmth lingering from the dryer. For a moment, the scent of fabric softener and clean cotton made me think of childhood afternoons spent in sunlit rooms, the hush of someone humming in another part of the house. I set the sock on the windowsill at home, beside Steve's ceramic coffee mug and the stray chopsticks from last night's takeout and felt a pang—a longing so gentle it could almost be mistaken for contentment.

That evening, as the golden-orange dusk settled against our kitchen window, Steve and I moved quietly around each other, sleeves rolled, hands plunged in soapy water. The dishwater was warm, almost comforting, and I watched the way Steve's fingers— broad, careful—circulated a plate beneath the suds. He glanced at the sock on the sill, the way a person glances at a note left just for them.

"What's with the sock?" he asked, not looking up, letting the moment linger like a question we'd both been circling.

"It was left behind at the center," I said, drying a glass. The light caught the rim, casting a delicate reflection onto the counter. I watched it flicker, found my hand trembling just a little.

Steve glanced at me out of the corner of his eyes; his brow furrowed in a way that always softened the longer he watched. He didn't just wait, his presence a quiet invitation.

I turned the sock over in my palm, thumb brushing the pale pink stripes. For a heartbeat, I let myself imagine a life where such a small thing might belong to us. A mess of toys in the corner, laughter echoing down the hall, the quiet comfort of being needed.

He leaned back, arms crossed loosely, a wet ring from the plate shining on his shirt. I felt him watching, but I couldn't quite meet his eyes.

"You're thinking something," he said, gentle as always.

I bit my lip, weighing words that felt bigger than the silence between us. "Maybe," I murmured, letting the sock rest atop the sill, caught in the last slant of evening light.

Steve didn't push. He just reached for my hand, his thumb tracing circles over my knuckles—wordless, steady. And in that hush, I realized how the smallest things—pink stripes, warm dishwater, the weight of a glance—could hint at the possibility of something more.

I took a breath, feeling the subtle vibration of the dishwasher humming beneath the counter, the warmth from the overhead light brushing softly across my shoulders. The faint clatter of dishes echoed in the quiet kitchen, and the scent of coffee lingered between us as we stood, hands trembling slightly.

It wasn't uncertainty I felt—it was certainty, tangled in hope, threading itself through the steady tick of the wall clock and the gentle press of Steve's presence.

"I've been wondering," I said slowly, voice barely above a whisper, "what it would be like… to have a family. A real one. With you."

Steve didn't blink.

He didn't freeze or fumble or change the subject.

Instead, he said, "Yeah. I've been wondering that, too."

My heart thudded, echoing in my chest.

"You have?"

"Of course," he said gently. "Not in a pressuring way. But I've thought about it. I've imagined you holding a baby. Or reading bedtime stories. Or getting too emotional at a school play."

A flicker of laughter escaped me. "I'd cry every time," I admitted.

"I'd keep tissues in my pocket just for you," he smiled, a spark of affection softening his eyes.

We stood there, the sock between us like a tiny monument, the weight of possibility thickening the air. The linoleum cool beneath my bare feet, the window glowing with the fading gold of dusk.

"I'm scared," I said. Memories of slammed doors and silent dinners flickered at the edges of my mind, reminding me why this mattered so much. "I'm scared of not knowing how. Of not being enough. Of becoming… them."

He stepped closer, his hands enveloping mine, thumbs tracing circles over my knuckles like he always did.

"You won't," he murmured. "Because you already know what it's like to feel unloved. And because you've spent your whole life making sure no one around you feel that way."

"But parenting isn't mentorship," I whispered, feeling the chill of the tile seeping into my toes.

"No," he said. "It's messier. But it's also made of moments—thousands of them. And we'd face them together."

I managed a smile. "You'd still love me even if I burned the grilled cheese?"

He grinned. "I'd consider it a rite of passage. Besides, I've got takeout menus on standby."

We were standing on the edge of something big— parenthood, in one form or another—and neither of us pretended to have all the answers.

Steve, my partner of five years, didn't sugarcoat it. He didn't promise ease or perfection or instant certainty. But he said "together." And somehow, that made all the difference.

We didn't decide that night. No promises, no plans. But we left the sock on the windowsill—a soft thing, faded from too many washes, its pink stripes catching the golden light as evening settled outside. It felt almost ceremonial, a quiet nod to possibility.

Over the next few weeks, the conversation continued in quiet pockets of our lives. At the supermarket, Steve pointed out a board book and said, "This one's got your name all over it." On a Saturday afternoon, babysitting for a neighbor, I caught myself singing softly to their daughter as I rocked her, the melody twining with the muffled sounds of traffic drifting through the window. Later, Steve smiled and said, "I didn't know you had a lullaby voice."

"I didn't either," I admitted. The vulnerability felt new, sharp as the cool breeze sneaking under the door.

We started asking deeper questions. Could we do this with our work schedules? Could our home stretch wide enough for someone else's laughter and tears? Would we foster first? Adopt? Try biologically? Would we be enough?

The question lingered between us, heavier than I expected. I wondered if anyone ever truly feels ready for this kind of leap—if doubts and hope always coexist in the shadow of change.

"I think love makes room," I said one night, watching the way the lamplight spilled across the worn kitchen table and the pile of dinner dishes.

Steve nodded, his eyes reflecting the warmth of the room. "And we've got plenty of that."

We toured a daycare center one rainy afternoon, uncertain and hopeful in equal measure. Days spilled into weeks, each marked by subtle shifts—a glance exchanged in the baby aisle, a hesitant touch on soft blankets, the growing weight of possibility between us.

We shared our childhood fear of becoming too much, his of never being enough. I remembered how my loudest laugh once drew stares at a family gathering, and how Steve's quiet achievements often went unnoticed, tucked away in silent pride. Those memories crept in unexpectedly, shaping the questions we asked and the answers we struggled to find. Would we offer a home that celebrated laughter, which cherished small victories? Would we be gentle enough with both our past and our future?

Sometimes, in the hush after dinner, we'd sit with the silence and talk about names. On Saturday mornings, stories would surface—ones we weren't ready to share with anyone else. Our curiosity became cautious commitment, each moment folding into the next:

laughter at a silly suggestion, tears at a memory, a deep breath before saying, "What if?"

One evening, as sunlight poured through the kitchen window, catching on the sock we'd left on the sill, Steve whispered, "You know, I think the bravest thing we could do is give someone a life full of the love." The golden light glowed across the faded stripes, making it seem almost new. I picked it up, tracing the worn fabric between my fingers, and felt the quiet promise it held.

I rested my head on his chest and said, "Let's be brave then."

Later that night, I opened my notebook and wrote:

#44   *Some choices aren't made in a single moment.*

       They grow over time—quiet, steady, and true.

       And when you finally say yes, you realize your heart has been making room all along.

Beneath the words, I drew a pair of tiny socks. One striped, one plain. Side by side on a windowsill, bathed in sunlight—soft, hopeful, waiting for what came next.

Chapter Fifty-Two
Double Blessings

The pregnancy test sat on the counter, a pale pink strip against cold, speckled porcelain. Above me, the harsh fluorescent light flickered, washing the bathroom in a glare that made everything—my hands, the quiet tile floor—seem sharper, somehow more real. The plastic test felt slick and fragile between my trembling fingers. My heartbeat thudded in my ears, mingling with the distant hum of the vent and the steady drip from the faucet.

I hadn't planned for this. There were no circled dates, no neat checklists, just the sudden vertigo of being late and then late again, followed by the chill of the drugstore parking lot and the crinkle of the paper bag in my lap.

The sound of Steve's footsteps echoed down the hallway, steady and slow, until he paused in the doorway. His silhouette cut across the bright, artificial light, and for a moment, we just looked at each other— the test between my knees, the truth suspended in the silence.

"Hey," he said softly, his voice a gentle break in the hush. "Everything okay?"

I held up the test. Two pink lines. The answer arrived, undeniable.

He blinked, then sat beside me on the cool tiles, shoulder to shoulder. The warmth of his arm brushing mine grounded me, as if anchoring me to the present.

And then?

He smiled.

We didn't cry. We didn't panic. We didn't leap up and down like people in movies. Instead, we let the moment settle around us, the air thick with possibility and the faint scent of lavender soap.

"We're going to be parents," I said, voice barely above a whisper.

"You already are," he replied, the words lingering in the quiet.

As Steve's reassurance echoed in my mind, a familiar ache tugged gently at my heart—Jaylen's name surfacing like a ripple across still water. The joy of new life mingled with the memory of someone lost in the system but never forgotten, weaving hope and longing together in the hush.

For a girl who once feared she'd repeat the past, the realization that I was carrying a future inside me felt like a quiet miracle. The thought of giving someone a home—one filled with laughter and small victories— made the moment bright with promise, even as it shimmered with the ache of memory.

And so, in the gentle light and the soft exchange of words, I understood becoming a parent meant making room for both hope and history, for what was and what might be.

Jaylen's name lingered, a soft reminder that love never truly leaves—it simply waits, ready to be welcomed home.

He was seven and had been in foster care since birth, never knowing the comfort of a permanent home.

I first met Jaylen through one of my outreach programs—he was sharp, sarcastic, and did his best to keep everyone at arm's length. Yet, even in his guardedness, there were glimmers of who he was beneath the surface. When he thought no one was watching, he'd hum softly and meticulously construct Lego cities, each building more intricate than the last. It was as if he was blueprinting the world he wished existed.

One afternoon, after a session, he lingered by the door, shifting from foot to foot. Without meeting my eyes, he asked, "Do people ever get picked twice?"

"Twice?" I said, pausing.

"Like, if the first people didn't want them. Can they get picked again?"

His words lingered long after he left the room, echoing in my mind as I drove home beneath the slow-fading light. "Can they get picked again?"—the quiet hope in his voice pressed against my chest, opening old wounds and unspoken wishes I hadn't realized I still carried. That single, tentative question rippled through my thoughts, haunting the space between memory and possibility, making me ache to reassure him that hope could survive, even after so many goodbyes.

Steve had watched me pour over pamphlets for weeks, his quiet support unwavering but his thoughts unspoken. He'd look up from his book and catch me tracing adoption forms with my finger, never rushing me, always there—a steady presence. He was the sort who believed in showing up, who understood that families were built as much by choice as by chance.

One evening, after dinner, Steve cleared his throat. "I've been thinking," he said gently, "that maybe this baby isn't meant to be our first child."

I glanced up and for a moment, we were both silent; however, our eyes met and the understanding between us was evident, unspoken yet clear.

"You too?" I asked.

"Yea- I think this baby will need a big brother." And just like that, the decision was made—it was revealed, as if it had been growing all along between us.

When we finally told him, Jaylen didn't smile. His fingers curled tightly around the strap of his backpack, knuckles pale, as if bracing for something he couldn't name. I could see his eyes darting from Steve to me, searching for reassurance in the quiet space between us.

He just blinked and said, "Even with the baby coming?" The question hung in the air, heavy with hope and uncertainty.

"Especially with the baby coming," I said, my own heart pounding as I spoke." There's more than enough love to go around," I promised him.

He paused—a brief flicker of vulnerability crossing his face—then nodded once and asked, "Do I have to share snacks?"

Steve grinned; a gentle warmth settled over the kitchen. "Only if you want to teach the baby how to steal cookies."

Jaylen thought about that, lips pressed together in careful consideration. "I might," he said, voice soft but steady.

After months of waiting, Jaylen was finally home with us, his new family. We'd worried how he'd react to sharing a house with strangers and a baby soon-to-arrive. The day we brought him home, he didn't cry, didn't run, didn't hug. He stood in the hallway of our little brick house, eyes flickering from room to room, searching for something familiar to cling to.

The house was filled with the scent of simmering soup and the faint musk of clean laundry. Jaylen breathed in deeply, then announced, "Smells like laundry and soup."

"Accurate," Steve said, a soft chuckle rising from his chest.

Jaylen nodded, gaze lingering on the streaks of sunlight spilling across the worn floorboards. "I think I'll like it." His voice was steady, but his fingers still gripped the backpack strap like a lifeline.

I watched him, heart aching with hope. It was the most honest yes we could ask for. In that moment, the quiet shuffle of Jaylen's feet in the hallway seemed to echo a promise: that here, in this house full of ordinary sounds and gentle light, something new and fragile was beginning.

Three months later, our daughter arrived. Ivy was perfect in every way!

The soft beeping of monitors blended with the gentle hum of conversation in the hallway, wrapping us in a cocoon of quiet anticipation. The air smelled faintly of antiseptic and something sweet—maybe the flowers on the windowsill, maybe the promise of new life. Steve stood beside me holding my hand, his grip steady and warm.

Jaylen lingered at the edge of the hospital bed, ears twitching at every unexpected sound—a nurse's shoes squeaking on linoleum, a distant baby's wail, the subtle rustle of sheets. He clutched his backpack close, hesitating before taking a careful step forward. His eyes flickered to Steve, searching for reassurance, and Steve gave him an almost imperceptible nod.

"She's small," Jaylen whispered, voice barely louder than the whisper of the ventilator.

"She's yours," I said, keeping my tone gentle.

He glanced from me to Steve, uncertainty shadowing his face, then back to the newborn. "You mean like a sister?" His words trembled with hope.

"Exactly."

He stretched out a hand—slow, deliberate, as if afraid the moment might shatter—and touched her tiny, curled fingers. She grabbed hold, her grip surprisingly strong. Jaylen's breath hitched, and a smile flickered at the corners of his mouth. For an instant, he and Steve exchanged a glance: relief, wonder, maybe even the beginning of trust.

Jaylen smiled bigger and said: "I think I like her.."

While at home and down the hallway. laughter ricocheted off the walls. Sometimes it blended with the sharp clatter of cereal cascading onto the counter, or with the gentle hum of lullabies Jaylen, insisted he didn't know. The air was thick with the aroma of strong coffee, the sweetness of warm oatmeal, and, faintly, the powdery scent of new baby skin. Light filtered through curtains onto a sprawl of storybooks and soft blankets. I sometimes found my elbows sticking to the kitchen table's honeyed surface— leftover syrup from breakfast, a small price for the mess of togetherness.

Steve became our quiet anchor amid the whirlwind—always within reach with a steady hand or a cup of tea, his warmth grounding me when I felt adrift. He brewed coffee with one hand while balancing the baby with the other, humming a tune that drifted from the kitchen to wherever I was trying, and sometimes failing, to write.

There were nights, after the children's breathing slowed and the house finally settled, when uncertainty crept in like a shadow at the edge of the lamplight. Curled up next to Steve on the couch, I'd whisper, "Do you think I'm doing okay?" The question was raw, heavy with the fear of not being enough. Steve would look at me—really look, soft and unwavering—and answer, "Makenzie. You're doing more than okay. You're doing magic."

I'd press further, my doubts bubbling up: "But what if I mess them up?"

He'd squeeze my hand. "We all do, sometimes. But we love them that's louder than any mistakes. That's what they'll remember."

Later, I'd jot words into my notebook, the paper cool beneath my fingertips:

#45   *Family isn't what you plan.*

      It's what you choose,

      What you carry,

And what surprises you when love makes room for more.

My hands gently cradled those of my newborn and my seven-year-old, their tiny fingers curled into mine. Their presence reminds me that love makes room to embrace each child fully.

Chapter Fifty-Three:

The Return

The letter arrived on a Wednesday, tucked among bills and flyers, but its weight was unmistakable. My fingers traced the edge of the envelope, feeling its roughness against my skin as my heart thudded in my chest. The name scrawled across the front—Mom—carried memories of slammed doors and silent dinners, of half-spoken apologies and years spent building walls around old wounds. Steve had always known better than to ask about my mother, respecting boundaries I'd built from hurt too deep to voice. Instead, he simply left a mug of chamomile tea beside me and pressed his lips gently to the top of my head, wordlessly anchoring me.

For a full day, I carted the letter from room to room, its stiff edges pressing into my palms, cool and slightly rough like dried leaves. Outside, the distant hum of a lawnmower drifted through a half-open window, mingling with the chatter of birds and the squeals of my children as they dashed past, their laughter ricocheting down the hallway and the scent of peanut butter & grape jelly thick in the kitchen. Yet beneath this familiar chaos, dread gnawed at me—my heart thudded against my ribs, my shoulders tight, each joyful noise feeling suddenly remote, as if I were drifting just outside the warmth of it all, the letter sending me back to a darker time and place.

That evening, once the children had fallen asleep, a nervous stillness settled throughout the house. The faint tick of the kitchen clock marked each passing second as I sat at the table, the envelope trembling between my fingers. My heart pounded with dread, every possible outcome racing through my mind as I hesitated before opening. Slowly, I unfolded the paper, the fibers whispering against my skin in the quiet, each movement weighed with anticipation and uncertainty. The note was brief, with no long explanations or apologies. Just this:

We've watched from a distance, unsure if we were allowed to contact you. We were wrong to leave. We know we can't undo that. But we're here if you ever want to try.

For three days, I said nothing. The letter waited on my desk, and each morning my eyes flicked to it as I passed, a small ache blooming in my chest. Steve never pushed for answers—just squeezed my hand a little tighter when he caught me staring out the window, lost in the swirl of what might come next. In the silence, I let the weight of memory settle and the possibility of forgiveness linger, suspended in the gentle pause between old wounds and new beginnings.

The soft morning light filtered through the kitchen curtains, casting gentle shadows across the tiled floor as I cradled Ivy in the quiet hush of dawn. Outside, the sky was streaked with crimson and gold, and the coolness of the morning air, drifting in through a cracked window, made me shiver. Birds trilled somewhere beyond the glass, their song a hopeful backdrop to the uncertainty swirling in my chest.

Steve moved softly around me, his silent presence remaining my constant anchor as ever. His steady warmth grounded me, especially now, when old memories threatened to sweep me away. When I finally whispered, "I think I'm ready," my voice fragile in the hush. He didn't ask for details, only wrapped his arms around my shoulders, and murmured, "You don't have to be sure of them—you just have to be sure of yourself."

We chose a park near the community center—a deliberate choice for neutral ground; quiet, public, and peaceful. That morning, the air was crisp with dew, and the scent of freshly cut grass lingered as we walked. Jaylen clutched my hand a little tighter than usual. He didn't know the story, but I'd told him we were meeting "someone important," and I watched the curiosity flicker in his eyes, threaded through with an unease he couldn't name.

Steve offered to stay home with the baby, but I shook my head. I needed my family beside me—needed the steady comfort of his familiar hand in mine and the love of my children as I walked toward a past I'd spent years avoiding.

As we approached the park, the sounds of distant traffic faded beneath the soft rush of leaves in the breeze. The bench came into view, sunlight dappling the wood. My heart thudded as we approached, each step echoing with questions I wasn't sure I wanted answered. Steve gripped my hand gently, while Jaylen looked up at me, studying my expression for comfort and picking up on my nervousness. I tried to steady my breath, feeling the tremor of anticipation in my chest.

They were already sitting there, older, a little smaller than I remembered, the years having settled hard upon their shoulders as they waited, bracing themselves, too, for what might come next.

Older. Grayer. Smaller, Tired.

My mom stood first. My dad followed, slower, his eyes tracing the ground before finding mine.

We stopped a few feet away, nerves tightening the space between us. Jaylen squeezed my hand, while Steve stood quietly beside us, his presence reassuring. My heart thudded in my chest as I waited for their reaction, the crisp morning air biting at my cheeks.

"Hi," I managed, my voice thin and uncertain.

They both echoed it, their voices cracking like dry leaves. My fingers trembled in Jaylen's grip, and Steve glanced at me, a silent reassurance shining in his eyes.

"This is Jaylen," I said, nudging him gently forward, "and this is Steve." My dad nodded, his gaze lingering on Jaylen—a fleeting look of wonder, tinged with regret.

My mom's lips parted in a trembling smile. "He's handsome."

"Jaylen?" I asked, trying to lighten the tension, my thumb tracing nervous circles on my son's knuckles.

She shook her head, glancing at Steve, then back at me. "No. Well—yes. But I meant your husband."

A quiet laugh shivered between us, breaking through the cold edge of uncertainty. Beneath it all, my heart fluttered—hopeful, fragile, and aching for what might come next.

We all laughed, nervous and fragile laugh, hovering between us like something easily broken.

We sat—space measured and deliberate. Not close. Not far.

No one rushed to fill the quiet with explanations or demands. The silence lingered, then the small talk began but led nowhere.

My mom's hands twisted in her lap, her knuckles pale with tension. She glanced over, lips parted as if searching for the right words.

"You look... happy." Her voice barely crested the hush.

"I am," I answered without hesitation.

She nodded, a flicker of relief and regret crossing her face. "I wasn't sure we'd ever get to see that."

For a long moment, I watched —uncertainty and longing mapped in the lines around their eyes. "There were a lot of years when I wasn't sure either."

Jaylen shifted, scraping his shoe against the gravel, drawing spirals in the dust. Steve's hand found my shoulder, a silent anchor.

My dad looked away and said, "You were always brave."

I hesitated before replying. "You never gave me much of a choice."

His lips pressed into a thin line. "No. We didn't."

My mom's voice fell to a whisper, words trembling. "We were drowning. We thought if we left... maybe you'd be better off."

A pause, drawn long by everything unsaid.

"You thought wrong."

"We know that now."

A beat passed. My pulse hammered—louder now that the words hung open between us.

Another pause.

"Do you hate us?"

I took a breath, feeling the air tremble in my chest as I searched myself for the truth—something raw and fragile. The old ache flared, a familiar burn in my throat, but it faded as I let the silence settle.

"No, I don't hate you - I don't hate anyone... I love my family! That's what truly matters. There's no place for hatred in my life."

Their faces shifted, hope flickering behind the exhaustion.

"I did," I admitted, my voice steadier than I felt. The words tasted sharp, but clean. "For a long time. It was easier to be angry than to wonder if you missed me. But dragging that hate around just kept me anchored in the unknown. I couldn't keep living there so I moved on."

Somewhere nearby, a swing creaked in the wind. For a moment, I noticed the sunlight angling through the trees and the way dust floated and spun in the breeze. My stomach knotted with relief and grief tangled together, impossible to separate.

Jaylen ran over to the playground, laughter bubbling up as Steve followed with his little sister Ivy perched on his shoulders, both eager to join in the fun.

That left me, alone with them.

"I'm not offering a clean slate," I said. "But maybe we can start with the corners."

My mom nodded, eyes glassy. A lump formed in my throat as I watched her struggle for words, and I realized how much I wanted to believe things could change.

"We'll take what you give," my dad said.

My mom approached and I allowed her to hug me. It wasn't a tight embrace or a lengthy one—just a gentle, brief hug.

But I didn't pull away. And that was something. Her perfume was faint—familiar but distant. My heartbeat faster, but I let myself breathe. The fabric of her sweater brushed my cheek, soft but awkward, as if it too were searching for the right shape.

As we parted, my dad gave an uncertain nod, hands fidgeting with his car keys. The breeze carried the scent of fresh-cut grass, mingling with the scent of old cologne and something almost like hope.

We walked back to the car, footsteps crunching on gravel. Jaylen glanced at me, his eyes questioning but gentle.

"Was that your mom and dad?"

"Yes."

Jaylen slowed his pace, running a toe through the gravel. "They seemed nervous."

I nodded, watching the clouds drift above the trees. "They were."

Jaylen hesitated, his brow furrowing as concern flickered in his eyes. "Why were they nervous?"

I didn't answer right away. Instead, I watched the way Jaylen's shoulders tensed, how he shifted uncertainly on his feet, waiting. Finally, I said, "I'll explain one day." I glanced away, remembering the promise I'd made not to reveal too much—not yet.

Later that night, the house bathed in the hush of late hours, I sat by my window and let the day settle inside me. The faintest trace of my mom's perfume still lingered on my sleeve, blending with the cool scent of approaching rain threading through the screen. My fingers brushed over the edge of a teacup—and for a moment, I let myself rest in that quiet, feeling both hollow and full. I thought of Jaylen's gentle question, the uncertain touch of my dad's presence, and the brave, trembling space I'd made for forgiveness.

With a slow breath, I opened my notebook and wrote:

#46   *Healing does not always arrive with fanfare.*

Sometimes, it finds you on a bench,

Or in the warmth left by a borrowed sweater,

Or in the hush that follows hard words.

It does not ask for everything—just hopes for something.

And sometimes, that is enough to begin.
Healing takes time.

Underneath, I drew three benches.

One empty—a quiet place of solitude, where I first learned to sit with my own sorrow.

One shared—a space of tentative connection, built from nervous laughter and the warmth of forgiveness beginning to root.

And one with two kids playing nearby—a bench transformed by joy, where hope and trust returned in small, playful echoes.

Each bench marked a step in learning to welcome others—and myself—into spaces once guarded by memory.

Because the past didn't get to define me.

But it could watch who I'd become.

And maybe, over time, even be invited in.

Epilogue:

Her Masked Identity, Unmasked

"Are you going to forgive them?"

The auditorium held its breath, the hush stretching until every cough and shifting chair echoed like a distant drum. I pressed my palms into the cool wood of the podium, the paper edges of my notes biting gently into my skin—something solid, something to hold onto.

My throat tightened as I considered the question. Was forgiveness possible? Did I even want it? My heart was a mixture of hope and hesitation, the old ache mingling with new resolve. I could feel the weight of every gaze, searching for my answer, searching for me.

A thousand faces waited. Some eager, some skeptical, some with arms folded—each person carrying their own history, their own reasons for listening. I saw the flicker of anticipation in a teacher's eyes, the nervous tapping of a student's foot, the soft rustle of programs in restless hands.

I stood at the podium, the warm spotlight flooding my face as my just published book trembled slightly in my hands. My heart pounded with excitement and nerves, each beat echoing the anticipation and vulnerability that filled the room.

On the cover: a pair of worn shoes, a girl standing back in a shadow and a notebook with the outline of a list just barely visible. The shoes mirrored my own journey—each scuff a story, each shadow, a secret I'd carried through years of silence and the list a blueprint for survival. The image wasn't just art; it was a confession, an invitation for the world to see the path I'd traveled.

Beneath the title: Her Masked Identity

And in the corner, my name. Makenzie Bennett.

Not hidden, not ashamed, whole.

It had been twelve years since I left the shelter. Eight years since I met Steve. Five since we brought Ivy home. Four since Jaylen started calling us Mom and Dad without flinching. Three years since I forgave myself.

Now, both kids sat in the front row, knees pressed together, the stiff fabric of their uniforms rustling every time they shifted. Jaylen's sneaker heels tapped against the polished floor in a jittery rhythm, a quiet percussion to match the thrum in my chest. Ivy tugged at her collar, wide eyes scanning the auditorium—her thumb tracing the corner of her book's cover.

Steve sat behind, wearing his favorite blue sweater. He gave a gentle smile—the very same expression he had when he first handed me coffee at the university coffee shop.

My parents were there, too, on the third row. As I looked their way, memories of our recent encounters surfaced. I recalled the awkward silences over mugs of strong, bitter coffee—the faint clink of spoons against porcelain echoing between us. My fingers curled tight around each cup, a subtle anchor as we took cautious steps toward trust. The familiar floral note of my mother's perfume lingered beneath the tense air, mingling with my father's careful, almost tentative attempts at conversation. Every small meeting stitched something back together, each detail—a nervous smile, a gentle touch, a shared glance—adding a fragile thread to the tapestry of our relationship.

Forgiveness was not a simple choice. For years, the idea of letting them back in—my parents, whose absence cut deeper than words—felt like inviting pain back in. I remembered the hollow ache of being left behind after their sudden departure, every shadow outside feeling like a promise broken. At night, I pressed my cheek to cold windows, listening for the creak of footsteps that never came.

My fingers trembled as I wrapped them around the cold, ridged shaft of the microphone. A faint static crackled through the speakers, mingling with the soft shuffle of papers and the nervous coughs scattered throughout the auditorium. The lights above felt hot against my skin, sharpening every sensation—the scratch of my blazer's sleeve, the thrum of my pulse in my ears. I drew a shaky breath, tasting the metallic hush of anticipation, and looked out over the rows of expectant faces.

"Good evening." I had begun my voice ringing out, thin but steady, echoing off polished wood and painted walls. I let the nervous energy settle in my limbs, letting it anchor me rather than unmoor me. "I used to be afraid of rooms like this. Afraid of people who might look too closely, ask too much, or see through the version of me I'd spent years perfecting." The words felt raw and true, echoing with the tremors of my past.

A gentle murmur rippled through the crowd. I felt its warmth, like sunlight on stone—an invitation to honesty.

"I've realized that bravery doesn't require loudness, love doesn't require perfection, and you can start over without having everything together." I paused, letting the message settle, listening to the hush of breath and the creak of auditorium chairs.

I shared pieces of my story—not every wound, not every scar, but enough to illuminate the path behind me for someone else to follow. Each detail—each admission—was a thread woven into the tapestry of the moment, creating a space where vulnerability felt safe and where hope, fragile but persistent, could take root.

How I was left at thirteen. How I slept in a Laundromat, listening to the echo of distant city sounds in the emptiness of night. How I walked into a shelter that smelled of bleach and brokenness and found Mr. Danner and Mrs. Grant, their faces gentle in the harsh fluorescent light. How I met Lila, who called me out and called me in, her laughter a lifeline in the quietest hours. How Lila taught me friendship, patience and unwavering, and Riley reminded me I could laugh and hop.

In those moments, I realized healing wasn't just survival—it was rediscovering joy. Each encounter shaped the person I became, leading me to moments like today—standing before a crowd, sharing my story, feeling the weight and the wonder of being truly seen.

I spoke about college: how the first day felt like walking onto another planet; how I learned the language of possibility, one hesitant "hello" at a time. About love—slow, sometimes stumbling, but steadfast. About Steve, the quiet anchor in my ever-shifting journey.

And I spoke about choosing family—twice. The first time, out of necessity; the second, out of hope. I paused, feeling the weight of the moment as the quiet hum of conversation faded. I looked around the room—Steve's hopeful gaze steadying me, Jaylen's nervous smile flickering in the soft auditorium light, my daughter Ivy, my "mini me," whose future fills me with pride and hope, and my parents' expectant faces met my gaze. "Will I forgive them?" I wondered aloud. I wasn't sure yet, but hope was beginning to outweigh old wounds. "The door is opening more and more," I said, letting the words settle into the hush that followed.

After the speech, the line for signatures curled around the edge of the stage, voices weaving through the bustle of the auditorium. Students approached—some with tears shining, some with curiosity bright as new pennies. The air buzzed with the warmth of shared vulnerability.

One girl—barely fifteen, her voice small but steady—stood silently until she whispered, "How do you stop being mad?" There was a quiver in her words, as if she held her anger close to her chest, afraid to let it go.

I pressed the pen I'd used on every page of my book into her palm, feeling the cool metal between our hands. "You write something new," I told her, the words soft but certain, hoping she could hear the promise in my tone—the invitation to begin again.

Later that night, I stood alone in our kitchen. The house was dark, but warm—the faint scent of night air drifted in through the open window above the sink, mingling with the gentle hum of the refrigerator. I felt the cool tile beneath my bare feet, and somewhere outside, a car rolled slowly past, its tires whispering against the pavement. Our son Jaylen had gone to bed late after asking if he could read just one more chapter. Ivy had fallen asleep against my shoulder, her hair smelling faintly of being freshly shampooed. As I rinsed a glass beneath the tap, a quiet gratitude settled over me, mingling with the night air and the hush of the house—a gentle reminder of how much these simple moments mean.

I held a copy of my book and traced the raised letters with my fingertips, feeling the smooth coolness of the cover beneath my hand. My husband Steve walked in, his footsteps soft against the worn linoleum, and kissed my temple.

"Proud of you," he said.

"Did I do okay?"

"You lived it, Makenzie. That's more than okay."

I glanced around our home—family photos on the wall, toys poking out from under the couch, a plant I hadn't yet managed to kill. I took a deep breath, letting the silence settle around me. The memories here were layered—some heavy, some light. The quiet wrapped itself around me, gentle and familiar.

And in the hush, I realized the most extraordinary thing I've ever done isn't just surviving.

It's letting me love this life after this life nearly broke me.

I opened the last page of my notebook—the original one, its first lines written on a park bench with nothing but a peanut butter sandwich and a quiet hope.

And I wrote:

#47   *You can survive in a world that forgets you,*

You can thrive in a world you create.

One filled with light, laughter, and people who never ask you to hide.

Beneath those words, I drew a heart.

Not broken.

Not patched together.

Just full.

For the first time, I realized that wholeness isn't about never breaking—it's about choosing to fill the cracks with hope and love. Fullness meant trusting that, even after the hardest nights, there could still be bright mornings with possibility.

Note From The Author

Even though Mackenzie's story is fiction, it's also the story of a woman who stepped forward—unmasked and unafraid.

And in this world she's created, every day begins with sunlight and ends with laughter shared with familiar friends who see her as she is. A Survivor!

But this isn't just a story of survival.

It's a story of learning to let love in—and, letting it stay.

LK Menzies